Vines of the Underworld

Book 1 of the Crystal Serpent series

PROLOGUE	4
CELESTE-THE ANCHOR	6
CYRELL-THE WARRIOR	13
DIAPHONUS – THE PRIEST	18
CELESTE - THE ANCHOR	24
TARCYLL – THE SPYMASTER	29
CELESTE – THE ANCHOR	33
CYRELL – THE WARRIOR	40
CELESTE-THE ANCHOR	47
CYRELL – THE WARRIOR	61
CELESTE- THE ANCHOR	75
CELESTE – THE ANCHOR	82
TARCYLL – THE SPYMASTER	94
CELESTE – THE ANCHOR	100
CELESTE – THE ANCHOR	108
DIAPHONUS – THE PRIEST	112
CELESTE – THE ANCHOR	120
DIAPHONUS – THE PRIEST	134
CELESTE- THE ANCHOR	147
TARCYLL – THE SPYMASTER	158
CELESTE – THE ANCHOR	162
CYRELL – THE WARRIOR	164
CELESTE – THE ANCHOR	179
DAIRELL – THE PRINCE	205

CELESTE – THE ANCHOR	212
DAIRELL – THE PRINCE	224
CELESTE – THE ANCHOR	230
CELESTE – THE ANCHOR	242
CELESTE – THE ANCHOR	267

PROLOGUE

When the primal magic at the universe's core became too dense, it exploded, scattering its shards and thus forming the Crystal Serpent.

The raw magic crystals dispersed across the aether, shaping a reptile carrying all the realms on its back.

Some domains were abundantly blessed with the gifts of the Serpent, and magic thrived in these lands, like Faëheim. Others were not so lucky, and their inhabitants had to carve their livelihood from barren soil, struggling for survival each day against the merciless laws of nature. Yet they succeeded against all odds without the mighty help of spellwork and wizardry.

For ages, Fae watched with condescension and dark curiosity as humankind fell, then rose and tried again. The magical beings of Faëheim seldom became involved in human affairs, allowing their fate to play out in all its torment, yet this was about to change.

The Siphons crawled out of their dark dimension and attacked, starved after eons of hunger, craving the might of pure magic.

The eternal radiance of Faëheim dimmed as the Siphons devoured the powers of its people.

With the last flickers of magic, the rulers of all Fae nations sent their most cunning heroes, their most skilled warriors, to find a means, a weapon, to defy the invaders and restore the brilliance of Faëheim.

And they discovered it in the most surprising place. The human realm.

Even though magic was scarce in men's lands, the Fae explorers realized that certain humans, the Anchors, had raw, untamed magic raging in their blood, as if the gifts of the Serpent were not distributed equally among all but stored in only a few.

These oddities weren't even aware of the rare, dormant power inside them.

The salvation from the Siphons´ invasion was now up to the four Fae Hunters, roaming the human world for decades. But how to harvest the power of the Anchors was a question yet to be answered.

CELESTE-THE ANCHOR

"This meeting could have been an email." I scrutinize my chipped black nail polish. *Should have booked an appointment to get my nails done today and save myself another trip downtown...*

"And remember, in servicing you, we service humanity!" My team lead Sandra wraps up the meeting with a fake smile. My colleagues reluctantly repeat the company's motto, some of them rolling their eyes when they retreat to their desks in the sterile, open-space office. The crowd and the cubicles give me the creeps. I usually work from home, but Sandra sabotaged my casual afternoon on my couch.

"Any plans for tonight?" Jasmin, my nerdy sidekick, startles me. I take in her round face and pierced lips curled up in a smile. She's wearing too much makeup today, her green eyes surrounded by the Goth, smoky eyeshadows she loves, the purple tips of her black hair styled into pretty curls.

"I don't, but obviously you do." A customer call interrupts us before she can answer. She presses the connect button on her headset and strolls back to her desk.

"Aeternus Medical Equipment support, you're speaking with Jasmin. How can I help you today?" Her words fade in the clamor of the call center.

My line rings before I can follow her and ask what she's up to.

Call after call, the day slips by in a blur. I crave the tranquility of my tiny apartment, the fairy lights over my bookshelves, the minuscule jungle of my houseplants, and the comfort of my gaming chair in front of the thirty-four-inch monitor. A glass of wine, a round of Skyrim, and then the cool sheets of my bed. This is my plan before Jasmin interferes.

Without listening to my protests, she drags me to a shady bar, where a band plays 90s music, and I try to convince my introverted nature that I'm having fun by quickly downing three toxic-looking shots.

Hours later, the singer is howling to "Creep" by Radiohead, Jasmin is in a deep conversation with a green-haired guy, and his friend is eyeing me, sipping on his beer, obviously gathering the courage to start a conversation.

My anxiety inches back in, despite the alcohol in my bloodstream, just as it predictably does every time I'm among people. The liquor doesn't help anymore, probably making it worse as I feel tension creep through me, forcing my shoulders to hunch slightly, my eyes darting away, toward my empty glass. As the anxiety heightens, suddenly the neon signs over the bar begin to spin, the faces of strangers crowding the space suddenly merge into an amalgam of features, and I start taking fast, shallow breaths, feeling watched and in danger. My fingers dig into the worn red leather of the stool to steady my shaking body, but it doesn't help. I'm in a full-blown freefall.

I grab my purse and murmur something in Jasmin's ear. She nods, understanding, though I've never informed her of my diagnosis and the pills I pop before leaving home to combat it. She's figured it out somehow, and I'm grateful she's not asking questions or treating me like a lunatic.

Agoraphobia and acute panic attacks don't go well with college and a successful career. So, I dropped out of school and started changing jobs whenever it got too tricky and demanding.

Outside, I zip my jacket up and gratefully breathe in the crisp, autumn air. It's past eleven, and I need to hurry if I want to catch the last train.

The fluorescent crescent of the new moon reflects in the street puddles, and the gaping darkness of the side alleys devours the clicking of my heels.

I've always felt safe in Chicago and know every corner of this neighborhood. But I sense a certain peril in the air tonight, like a distant whiff of gunpowder before a sea battle, the crackling thickness of the sky before a devastating storm. It's as if malevolent, eerie eyes follow me, and I look over my shoulder. Empty cans roll on the street, picked up by the wind, and a couple walking a dog talk in muffled tones. Anxiously fishing in my purse, I find my medication and pop two pills. My doctor warned me against mixing it with alcohol, and also against taking too many, yet I bet he never had a problem breathing when he was in a room with more than three people.

Relieved, I dive into the underground maze of the subway and head to my platform.

It's crowded with strangers, and it doesn't help. I inch closer to the tracks, when a particular group of young men catches my attention... and they reciprocate my look in an alarming way.

Drunks, I note mentally and take another step toward the tracks, ready to hop on the train when it arrives.

The men ogle me, something I'm used to. Jasmin often tries to convince me that I'm beautiful, yet I don't possess the plastic perfection of social media models. I perceive myself as mousy, as my long, chocolate-brown locks are never styled, and I seldom put on any makeup to conceal my freckles. My full lips, heavy breasts, and tiny waist do the trick, my friend explains. "And if men look away from your hourglass figure, they'd find that you have quite interesting eyes, too!" she had said earlier today, trying to convince me to join her at the bar.

Well, these men seem to be interested in what I offer, even as I curl further in on myself, as one of them, a tall and bulky guy looking like a textbook example of a school bully, approaches me, accompanied by the cackling of his friends.

I shuffle nervously, looking around for a way out or help. Finding nothing, only distracted strangers´ faces, suspiciously focused on minding their own business. Just two feet away are the tracks, their metal bones faintly reflecting the light. Beyond them gapes another tunnel, or God knows what—boasting black emptiness.

Warily stepping to the side, I hear the welcome sound of an approaching train and rejoice at the squeak of the breaks and the headlight slicing the gloom before me. The tracks vibrate and moan with the weight of the carts, and I can see the cockpit and the man sitting there.

Our eyes briefly meet, and I see his widen with terror just as I feel a powerful, bruising shove in my back.

I land on the tracks, hearing the cackling and the shouts of *"Take that, bitch!"* from the drunks, swallowed by the rumble of the machine.

The landing is rough, the adrenaline rush suppressing the pain of my injured knees and probably dislocated right wrist. Perplexed, I stare at the blinding headlights of the train, approaching at breakneck speed.

Steely hands grab my forearms, my bones screaming in pain as a superhuman force pulls me out of harm's way in the blink of an eye, a millisecond before hundreds of tons of metal turned me into a bloodied pile of minced meat.

I become a passive spectator of my own life, watching the massive steel wheels whizz by, inches from my thigh, and the metal monstrosity stops huffing and screeching. The whiff of oil and overheated machinery sobers me up, and I look around, hardly believing the last few seconds even happened, a nightmare of a moment that has me numb.

But I'm alive. And I turn to face the person responsible for that miracle.

The stranger's fingers are still clutching my arms, bruising them, and feline green eyes, glowing in the dark, stare at me, framed by loose silver strands. The rest of his hair is tied up in something resembling a man bun, and he's wearing—wait a minute, is there a Comic-Con or some cosplay event in the city tonight? Because this man, who studies me as I take in his appearance, white eyebrows knit together with concern, wears exquisitely crafted leather armor. It accentuates his broad shoulders and descends to a narrow waist. My gaze drops down to his hands, gloved in gauntlets encrusted with large, faintly glowing crystals.

The mysterious man parts his lips to say something, but a massive four-legged shadow resembling a car-sized dog emerges behind him. The flash of metallic tubes and sound of a smoothly running engine don't add up to the pair of red glowing orbs of the mechanical monster. It freezes behind the stranger's back, staring at me, too.

Then the tunnel explodes in light and sound, emergency lights blinking, warning signals deafening me. People with flashlights swarm the train track, checking the train bumper and shouting at each other. Looking back to my mysterious savior and the odd machine dog behind him, I stare at an empty space. The man has disappeared so fast that I speculate if the adrenaline or the alcohol mixed with my meds has made me imagine the whole thing.

Yet the purple prints of his fingers on my forearms confirm that he was there, and he saved me from certain death.

CYRELL-THE WARRIOR

"As above, so below." I was so surprised that this saying exists in the human realm, too. Some concepts make it beyond the barriers of time and space, I assume carried across the universe by the pulse of the Crystal Serpent.

I grew up in the dark tunnels of the Lower Lands, surrounded by the steam of our machines and the glow of our magic, so I headed to the bowels of the human world as soon as I set foot in this realm. It was the only place where I felt safe, less exposed. Men have built extensive mazes of passageways deep beneath their cities, with hidden, dark places where I thrive.

Cerberus and I found the frail magical tread that led us to the Anchor. Perhaps it had been my warrior instinct, my sharpened dark elf senses, or the gentle support of Cerberus, who is strangely fascinated by humans, but I had caught the pull of the magical anomaly long before the other Hunters, just as I had hoped.

We dark elves are the most depraved of the four kingdoms regarding arcane gifts, but what we lack in magic, we compensate for with technology. Our refined machinery is praised all over Faëheim, and our weapons never fail.

If I manage to capture the Anchor, harvest or subdue her essence, and return to my people, my home will have a more significant chance to stand against the Siphons than the rest of the Fae kingdoms.

All Faëheim Hunters track their prey alone; none of my rivals would share their intel or suggest cooperation, as each is trying to ensure the survival of their kind, of their own lands. And this is the way of Fae. Indeed, there are rumors about some twisted partnership—even friendship—between Tarcyll the Spy and Diaphonus the Priest, yet I take it with a grain of salt.

The last Anchor I'd discovered and stalked had been a large man in a cold human kingdom in the North. It took me years to catch his scent and find him, only to realize that the potent magic had drained all sense out of him. Maddened by a power he could not understand, he took his own life.

Cerberus and I spent years after that devastating failure exploring humanity, studying their machines, observing their ways from the shadows while keeping watch for the next Anchor manifestation.

I expected another bulky man shining bright like a beacon in this magic-deprived world. Yet that cool autumn night had a different treat in store for me. The magic trails had lured me to a tavern, where I stood near the entrance, music, light, and the stench of cheap alcohol contaminating the sacred twilight. Then the blinding radiance of the primal gift of the Serpent poured out into the night.

A stunning female, her proportions more lush than a succubus, her face more serene than a high elf, and her hair a graceful mess, passed by us, eyes concentrating on the cold ground before her feet as she rushed into the night. I patted Cerberus's neck, ensuring I was not dreaming, and my companion huffed in understanding. My discipline and focus kept me from lunging after her. Traits that have served me well and helped me to survive the raw challenges that each dark elf warrior must face at their initiation. Yet the life-giving light that glimmered within her, the sensual sway of her hips when she descended the stairs to my underground hideaway, the dreamy look in her eyes... I was enthralled by her delicate beauty. Dark urges stirred within me, and heat rushed through my core. I have lain with many females, yet this human was something special. I felt my flesh hardening at the thought that soon she would be at my mercy, in my hideout, and then I could make her scream with pleasure.

Yes, she would scream, I remind myself sternly, but for another reason. The Elders' instructions were to attach her to the Extractor: a unique machine that would drain her magic and store it to be safely transported to our realm.

What would happen to her body in the process? Nobody knows.

And I shouldn't care, I decide, thinking of the darkness that flooded my homeland's tunnels after the Siphons´ attack. I force myself to sober up from my lusty daydreaming by thinking about the last time I saw my sister and her offspring—crying and begging me to stay, terrified that they might never see me again.

My mechanical friend and I followed her through our secret underground passageways and watched her descend into the marble palace they call the subway.

Then I saw drunken men taunting her, and my first instinct was to draw my blade and finish them off. A gentle nuzzle from Cerberus brought me back to my senses, reminding me that we had to remain hidden. *"Fae keep out of human affairs,"* the Elders had retorted during my mission preparations. We had been the most powerful race, yet the Siphons devoured our magic and left us vulnerable. The humans, on the other hand, invested in science and weapons, able to turn kingdoms to dust in the blink of an eye. They have become respectable opponents we do not wish to see on our doorstep.

So, I lingered in the shadows, prepared to jump on Cerberus's back and follow the train as soon as she boarded it.

A moment later, I saw her plunging to her death, and saving her had been instinctive. Not only because of the raging magical power in her delicate body but because she was a female in trouble. In other circumstances, I would have introduced myself and even courted her. Yet I am but an exile in a foreign realm, a hunter on a mission, and before I could do anything, her world claimed her back, the sirens and shouts numbing my senses. I hid in the darkness, aroused by the memory of her softness in my arms.

Now, I wait patiently for the officers to complete their job and the paramedics to examine her. Then she leaves, and my loyal Cerberus helps me track her. I watch the tiny human female paying for her transport from the thick gloom of a deserted side alley. Darkness is an ally in this strange world, as human eyes cannot pierce it. I take a step to memorize every detail of the building she lives in, a multistory abode she shares with many. These living conditions are so similar to ours in the Lower Lands that nostalgia squeezes my heart again.

Now, I know where the Anchor lives, and my lips draw into a smile. The best part of the Hunt begins.

DIAPHONUS – THE PRIEST

I know the ways of magic. Nobody in the four Fae realms is more skilled in reading its ebbs and tides.

I follow its gentle stream, which leads me to a busy street with many glass and steel buildings piercing the clouds.

I take out my utensils, arrange my easel, and line up my charcoal pencils and paints, sitting in a tiny green oasis between two busy roads packed with cars and poisonous fumes. The trees around me provide air and shelter for the few birds that stubbornly refuse to leave this contaminated land.

I whip my blond braid back and smile at a few girls who have stopped to stare at me. They giggle, blush, and walk away, the bravest one taking her phone out and snapping a picture of me. I've spent enough time among humans to know that it will probably go viral days later, circling the social networks with hashtags of #hotartist, #hotart, and some indecent comments. So much for remaining discreet.

I roll up the sleeves of my linen shirt and start painting, keeping an eye on the building that harbors my hope.

Autumn leaves spiral to the pavement, birds gathered in the branches above, and I finish my first sketch just as the massive glass door draws my attention.

Light, brighter than a flash of lightning, pierces the dull landscape. *Magic.* More brilliant than the beacons of the Bone Coast. So mouthwatering powerful that it pulls me, an invisible thread stretching between me and the Anchor.

The most alluring woman I have seen in all my long life steps out of the building as the glass doors close behind her. She stands in the last rays of the late autumn sun, head cocked, as if listening. Then her gaze takes in her surroundings... and meets mine. A finely shaped eyebrow flies up as she studies me, then she is gone before I can react, and I wince as if shaken awake from a beautiful dream.

Did she feel what I felt? The scorching connection between us, the soundless roar of magic colliding, the clash of two powers that, if not controlled, could destroy her and me both?

It takes me days to learn more about her habits and routine. A week later, I wait for her in the park, where she exercises.

I have learned that the Anchor values her solitude; she prefers to be alone and runs among the city's scarce area of nature, a rare spot of green in a world of steel and concrete. This makes me uneasy. What if another Hunter spots her and gets her before me? Tarcyll knows that I am one step ahead of him but doesn't seem troubled by it. He enjoys the human realm too much, sometimes making me wonder if he has forgotten how vital our objective is.

As expected, she shows up for her run. The park is empty so early on Saturday, which serves my plan. I stand next to a bench, wearing these ridiculous human exercise clothes, and pretend to stretch. Then I feel the pull, the radiance streaming from her, like the sun coming from behind the clouds in all its glory. She approaches, petite and fragile, her tight clothing seductively displaying the generous curves of her breasts and her snatched waist, her hair up in a bouncy ponytail. Today she looks different. Dark circles surround her eyes, and her face has a haunted strain to it. Have some of the other Fae Hunters already reached her? No, it isn't likely. My sensitivity to magic gives me leverage over the multitude of other males after her.

She spots me immediately. Most likely due to my height and frame. Humans are quite small compared to us high elves. People ogle me with curiosity, especially the females. Tarcyll has similar experiences, but he shamelessly takes advantage of our superior looks. I have always chastised him for bedding humans, yet right now this prospect seems incredibly tempting.

The deafening rumble and the screams of terror when the Floating islands of Taer Vallhen crashed to the ground still ring in my ears, reminding me why I'm here. We lost many lives the night the Siphons attacked and almost depleted the magic of the four domains. I was one of the few still able to cast spells, yet not strong enough to prevent the downfall of our floating islands.

I push the painful memories away and focus on the task at hand. To save my people, I need to get to the Anchor first, and I must find a way to harness the magic singing in her veins. Of all the Hunters, I have the best chance to solve her riddle. With active magic at my disposal, I would use the arcane force to unlock the treasure chest she is, even if I have to crush her mortal body in the process.

Clenching my jaw, I promise myself not to become distracted by the fleeting beauty she possesses. She would be nothing but a whisper of a memory in a hundred years, while the hanging gardens of the cloud cities would rise forever.

There she is, within my reach, fragile as all mortals are, and I need to get close enough to throw the enthralling spell and take her to my hideout, where I can study her undisturbed. Shameless visions heat my loins and flush my face. The bright, intoxicating presence of the human female stirs a longing inside me, snuffed long ago by ages of celibacy.

Does she remember me? She measures me with a look I'm used to receiving from the females of this realm, and I know it is time to act. We are alone on the narrow gravel path, meandering among the trees in the heart of the tiny forest, hidden in the city, with only the clear blue sky and the chirping birds bearing witness to what I am about to do.

I have concealed the slope, making the alley appear smooth and even, and tense up when the woman stumbles and rolls in the dust. I am at her with one leap.

"Are you hurt?" I ask, concerned, wrapping an arm around her shoulders and helping her to a strange sitting position, where she leans against my chest. I note that this is a little bit too close, yet it is too late, as her scent—a sweet elixir of heat, salt, fear, and blooming hyacinth hits me, and I fear that she might hear the loud thumping of my heart.

What is wrong with me?

All Fae know that humans are infectiously promiscuous due to their short lifespans, yet how is the High Priest of the First Light Order fooled so easily? Reining myself in, I lower my gaze to her.

The human rubs her ankle, pain distorting her serene features. It is the first time I have looked into the eyes of a mortal so up close. Hers are warm amber sprinkled with gold and green, full of concealed melancholia. It's the burden of living only a few decades, I conclude while preparing to enthrall her and take her to my car parked nearby. In this realm, I avoid using magic, as it may draw the attention of the other Hunters. And I want this Anchor only for myself. I want the Floating cities of Taer Vallhen to rise again, their waterfalls casting rainbows into the lavender skies of Faëheim.

And the raw magic contained in this lithe body would be enough. If I manage to harvest it, it would be sufficient to erect mighty protection wards against the Siphons and restore the arcane network fueling our daily lives.

I feel already the magic sparks for the tiny spell gather around my fingers, when a sudden shift in our surroundings alerts all my senses. Something is approaching.

The shadows under the bushes thicken and lengthen. The branches toss about in a powerless rage, and the leaves scream with a thousand voices, a wordless symphony of terror. Darkness creeps up on me, ambushing me while I'm wasting time, drunk on the fleeting charms of this human.

I know this presence. Everyone in Faëheim knows it.

The Dreadful One, the Lord of Darkness, the Prince of the Underworld himself, has joined the hunt. And I know what he's after—the living, breathing, magical artifact in my hands.

Drawn by my magic like a moth to the flame, he can sniff the trail of my spell across realms.

The Abyss swallow you, Dreadful One!, I curse softly. I need urgently a new plan.

CELESTE - THE ANCHOR

A good run to clear my head. This is what I need to filter out the hallucinations, because it's impossible to see what I saw last night on the train track, right?

Or did a white-haired man, looking like a CrossFit fanatic, save me from getting killed? And what exactly was his sidekick? Was it a machine like those Boston Dynamics robot dogs? Or a clever costume? Was this the most elaborate prank of all time?

I wince when I relive the scene, drenched in the red light of the train track's emergency lights: the glowing eyes of the stranger who saved me, his angular features, and the chiseled body under the exotic armor.

I decide to take the healthy approach and blame it all on the alcohol, except for the douchebag who pushed me on the tracks. They got him and his friends, the police told me. Godspeed. I'm sure he'll have plenty of fun in prison.

Telling Sandra how I almost got killed was good enough to obtain permission to work from home in the coming days. It is precisely what I need: to be by myself among my tiny jungle, the soothing fairy lights, my cat, and my amazing espresso machine.

A morning run has always helped to clear my head and re-align myself. I picked up the habit when my mother lost herself to alcohol. I did anything to get away from her and avoid her torturous self-victimization episodes. Matching my breathing to my steps was my meditation, and soon I disappear into the golden oasis of the park next door.

I find my pace, and the world around me blurs into a pale background of leaves rustling, birds chirping, and branches crackling. Then something catches my eye.

Next to the narrow path stands a man, busy warming up. He's tall, his long blond hair tied in a messy braid that snakes down his broad chest. Azure eyes the color of the summer sky over some tropical island pierce me. He's the type of handsome that makes you daydream when you see him on social media or in an Avengers suit but makes every girl with a grain of common sense run away, because beauty like this means trouble. It means loads of girls at his feet and stress I don't need in my life. But looking is allowed, and I appreciate his biceps as they swell and the curl of his sensual lips. The stranger also stares at me, his defined jaw clenched, eyes narrowed, as if waiting for something. His odd fixation on me almost makes me reassess my "not worth the trouble" philosophy, when I feel the ground beneath my feet give in, and I roll on the gravel, the pain in my ankle sharpened by humiliation.

He's suddenly nearly on top of me, making me think I probably blacked out for a few seconds, because no human can move that fast. He helps me sit up and awkwardly holds me against his chest so that I feel the hard contours underneath. I turn to face him and meet his gaze. I am lost, drowning in the alpine lakes of purest cerulean.

"Are you okay?" His voice is low, and he drawls the vowels in a strange way. I can't look away from his lush, perfectly shaped lips, and I swallow before opening my mouth to answer. No words come out as some odd gust of wind appears from nowhere, whirling the dead leaves into a mini tornado of dread.

A shadow passes over the stranger's face, and suddenly he lifts me as if I weigh no more than a child. I struggle to catch my breath as the man bolts toward the thicket, pressing me firmly to his chest. Looking back, I see the silhouettes of three enormous black pit bulls, unleashed, growling, and baring their sharp teeth.

The dogs don't bother to chase us, I notice with relief, and soon we reach the more crowded area of the park. People stare at us, and he gently lowers me to my feet.

"What was that?" I blink, confused, still unable to process what happened. Were we close to being attacked by these vicious dogs?

"Can you walk?" he asks instead of answering. "That fall looked pretty painful. My car is over there; I would be happy to give you a ride home."

Well, it seems like my savior isn't from around here, obviously not knowing the most basic safety rule for women—to never get in a car with a stranger.

His arm is still around my waist, and he looks at me with concern. It's so disarming that I almost consider his offer.

"No need, I live nearby. If you can help me… limp my way home, that would be great," I mumble instead, wondering what happened to my common sense. Today is obviously about breaking safety rules. At least I have a gorgeous six foot six reason for it.

He nods, and we walk, his arm slung around my waist. Heat flushes my face when I realize that his palm is almost the size of my waist, yet he holds me delicately, as if I might break. Passersby stare at us, probably wondering how a gray mouse like me could get such a specimen.

We chat to smooth the awkwardness, and I learn he is Diaphonus—what an odd name. Definitely a foreigner. He is a painter living nearby, and I seem to be in luck, as he is holding an exhibition this weekend. He gives me a card with an address before I disappear into the entrance of my building, asking me if I would come for the opening.

My heart skips a beat when he looks down at me.

Trouble, I remind myself, yet I take the card and consider what to wear while climbing the stairs to my apartment. Glancing back one last time, I see him still standing beyond the glass door; head cocked, as if listening to something only he can hear.

TARCYLL – THE SPYMASTER

Humans can deliver pleasure in ways unfathomable for us Fae. It's the heat they are constantly in, pressed by the urge to procreate now, as tomorrow might be too late. Their fleeting, rushed existence makes them eager and intoxicatingly promiscuous.

Their hearts beat faster, their bodies are warmer than ours, and they are curious, always willing to experiment. Unlike the thoughtful and delicate Fae females, who have seen and tried everything in their long lives, and also lost a portion of their appetites in the process, human women are glowing with lust, the carnal heat of their desires hitting me in waves in the sticky air of my nightclub.

I send another girl who asked if I would like a lap dance away, the fourth one this evening, though my length strains with desire when I glimpse her perfectly rounded, bouncy breasts. The sight makes me growl. Curves. The other thing that made me fall in love with human women. Something in these spheres, in these proportions, awakens primal hunger in every male. I wonder if the other Hunters feel the same way.

Yet I discipline myself, as tonight is not about fun but work. My informer promised to be here around midnight with some valuable intel about my target.

The Anchor. The salvation for my people. The only hope for my realm—the Kingdom of Verdant.

I quickly realized the potential of my experience as a spymaster in this world and teamed up with Diaphonus at the beginning of our mission decades ago, yet my ways quickly drove him away. He found my dubious status here tasteless.

You need to be creative when you don't have piles of magic at hand as he does.

So, I started working, taking odd jobs in the criminal underworld, where my skills were quickly noticed and praised as supernatural, my moral code and principles earning me the reputation of a ruthless, powerful, and reliable ally. Feared by some, respected by others, money quickly followed, and connections, too. Without planning it, I am now operating a small underground empire focused on transporting risky goods, espionage, and extortion.

The sole purpose of everything I do here is locating the Anchor that resides in this town.

Valter, my employee charged with following Diaphonus, finally joins me in the VIP section. Twirling an amber drink, he casually looks at the seductive tangle of supple flesh on the dance floor.

"And?" I ask, eyebrow arched, and the man knows he is abusing my patience. He drops a stack of high-resolution photos on the table before me, and I eagerly grab them, not bothering to conceal my curiosity.

Then my jaw drops. I can feel the Anchor's pull even through the paper, her magic so raw and tempting for my abstinent soul. My fingers shake as I take in the delicate features and fleeting, melancholic beauty of the human female. The promising curl of tempting lips, heaviness of her breasts, and tiny waist, the casual ponytail swung over her shoulder as she warms up for exercise. I feel my pants getting tighter when the following picture shows the mouth-watering arch of her behind as she is bending over to reach her toes in a stretch.

I must remind myself that this is the Anchor and that this tempting body is only a package for the arcane force within her. A power I need to unlock and leash, even if I have to crack the mortal shell containing it. I trace my thumb over her face. It's distracting that she is a beauty, yet my loyalty lies with my king and my people, and I will deliver her to them and let them extract her essence. Yet she should not suffer. Not only because, had the circumstances been different, I would easily fall in love with her, but because of my principles. Never in all the long centuries of my life have

I caused suffering or raised a hand to a female or a youngling. Never have I forced myself upon anyone.

I curse softly when the following pictures show Diaphonus holding her, his face frozen in a mask of surprise and longing, just like mine. Did he also contemplate how things might have been if she were not the Anchor?

"He just walked her home after," Valter's impassive voice was somehow louder than the music.

"Tell me what you saw," I demand, but he gestures to the pile of pictures.

"See for yourself, man. I can't explain it. Some aggressive dogs appeared from nowhere, then, suddenly, puff! The beasts were gone. Disappeared into thin air. And before you ask me, no, I've been clean for seven months already."

Diaphonus´ tricks. But why did he use magic to draw her away from this place? Why risk detection by the other hunters?

It's time to visit my old friend.

But before that... the Anchor's picture still in my hand, I gesture to one of the lap dancers. As soon as I unzip my pants, she knows what to do. Thrusting my cock deep into the wet heat of her mouth, I can't suppress a smirk.

I have always loved hunting—especially stunning prey like this.

CELESTE – THE ANCHOR

Three pills should do it. It's what I usually take before visiting my mother in rehab.

It's a beautiful November morning, the air clear and the birds weaving invisible nets in the spotless sky.

The street below my window slowly wakes up, like always on the weekend. I finish my coffee on my tiny balcony, hidden in the soothing emerald green of my plants, and go inside to dress.

The rehab is a cozy farmhouse a two-hour drive from the city. My father left when I was seven, yet he never stopped generously supporting us. My mother led a modest life and saved as if already knowing that her fragile mental health would drive her to addiction.

Navigating the road toward the rehab, I listen to loud, cheerful music, trying to exorcize the demons of the past. A pair of beautiful pearl earrings lie neatly wrapped on the seat next to me. A birthday present that would probably end up being given away to one of her friends, sold, or discarded. For some reason, my gifts are never good enough.

A couple hours later, I sit in the sun-drenched garden, listening to the same old stories of my mother's eternal crusades against the world. Whatever happens, it's always someone else's fault, the entire universe plotting against her well-being.

She briefly asks how I'm doing but switches to rant about the rehab's food before I can open my mouth to answer.

I listen and nod, counting the hours till I drive back and escape in the blissful oasis of my voluntary isolation. As the afternoon rays stretch and bathe the bench in liquid gold, I interrupt the monologue and bid farewell. Annoyed by my decision to leave, my mother snatches the blanket from her lap and disappears into the house. The earrings I bought her, unpacked and untouched, remain on the bench. I pick them up with a sigh.

The foreboding throbbing of a headache builds up in my nape as I reverse my car and head back home.

The first stars glimmer over the deserted road, when diverse lights start blinking on the dashboard. I expected my tiny twenty-year-old Honda to abandon me one day, but does it have to be here? There are only trees around, and calling a tow truck would cost me a fortune. I decide to press on, when the car starts making terrifying noises, like a dying creature taking its last breath. I manage to pull over on an overgrown side road just as the engine light comes on, and my loyal ride since college dies on me.

Great. It's already dark, and there are no other cars on this lonely highway. The thin moon mocks me from the indigo sky, smiling like the Cheshire Cat.

Well, Celeste, you've been through worse! I try to cheer myself up and pull out my cell phone. Why am I not surprised when I see no signal on the screen? As if this mishap has been perfectly orchestrated by some higher power, to what purpose, I do not know.

I step out and open the hood, the crisp autumn wind throwing a handful of leaves in my face. The universe is set to ridicule me tonight, I note, while examining the motor with my cell phone flashlight. The fresh, inky air thickens around me, shadows stretching bony hands from the trees, and I shudder. Night birds of prey commence their lonely calls, like lost souls searching for direction. Slowly, a foreboding creeps into my gut. Something will happen, I'm sure of it, and it won't be something pleasant. My instincts tell me it won't be a story I'll tell Jasmin about and laugh. I snuggle in my beige raincoat, bracing myself for whatever's is coming.

Then I hear the sound of a motorcycle approaching, and before I can wave them to stop, the leather-clad rider pulls over and dismounts the powerful machine. He must have seen the emergency lights of my car on the overgrown side road.

Oh my God, how tall is he? Icy terror floods my belly when he approaches, walking with the casual grace of an athlete. Without realizing it, I take a step back, away from this stranger that I know in my guts will do anything but help. I lose sight of the reflection of my horrified face in his black visor as he removes his helmet.

How many pills did I take again? And was their effect supposed to last this long?

White, shoulder-length hair, halfway up, tied in a casual man bun. Glowing, fern-green eyes, fluid feline movements, fine lips curled upward in something intended to be a smile. A grin of a predator, bearing the tips of razor-sharp fangs, this is how he appears to me.

He steps toward me, stretching out his hand, his combat boots kicking the gravel.

I prepare to bolt into the thicket, yet social conformism wins the battle over my gut instinct. You can't just run away from strangers trying to help only because they look similar to…

"I see you require my assistance *again*." He speaks in a low voice, dragging the "a"s in an alien way that sounds somewhat familiar.

That ominous "again." So it was *him*. The mysterious stranger who saved me from the train.

"Car troubles, I see. Let me take a look."

He takes another step toward me, and I know something has irreversibly changed in my life. If there is a path for everyone written among the stars, I have just taken a dangerous, forbidden detour. And there is no way back.

The stranger approaches me, his scent of leather, machine oil, and some unknown incense wrapping around me. He still smiles, looks at me like I'm his dinner, and leans over the engine.

Swallowing dryly, I finally gather the courage to speak.

"Thank you for saving me, then," I stammer, avoiding the elephant in the room and holding back the flood of questions on the tip of my tongue. What was he doing on the tracks, why did he disappear into the tunnels when people came to help? What was that mechanical monstrosity with him? And how the hell is he here now?

He turns to face me, a cold smile on his thin but beautifully shaped lips. I could barely see his face back then, and the light is scarce now, yet he is strikingly handsome in a stern, masculine way. A few loose strands frame his angular jaw, his high cheekbones bearing scars, one snaking around his lips to his chin. I realize I find them intriguing, and each one has undoubtedly a blood-curdling story. I take a step toward him, ignoring the clamor of alarm bells in my head. His eyes are still fixed on the engine, yet I see his nostrils flare and his massive muscles tense, a beast of prey preparing for a leap.

Transfixed, I stare at him, my lips half-open, unsure what to do or say next or why this whole situation hardens my nipples and sends heatwaves to my core, when, suddenly, the impossible happens.

Darkness descends upon us, consuming the meager light of the night sky, just as a monstrous human shape with black wings dives from above, a gush of wind from the mighty wings almost knocking me to the ground.

The white-haired stranger, my mysterious savior, shouts a warning, grabs my wrists, and drags me to his motorbike.

"The Dreadful One is here!"

When the creature lands with a loud thud on the roof of my car, I'm already sitting behind the strange biker as he speeds down the road, instinctively clinging to him as he accelerates. I'm too stunned to react, too terrified to fight.

I shiver in my thin beige raincoat, the cold force of wind pulling my hair and stinging my face. Did I fall asleep behind the wheel and end up in some twisted afterlife? Or is it some side-effect of my medication cocktail? The rugged outline of the stranger's back I'm clutching is a solid reality. So is the landscape that appears fleetingly familiar. The freezing draft that buffets me as we push against the night air steals the words from my mouth. *Where is he taking me?*

Squeezing the man's waist, I look back. Nothing follows us. It seems like the demon has given up the chase, but I spot the grotesque figure standing on top of my car, head cocked, sniffing. The Dreadful One? What does that even mean?

A myriad of questions buzz through my head, when I notice that we've reached town, and the motorbike halts to a stop at my street, at my door. I hop off the leather seat, yet hesitate to rush to the building's door.

"What was that?" I demand, voice trembling.

The man jumps off the bike with a graceful move that makes me wonder if he's a dancer, "You are hunted, Celeste," he declares simply, and I'm so flabbergasted that I don't even think of asking how he knows my name or where I live.

And then I do the craziest, most irresponsible and yet somehow logical thing in my life.

Strangers try to kill me in the subway, the hounds of hell chase me in the park, and a winged demon attacks me in the middle of nowhere—I clearly need to find out what exactly is happening.

"Come in," I utter, "I have some questions."

CYRELL – THE WARRIOR

I made my home in the underground labyrinth of this megapolis, among pipes, power cables, rats, and cockroaches the size of my palm, down below the surface where people dispose of things they don't wish to ever be found again.

For each alley above, there is a path below. For each avenue, there is a wide sewer tunnel. For each building, teeming with people, there is a settlement of creatures, born and raised among eternal darkness, blind, elusive, deadly.

It reminds me of my home, of the Lower Lands, as it used to be in the times before my civilization flourished. When the dark elves were nothing but a handful of desperate exiles, cowering in the relentless gloom of the Underworld, surviving on the only nutrient available in that inhospitable environment—the blood of their brethren.

Those times are long gone, and the Lower Lands flourish, the clever creations and engineering achievements of my people turning the damp tunnels into a mechanical garden of Eden. In this clockwork paradise, birds of bronze sing among trees of titanium, and a crystal sun reflects the light from the surface, setting in the evening, giving way to a pale moon of diamonds and neon. Oh, how I miss the opulence of the carefree days before the Siphons' attack, when my mind was obsessed only with honing my warrior skills to multiply the glory of my people. And I had many chances to do it, to prove myself, establish myself as the best of the best, a chosen one, a knight and superior warlord of the Lower Lands. I survived a thousand skirmishes against the hordes of the Dreadful One. Living at the doorstep of his wretched domain has never been easy. What an honor it is to be chosen by the Elders for this mission; what an opportunity it is to save not only my beloved sister and nephews but our entire realm!

Unlike the other Hunters who become distracted by the wonders and opportunities of the human world, I remain loyal to my mission. I follow trails, dig tunnels, scavenge, scout, and map.

I found the Anchor and hatched a plan. Sabotaging her car was easy—it was parked in front of the old five-storey building, her home. Yet darkness followed me into this world, and the Dreadful One attacked.

I need time. Time to reconsider and recalibrate my plan, so I follow the woman into her home, bemused by her bravado to invite me in. If only she knew how dark elves are—still feasting on the blood of our enemies in the frenzy of battle, remembering those barbaric times that shaped us into who we are. If only she knew my intentions, what I am—

a creature of twilight, an alloy of loyalty, discipline, ferocity, and power—she would run.

Yet she doesn't know, and she invites the monster into her home. I follow her up the stairs, my nostrils flaring as I take in her sweet scent—a fresh spring flower about to be crushed, my eyes scanning the curves of her body. I feel strange hunger rumble low in my gut, a carnal need, an abstinence howling to be satiated. Her long brown hair hangs tousled down her back, the belt of her coat accentuating her minuscule waist. The heat of her fleeting, rushed existence hits my face, and my senses, trained in the eternal darkness and silence of the Lower Lands, perceive the thumping of her heart, the rush of her hot, mortal blood. I feel my fangs extend, my mouth water, and only ages of raw, rigorous training help me restrain myself, to not to leap on her and sink my teeth into the soft, inviting flesh.

She unlocks the door, inviting me in with a gesture. I fill the doorframe, and the scent of damp soil and blooming plants overcome my senses. By the Serpent, her home is a lush garden, a tamed jungle. Plants hang from pots dispensed from the ceiling, orchids bloom on every surface, and magnolias spread their intoxicating scent. When a tiny furball rushes to my feet, I cannot help but chuckle. It seems the beast is wiser than its mistress, as it arches its back and hisses at me before turning and disappearing into the vegetation.

"Catherine, come back!" my host calls, "Catherine Earnshaw, where are your manners!" she chastises the cat while I scan my surroundings.

It is the first time I've entered a human dwelling invited; honestly, it's not as bad as I thought.

"Do you want a drink?" she asks, and I nod, assuming this is expected from me.

She comes back with a glass of fizzy amber liquid, cool on the tongue and soothing on the throat, that makes me forget the eerie hunger I feel when I look at the Anchor and quenches the dangerous thirst inside me.

She kicks off her shoes and settles in a comfortable-looking, plush armchair, motioning for me to do the same. Catherine observes me with suspicion from a dark corner of the room, her tail twitching.

We sit in silence, and I enjoy the dance of the freezing bubbles of the drink in my system, my eyes strangely drawn to her tiny, bare feet—so fragile and tender. I clench my jaw and look away, reminding myself that this human is destined for the extractor and that she is the only chance for my people to survive.

"How do you know my name?"

Our eyes lock, and she shuffles uncomfortably as if finally realizing she has let a monster into her home.

I am a curious male. Centuries of life in the scarce light of the Lower Lands don't provide much entertainment, so I grasp every chance presented to feel alive. Curiosity makes me answer her question, and that strange warmth gathers in my gut (for that, I blame the drink she served me). So, I tuck away the bracelet spiked with tranquilizing needles under my sleeve and cross my legs, preparing for a long conversation.

"Like I said, you are hunted, Celeste. And I am one of the Hunters."

Emotions flit over her face as I watch, mesmerized. Humans can feel so intensely!

"Why am I hunted? And who are you?" she finally utters.

I take a sip of my drink, starting to feel slightly light-headed. Is she poisoning me?

"Imagine that you have something very rare, Celeste, something incredibly precious that many desire. A key to surviving our doom." Her brow furrows, and she shuffles again, her eyes appearing black in the soft light, full of fear and doubt.

"As for who I am," I carefully put my glass on the tiny table next to my chair and rise to my feet, squaring my shoulders, "I am the Hunter who found you first."

I stalk toward her, and she squirms in the armchair, trying to pull away, to escape. I imagine I look frightening, with my imposing height, my body clad in black rider leathers.

I look down at her, head cocked. She has removed her coat and wears only a long green dress with deep cleavage. The spheres of her breasts heave as she pants in fear, and that dark thirst possesses me again when I sweep my gaze over her marble flesh.

The dark side of me wishes she were a spoil of war or a maiden of the lowest dark elves´ cast. A concubine, gifted to me by the Elders. My fangs extend at the thought of the delicious opportunities. But the human before me is a powerful, magical anomaly, my kind´s only hope to survive the Siphons.

Her scent hits my senses, fear, doubt, and... has the taint of this world messed up my perception, or is it arousal? The peaks of her nipples straining against the soft fabric of the dress confirm it. I am aware of how my looks, stature, and skills affect females, yet this is utterly unexpected. Is it the presence of a powerful male in her living room making her desire pool, or is the danger we have just escaped? What a fascinating creature this human is.

I slowly lick my sharp fangs and cup her face. She freezes, terror and curiosity swirling in her gaze.

"Fascinating…" I murmur as the tranquilizing needle stings her cheek.

CELESTE-THE ANCHOR

I wake up in my bed, neatly tucked in, Catherine sleeping at my feet, experiencing the worst hangover of my life. Slowly, visions of last night flood my tormented brain, and I wince. Was this all a dream? I stumble toward the living room, and there is the proof—an empty beer glass next to the armchair. I didn't imagined last night's visitor. Or the demon.

My car! Still abandoned in the middle of nowhere. I get myself together, pushing aside the screaming questions that bombard my aching mind. First things first. I make a phone call, take a shower, letting the water wash away most of the grogginess as it slips down the drain, then I force down some toast as I mull over the night before.

A few hours later, the tow truck delivers my dead Honda to my doorstep. A ding from my phone alerts me to a text.

What are u wearing tonight?

Jasmin's question startles me.

Pajamas? I reply, unwilling to get into explanations about my weird night.

Pajamas? For the exhibition of your super-hot Viking artist friend who saved you from the feral dogs?

I curse softly as another text comes through. **Will pick you up at seven. Put something nice on. We're getting you laid tonight. Doctor´s orders.** I groan and prepare myself for an evening out, squirreling away the fear and confusion regarding whatever the hell happened last night. *Was it even real? Too many meds? But what about the beer...?*

With no answers forthcoming and no logic to explain it away, I decide ignoring it is the only real option.

Diaphonus´ art is haunting, detailed, and otherworldly. Floating cities over jungles teeming with alien beasts, ghosts of lost civilizations in the turquoise depths of unknown oceans, creatures generated by a Victorian explorer's absinthe and opium-fueled mind. The atmosphere in the gallery matches the exposition, soft experimental jazz buzzing, the cream of the art society chattering, servers dressed in skin-colored tricots generously refilling our glasses.

Jasmin's striking eyes, contoured with lapis lazuli kohl, widen.

"Is that him?" The crystal bracelets on her wrist clank when she motions toward the man I briefly met at the park. I nod, embarrassed, as he catches us staring.

"If Thor and King Thranduil had a baby—" she starts, and I almost choke on my gin and tonic. Our host covers the distance with three giant steps and looms over us.

She's right. Diaphonus is breathtaking. He's wearing a casual gray jacket with a plain cotton t-shirt and jeans, accentuating his fit legs, an emanation of Scandinavian minimalism. The colors bring out the cool sparkle of his eyes, and his blond hair brushing his shoulders frames his chiseled features.

"Celeste, I'm so glad you made it," he declares, his accent making Jasmin curiously cock a brow, "and who is your charming friend?" He turns to her. Jasmin beams, flirtatiously stretching her hand. He distractedly squeezes it and faces me without bothering to wait for her answer.

"I would love to show you my... more private work," the artist declares and leads me through the crowd, leaving my disappointed friend behind.

Soft warm light fills the side hall he takes me to, his large warm palm on the small of my back sending sweet trembles along my spine. I can feel the pressure he applies, his confidence, his desire to be alone with me in this room.

These paintings are more intimate and more abstract. As if Diaphonus was trying to perpetuate an idea, an unclear concept. Feminine curves and tangled bodies, hands squeezing flesh in a bruising caress, lips open in ecstasy, tongues entwined. There is a striking similarity between all the female faces, distorted by pleasure, and I gasp. Maybe I'm imagining it, but these models look a lot... like me! Indeed, the hair colors are different, yet the way their lips curve, the way their lashes flutter...

I turn to my host and find him smirking, his broad chest heaving mere inches away from me.

His eyes make my knees weak. Rivulets of pristine water trickling down alpine glaciers, clouds over Caribbean waters, lighthouse lights over dangerous tropical reefs, inviting pools, tempting with the promise of bliss. He cocks his head, watching me, and I forget what I am about to ask. I raise to my toes, lips half-open, ready to follow this siren call, to dive into these clear depths, and he leans in.

Heat pools between my legs, my body forgetting all the warnings, ignoring my "too pretty means trouble" motto. The hot huff of his breath brushes my face, when—

A dramatic, annoying clapping in the background. The real world sucks me back in, and it's beyond frustrating.

"Diaphonus, old friend! I am so proud of you! Do you see? You made it! And who is this?" The male voice turns husky at the last syllable.

A disappointed growl escapes Diaphonus as he looks away from me.

"Tarcyll! I see you made it, too, friend, even without an invitation." The word *friend* sounds forced, and I turn around to face the intruder.

Sweet Lord. What is it with me and the men I'm meeting lately? Is the Universe compensating me for decades of lame relationships, mediocre sex, and below-average-looking boyfriends?

This specimen is as tall as Diaphonus, a solid six foot six at least, with inky, messy, cropped hair, pierced ears, dark eyes, and lashes so thick it appears as if he wears kajal. Strange, tattooed symbols crawl from the visible part of his chest up to his neck, covering most of his skin. The sleeves of his perfectly fitting white shirt, which screams quiet luxury, are rolled up, displaying inked, sinewy muscles, a healthy tan, and a Patek Filipe watch. If Diaphonus would be the highlight of each Calvin Klein underwear show, this man was born to steer a yacht somewhere in the Mediterranean, sipping on a 2600-dollar bottle of champagne while models claw their faces over him.

Black eyes pierce mine, the right angle of his lip curling up, drawing my attention to his stubble, and he stretches out his hand.

"I'm Tarcyll. Nice to meet you. Don't mind Diaphonus. I'm pleased to witness the triumph of a friend."

I shake his warm, hard hand, wondering where he got those calluses. Fencing? Working out? Steering a ship?

"Celeste," I mumble when I notice a familiar flushed face in the background." And this is Jasmin, my friend," I add. The dark-haired man smiles wider, displaying predatory, unnaturally long, and sharp canines.

"A pleasure," he purrs, "Diaphonus, we are in for one hell of a night, old friend."

Jasmin calls them Ying and Yang. They're so different in manners and looks yet work well together somehow. After the pretentious mingling with the art society, we head to the nightclub owned by Tarcyll. It's my first ride in a Bugatti, and, honestly, it's a little tight for four. Jasmin sits beside the driver, and I'm squeezed into the backseat with Diaphonus. His hand casually rests on my thigh. The cocktails I downed make his touch appear natural. The shots of absinthe and some "secret ingredient" later mixed with a couple of pills I popped do not improve my judgment.

We sit in the VIP area, overlooking the dance floor, the lights flashing over skimpy, glittering dresses, seductive bare flesh, hungry eyes, and unruly hands. The music makes it impossible to hold a conversation, yet Jasmin sits next to Tarcyll on the luxurious, soft couch opposite us while I feel the firm heat of Diaphonus´ thigh pressed against mine.

My world spins as a waitress wearing only tassels on her nipples brings another round of shots and gracefully bends over to refill Tarcyll and Jasmin's glasses with Dom Perignon vintage, offering us a view of her transparent black thong.

She leaves, and my gaze shifts back to the couple at the other side of the table. Jasmin is kissing Tarcyll's neck, but his eyes, those black, bottomless wells holding a promise of sweet torment, delve into mine. He doesn't look away when my friend murmurs something in his ear and bites his earlobe. He only smiles wider, and his pearly fangs flash ominously.

Jasmin is under his spell. She shamelessly spreads her legs and moves her panties aside. I choke on my drink and leave a mental note to myself to speak to her about it tomorrow, yet what happens next drains all the blood from my brain and directs it to other regions.

Tarcyll's hand reaches between my friend's legs. I can clearly see the glistening rims of her sex, and it's impossible to look away, hypnotized by the moves of his digits circling her opening, gliding along her folds, then dipping into her slit. Jasmin gasps, throwing her head back, as the man slides his massive, ringed finger in and out of her drenched hole, his dark burning eyes locked with mine. I feel the heat of Diaphonus next to me, the warmth of his breath as he leaves a trail of soft kisses along my neck. I don't resist as he gently lifts me and places me on his lap, making sure I feel the massive bulge of his erection against my ass.

I stare as Jasmin's opening devours one, then two, of Tarcyll's fingers. Her breasts have slipped out of her dress, and she's rubbing her nipples.

The dancing crowds around us disappear, and the topless waitress knows better than to linger when her boss is occupied.

I turn to face Diaphonus and catch him staring, chest heaving, not at the shameless display unfolding before us but at me. His sapphire eyes are burning, his lips parted, and he looks like he's about to lose control.

I take a deep breath.

The joke's on you, Universe! My last boyfriend dumped me via text, and now these two twenty-out-of-tens are staring at me, drooling, while one is fondling my friend. This right here is my epic payback for all the ghosting, all my messages left on "seen" and unanswered, all the gray mediocrity of my life.

The air between us crackles with tension, as if the loud music, the flickering lights, and the heavy cocktail of perfume, sweat, and smoke disappear. It's only the four of us now, and the two men stare at me with an intensity that starts to feel unnerving.

are You hunted, Celeste. The words of my strange white-haired savior from the previous night echo in my mind.

Cool, graceful fingers brush along my jaw, and the blond artist tilts my face toward him. Sparks shower over us—I definitely had one shot too many—and suddenly his lips draw me in, a siren's call pulling the strings of desire I'm not even aware I had. Heat rushes between my legs, my breasts swelling with lust, and I part my lips. His large arms draw me to him, and his mouth crashes onto mine, the depths of his silvery irises consuming me.

I let his tongue explore my mouth, hot, daring, and curious, feasting on me and my desire while stars shower around us.

His flavor... so otherworldly and exquisite, so craved.

A rough pull shatters the moment, and I look up to a furious Tarcyll. It seems like our kiss has outraged him, and he has abandoned his ministrations, leaving a disappointed Jasmin sprawled on the velvet couch.

"You've glamoured her!" the dark-haired man barks, his hand subconsciously reaching to his left hip as if searching for a blade to draw. "How dare you glamour her?" he repeats in disbelief, his tone solidifying to a cool rage. Diaphonus rises, and the air around both men glows with tension. He is slightly taller than his dark-haired friend, yet he has the refined body shape of a professional swimmer with long, graceful limbs. Tarcyll is bulkier and, from what my hazy brain has witnessed, can move with a supernatural speed.

"You know why we don't use magic in public, Diaphonus." He pokes his chest with an accusing finger, "Are you that desperate that you use cheap tricks to snatch her away from me?"

What the hell?

"Glamoured me?" I try to grasp the meaning behind this word when security guards swarm the VIP area, alert and ready to act.

The tall Viking clenches his elegant fingers into fists, and I notice swarms of tiny lights gathering around them. I blame the shots.

"You know what's at stake, spymaster. And I will use all the tricks I have at my disposal," the blond man declares coldly, squaring his shoulders.

"Over my dead body, Priest."

What the actual hell?

They stare at each other, and I notice the first signs of hyperventilation just as my surroundings begin to spin. I have to run. Solitude is my only escape, my safe space.

Without a word, I leave the area and rush to the door, making my way through the security guards, pushing through bodies tangled in the primal rhythm of the music.

I need air; I need to get away from all these people. If these two men have a problem, I'd rather let them sort it out without me.

The autumn night welcomes me with darkness and a fresh waft of cool air promising relief. The parking lot is full of cars, and groups of people hang out at the entrance, smoking in groups, chatting, or making out.

Reminding myself of my therapist's instructions, I take several controlled breaths. The crescent of the moon lures me deeper into the parking lot, frowning upon my poor life choices.

What is happening with my well-controlled, dull, but safe life?

I walk away from the lights, the people, and those two strange men who threaten to destroy the fragile balance of my life, meandering between the rows of cars and sinking deeper into the shadows with no clear direction or plan.

Hasty steps echo behind my back, and I don't need to turn around to see who it is.

"Celeste," a dark, velvet voice calls to me, and I curse myself for leaving without my purse—my keys are inside, and I need my phone to get an Uber.

"Celeste, let's talk," the husky voice of his friend joins in from the open doorway.

I ignore them, taking a few swaying steps into the darkness at the far end of the parking lot, the cold night air biting my bare shoulders. Frantically considering my options, I'm about to turn around and head back to collect my things and Jasmin, who is clearly incapable of making rational choices, when it starts drizzling, my black dress quickly clinging to my body. It's freezing. Better get some air and return to fetch my things, hopefully both men have cooled off already.

Then a slight movement catches my attention.

Away from the neon lights, in the hazy darkness of the alleys beyond the last row of parked cars, something stirs.

A stray cat, or worse—probably a giant rat exploring the piles of trash.

Yet I somehow know it's something else. Dread squeezes my gut with an iron fist. The darkness thickens, the ink of the night becoming dense, and primal gloom pools at my feet, rippling around my ankles, rising to my waist like a black geyser. My jaw drops as it starts taking the shape of a blurry male figure.

Hasty footsteps clatter behind me, and Diaphonus protectively pulls me behind him, Tarcyll next to him, feet apart and firmly on the ground. A warrior's stance. His black brows are knit together, and he pulls out a gun. They bark at each other in a language I hear for the first time.

Tarcyll turns to me. "The Dreadful One is here, Celeste! On my command, run back to the club!"

I watch in disbelief how the condensed darkness forms an imposing male silhouette with massive black wings. His eyes—two flames among the shadows—fix on me, and I stumble, walking backward.

Tarcyll fires at the entity without causing any visible damage, while sparks gather in Diaphonus' palms and he throws a shimmering ball of energy toward the dark entity.

My jaw drops so low that I hear it click.

Am I in some dark and twisted version of Avengers?

There's no time to wonder what exactly was in those shots or if someone has spiked our drinks with something hallucinogenic. Maybe I'm just dreaming, or my body has finally rebelled against the onslaught of medications and alcohol I've subjected it to for years.

I leave these questions for a more fitting time and bolt between the cars, dead-set on reaching the club, grabbing my purse and my intoxicated friend, and getting the hell out of here.

Yet fate has other plans for me. The sound of an accelerating motorbike makes me whip my head just in time to jump aside and avoid getting hit by a familiar rider. Before I realize what's happening, he hops off the bike with superhuman agility, grabs me, and loads me onto the seat as he jumps back on.

"Hold on to me!" His voice thunders louder than the engine, and we speed off into the city night, followed by gunshots, muffled explosions, and shouts in that strange language.

The needles of the freezing wind and rain pierce my soaked skin, my hair glued to my face, and I hold on to my mysterious knight. It seems he is always there when things get rough. Is trouble following him, or is he by some miracle always around to save me, I wonder? Another question to ponder on later. For now, I'm grateful to be leaving that mess behind and for the warmth his broad back provides. Though the memory of the man I'm clinging to warning me *"I am the Hunter who found you first,"* whispers through my mind as he races us into the night.

CYRELL – THE WARRIOR

Another Hunter has used a spell on her, and the raw power in her veins responded; that is my guess. And her reaction was so powerful that it drew the attention of the Dreadful One. He is always there, lurking in the shadows, in the blurred contours of this world, waiting for the right moment to strike. And the other two Fae lit the beacon of magical light that drew his cold, restless eyes.

The magic within humans is rare, savage, and untamed. It clashes with their mortal nature like the surf crashing onto the steep rocks of the ocean shore. This collision echoes across the realm, and creatures, starved for magic, can hear it even from another continent.

It is a miracle that the Siphons have spared this world, yet I bet that it will catch their eyes as soon as they are done devouring my home.

I feel the human's arms around my waist, pale and shivering, her grasp loosening. It's too cold for her out here.

The rain picks up when I speed up through the night, but soon we reach one of the many hidden entrances to my hideout. I park the bike, hop off, and help her off the seat. I was right. She is glamoured. Her eyes glow unnaturally under the long, wet strands of hair glued to her face, and I smell her arousal. I clench my jaw, pondering who might have done this to her. Was it the high elf priest with the largest amount of magic at his disposal of all the Hunters? Or was it the spy?

The woman staggers, and I sling an arm around her waist. She is also intoxicated. Unclean.

I curse while I unlock the heavy service door leading down into the forgotten depths of the city, the only place I feel at ease.

I will have to cleanse her before attaching her to the Extractor and draining her magic. A mind blurred by spells or toxic substances is a lighthouse without light; it is still there but useless. She is of no use to me in this condition.

I drag her down the dusty stairs, rats dancing around our feet, spiderwebs, undisturbed for decades, draping over our shoulders.

We are crossing a sewer, and I suddenly feel her weight on my arm. Is it the drinks, the barbaric spell, or the miasma of the place that knocked her out? I sweep her in my arms and splash through the shallow water. The tunnels intertwine into a maze, but I follow the marks I have left, carefully avoiding the traps I have strategically placed.

Soon, I cross a stream of clear water, then a tiny oasis of moss and mushrooms marking the entrance to my hideout. Cerberus stands dutifully on guard. The soothing sounds of his engine when he approaches me, metallic tail wagging, is music to my soul.

He gently sniffs the loose hair of the unconscious human in my arms, and I tense up. Seeing his eight-inch steel teeth that can bite a head clean off so close to her delicate face makes me nervous. He notices my protectiveness and withdraws, and I enter my den.

I make my way between the piles of parts and machinery, through my exercise field, and reach my sleeping quarters, where I gently lay her on the bed and rub my chin thoughtfully.

I must keep her here until she sobers up enough for the Extractor. She is still dozing, her lavish breasts heaving, her simple black dress rolled up, exposing her thighs. Her silky skin, still wet from the rain, glistens in the dim candlelight. She has lost a shoe during our flight, and there is something endearing in her tiny toes and the arch of her foot. My gaze wanders up, and I feel dangerous flames rise below my stomach. Her hips are almost bare, and I devour the transparent black undergarment covering her sex. It's drenched with her arousal, and my fangs extend in response to the inviting scent. Other parts of me extend, too, yet I have enough self-discipline not to indulge in these tempting but dangerous thoughts. Mating with a dark elf would surely kill her, even if I hold back, as my kind is not known its gentleness.

We are survivors, warriors, the shadows of the Lower Lands, the last line of defense between Faëheim and the abode of the Dreadful One. Our women are sinewy and drained of color, the lack of light has turned them pale, and they emphasize their beauty with sparkling gems and clever makeup. Yet the beauty that lies before me does not need any garnets or emeralds to shine. It glows so brightly in the murky darkness that my heart squirms with longing. Her hair has the color of tree bark, her lips the crimson red of fresh blood, her lashes the ink of the moonless night, her cheeks the flush of fragile spring blossoms.

I debate tasting her, my tongue feeling the pins of my sharp fangs, it would be practical, as I would know precisely how tainted she is and how long it would take to purge the poison from her veins, but it would mark her as mine.

Mine.

Brow furrowed, I lean closer to her, her scent destroying any reason in my thoughts, when her lashes flutter, and our eyes meet.

The human looks around, startled, then she recognizes me and relaxes. I bitterly smirk when I realize that she trusts me. She trusts the one sent to consume her then discard her empty shell.

"Where am I? What happened?"

Those are questions I can work with.

"You are in my hideout," I answer simply, spreading my arms, and she curiously looks around. Cerberus always has the worst timing. He peeks behind my back, and her breath catches.

"He will not hurt you—he knows you are with me," I reassure her while the metallic beast with razor teeth, bronze bristles on his back, and various pipes and turning cogs in his torso cautiously approaches her and nuzzles her hand.

The human is scared but doesn't show it, and I'm impressed by her resolve.

"Go guard the entrance, Cerberus!" I shoo him, and my friend leaves with a hiss from his pipe that sounds like a disappointed sigh.

"What is he?" Celeste asks, and I can barely hide my smile. Instead of inquiring about my intentions, her eyes curiously wander around, studying the treasures I have hoarded like a cave dragon during my years in her world. "What do you want from me?"

"I am afraid that this is a longer story, Celeste." I gallantly stretch my hand to help her up and lead her to the massive dining table.

She throws herself over the meals I place in front of her, the salads and sauces, the crispy bread, the cakes, and the crunchy appetizers.

"Mmmh," she moans, eyes closed in appreciation, and this reaction sends a jolt of pleasure down my spine. "Where is this abundance coming from?"

"I believe you call it dumpster-diving." I grin as she chokes. "Humans tend to discard so many things that are still useful."

"Humans?" Her tone is flat, her brow furrowed, and she avoids my gaze, as one does when talking to a madman.

Well, it is time for the longer story, then. The woman will be attached to the Extractor in six hours and probably dead in seven, so she deserves the truth.

"There are... other worlds out there, Celeste, with ancient and powerful inhabitants. Humans are not alone."

"Like-like other planets?" she asks, a twirl in her tone betraying her doubts. Doubts about my sanity, I am sure.

"You can call it that. Faëheim, it is where I come from. A realm of wonders and magic."

"Faëheim, like Fae? Like Faeries?" Her delicate eyebrows arch. I nod. Humans turned out to be more intelligent than I expected. Their fascinating technology, their theories of the universe, and the path of the firmament spheres, even if not entirely accurate.

"Like that, yes. Our kind left a trace in your folklore, yet we lost interest in the dealings of your people ages ago." She pierces me with those eyes, the color of autumn leaves carried by a mountain stream, and I feel that pull, that dangerous thirst again. Not to mention the uncomfortable shift in my pants.

"And now you are here again? You and that strange mechanical creature."

"Cerberus is my mount and a loyal friend. He has been with my family for generations..." My voice trails off as I remind myself that I should be more reserved. She will be dead soon. No need to fraternize.

"Who are you? And why are you here?" she shoots, trying to keep her tone calm, though the last syllable sounds squeaky. Admirable, though.

"They call me Cyrell. Cyrell Lancebearer." I proclaim this as if ancient dust from the tunnels of the Lower Lands swirl around us when my honorable name reverberates in this strange world. "My realm was invaded. The Siphons are consuming all magic in our world, our lifeblood. We are here to find a weapon, a way to oppose them."

"We?" She raises a brow, chewing on a broccoli flower.

"You have already met the other two Hunters. They were fighting the Dreadful One."

She nods in understanding, her gaze still dizzy from the alcohol. "Diaphonus and his tattooed friend are from your world too?" She leans her chin on her palm.

I nod. "Diaphonus the Fair and Tarcyll Nightshade are from Faëheim as well. From other kingdoms." It seems like I have confirmed something she has already suspected.

"And you are hunting what, exactly?" I study her with concern. How would she take the truth? "What is my role in all this?" she insists.

There it is. The moment I have dreaded. Fae cannot lie; every human child knows this. It is our deal with the Crystal Serpent, I guess. We are blessed with almost unlimited power, but we must be fair and honest while wielding it. I put my hands on the table and tense up.

"You have something precious, Celeste. Pure and primal magic, directly drawn from the source. You call to us, the magic-sensitive beings, and we crave the power that sings in your body."

"So you are hunting *me*," Celeste whispers, and I nod. I wish I could change the situation and her fate, yet she is the Anchor, our only hope. "And the Dreadful One, is he after me too?"

"Yes."

She is pale, and I can see that her muscles strain. Her foot slips out of her single shoe. She is preparing to run.

"And why am I here? With you?"

I sigh.

"My Elders have charged me to extract the magic essence from you with this device." I look at the Extractor, and she follows my gaze. Indeed, the apparatus must appear terrifying to her human eyes. A box of solid bronze, tangled cables ending in cruel needles or hungry metal jaws, resembling gaping bear traps.

Celeste bolts to the closest door. It is as I feared. I will have to use violence. I follow her, aware that she will get lost in the dark and deadly labyrinth outside. I breach the distance between us with a few steps and find her feeling her way into the gloom beyond the door.

My eyesight is designed for this, so I can perfectly see her trembling, slender silhouette, her pale skin, and the sharp piece of glass she is pressing against the tender skin of her neck when she hears my steps. She is taking sharp, shallow breaths, and I know that in such an aggravated state, she could harm herself.

"I have something valuable, you said. One more step, and I will slit my throat."

"Come back with me, Celeste. It is more dangerous out here than you think. It is a place where people discard things, hoping them never to be found again."

The human shakes her head.

I rub my temples. The vision of her bleeding out at the bottom of the sewer unnerves me, and I need her healthy and sober for the Extractor.

Out of desperation, I use a dirty trick just like Diaphonus. Nothing magical, though, pure nature.

How do male dark elves attract females in the eternal gloom of the Lower Lands? With pheromones. We have the most disarming, potent pheromones in all Faëheim, and mine could drive each female mammal within a mile in heat.

It would give me an edge, and I could convince her to drop that glass and her ridiculous plan.

So, I cross my arms, smirk confidently, and do my thing.

She freezes. Her nostrils flare, and her long thick eyelashes flutter. Then she drops the glass.

In other circumstances, I would have laid my claim on her. The temptation is so strong that I see red. My fangs elongate, and I breathe in her alien, intoxicating scent. Like an exotic fruit, ripe for tasting, like a well-aged liquor, like a sweet perfume lingering in the air. I salivate.

The woman's eyes glitter, and she staggers toward me. I can smell the chemical adjustments in her body when it processes my message.

She approaches me slowly; her pupils dilate, and she halts just an inch away from my heaving chest. I grab her hand and prepare to lead her back, when she props herself on her toes and kisses me.

It is a tiny, harmless kiss on my chin, as she is much shorter and cannot reach my lips, yet my reactions are faster than my senses, and I respond. I lean in, brush my lips on her neck, grazing her satin skin with my fangs. She moans and presses herself into me, and I pull her closer, craving her warmth. Her eyes seek out mine; her lips parted, an unspoken question lingering in the air.

It is wrong, and a distraction to my mission, yet my perfectly trained and disciplined body cannot resist. I realize that a mortal would barely survive mating with a dark elf. Humans are so fragile they couldn't endure such a union with any magical being. And yet the power of her blood, the magic in her core, calls to mine, a mighty primal song that I cannot resist. My whole being is drawn to her, to her otherness; I am aching for contact, my arousal already visible under my leathers, and I capture her lips in a rough, bruising kiss.

My tongue explores the depths of her delicious mouth, savoring her flavor, demanding surrender. It's not enough, and I grab a fistful of her hair, drawing her even closer, if that is possible, while my other hand roams over her body. Those curves...

The instant my palm cups her breast's supple rounded flesh, my mind goes blank. The little human taunts me and leans into my touch, molding her warm frame to mine. A warning rumble escapes my chest, my fangs aching, craving to sink into her flesh.

This has to end now, or it will go very, very wrong. With the last spark of common sense, I sweep Celeste off her feet, swing her over my shoulder, and carry her back to my hideout. The scent of her arousal just inches from my face, the rounding of her backside under my palm, is so intense that I feel my thick shaft throbbing.

Before she can react, I kick the door open, throw her on the bed, and with one swift pull, take off my belt and use it as a restraint. With my large hand at her neck, I pin her to the bed while pulling her arms up and tying them to the headboard. She watches me through half-lidded eyes, assuming this is some kind of foreplay. I whirl about the room and search for some tape for her legs. Touching her bare skin, seeing her helpless at my feet, stokes the flames inside me to an all-consuming fire. My ache for her is so overwhelming that I contemplate betraying my peoples' hopes for an instant of bliss inside her. The Elders have chosen the wrong hero...

I know that I have to run. Otherwise, I'll give in to this dark-haired temptation and ruin my peoples' chance for a normal life.

I finally find some discarded tape and tie her ankles, brushing my fingers over her smooth skin, and she purrs in delight, squeezing her thighs. Our eyes are locked, and she can read all the dark instincts rearing their monstrous heads inside me. Oh, how I crave ripping this wretched gown apart, sinking my fangs into the sensitive flesh of her lush breasts, whose nipples strain beneath the fabric, and burying myself to the hilt into her intense mortal heat. Yet I know better.

At that point, the woman senses something is off and starts pulling on the restraints.

I rise and leave my hideout with quick steps, not looking back, fleeing the sweet poisonous promises of her body. I give Cerberus an order to guard her and disappear into the gloomy labyrinth of my new home. I will be back in the morning to commence the extraction.

I lose myself in the darkness, then wrap my fingers around my thick cock. Visions of Celeste bare and spread before me, her heavy breasts bouncing with my every thrust, torment me. My thirst is not quenched when I spurt my seed into the darkness, and the tunnels echo my roar.

I hunger for more.

CELESTE- THE ANCHOR

All my attempts to free myself remain futile.

My captor knew what he was doing.

Who is he really, and how did I end up in this mess? Am I at the mercy of some psychotic serial killer who likes to taunt his victims with fantastic stories?

Yet I believe him. The last days' events were way too weird to chalk it all up to randomness.

I look around. The warm light of the candles and lanterns reflects on the piled-up parts and machinery. It seems like the workshop of a steampunk-obsessed engineer who also enjoys swordsmanship and martial arts.

The metallic behemoth my captor called Cerberus is nowhere to be seen; it probably waits outside, following Cyrell's order.

What is wrong with me to throw myself at him without restraint? Nobody had ever kissed me like that. Diaphonus' kisses held the promise of a tender and devoted lover, but Cyrell´s were the claim of a conqueror, of a ruthless warlord. Squeezing my thighs together, I feel my panties dampen at the thought of him. Surely he is one of the most attractive men I have seen in my whole life, yet that behavior is so not me. I was running away from him, terrified by his cold and menacing demeanor and that evil machine he called the

Extractor, but suddenly, something changed. I think there is a name for that. Stockholm syndrome. Or was it some magical Fae trick?

A loud rumble reverberates under the rough concrete ceiling, and I freeze. The heavy fire door at the room's far end flies open, and two familiar silhouettes burst in. Diaphonus and Tarcyll, still wearing the same clothes from the nightclub, spot me immediately. Stumbling over the piles of clutter and books strewn on the bare concrete floor, they rush toward the bed I am tied to.

Relief is the last thing I expect to feel when I see these two, who bring nothing but havoc into my life. Yet they are a far better option than the white-haired maniac who makes my sensitive parts twitch on command but fills my heart with icy terror. And an odd, unhealthy curiosity. The combination seems contradictory to my body, as I feel my nipples stiffen again.

Right on time to draw the hungry gaze of Tarcyll.

While Diaphonus scans the surroundings, he takes a moment to savor my restrained body, his dark eyes clouding with desire.

"Hurry!" his blond friend urges him, and he loosens the belt restraining my wrists. I rub my irritated skin while he works on my feet. Then I hear metal paws carrying a one-ton body galloping our way.

Tarcyll turns around to face the metal beast who just entered the hideout with a hiss of steam. He pulls his gun out and opens fire before I can open my mouth and scream. Diaphonus throws something like a smoke bomb, and suddenly a thick haze enshrouds my surroundings.

Panicked, I pull on the tape to free my feet, cursing my savior, who spent too much time staring at me instead of releasing me. Thank God, the duct tape gives in.

I feel my way around to the door I used for my first escape, wincing at the sounds reverberating behind my back—scraping of metal against concrete, heavy thuds, gunshots, clanking of steel. I'm not sticking around to see who will win. I'm also not sure who to root for.

The underground tunnel wraps me in heavy, suffocating darkness, and a distant reek of sewage water stings my nose. My feet splash in invisible puddles, and tiny bodies brush around my ankles. I press a palm against my mouth to choke a scream. *Rats!* Most likely rabid. Still a better option than going back to that room. What expects me there? The crazy pack calling themselves "Hunters"? The aggressive metal monster the size of a small car?

There should be a way out, a tunnel leading to the surface. The noise of the clash and the gunshots fades behind my back. I can hear flowing water somewhere ahead. Short of options, I decide to follow the stream. It's what survivors do in the wild; surely the same logic applies here?

Murky light filters through some openings in the walls high above my head. At least I can see where I'm going. The tunnel widens, trickles of water gathering in the middle of the floor, forming the lazy rivulet I follow. The bottom is slippery, and I shudder with disgust. The lukewarm sluggish water reaches up to my bare ankles. I don't flinch anymore at the presence of the rats. They stare at me with beady glowing eyes but keep their distance.

Heaps of trash litter the floor. Random objects like plastic toy parts, glass bottles, cutlery, and paper tangle into surreal monstrosities that look alive in the scarce light. I tread carefully; cutting my bare feet here would bring me a nasty infection.

A place where people discard things, hoping never to be found again. I remember the words of Cyrell, and a chill crawls down my spine. Who knows what lurks in these depths? What kind of beasts—far more terrifying than rats—have established their domain here? A draft of cool air and an impossible stench hits me when the rivulet turns into a wide, slow creek, the dark waters stretching from wall to wall. I press my back against the sticky, humid masonry and suppress the urge to vomit as I move forward. The heavy waters are getting deeper, touching my mid-calf with unclean fingers. Just a few more feet to scout what lies ahead. If there is no safe path, I will retrace my steps and take another tunnel I passed earlier. The stench brings tears to my eyes, and I brave my way through the repulsively warm water, trying not to contemplate all the diseases flourishing in these unsanitary conditions. A cockroach of terrifying size scatters over my hand, and I scream.

My voice rushes down the hidden depths, gains momentum, and bounces back, multiplied by unseen tunnels and niches ahead. Then silence reigns in. Blood-curdling, unnatural silence, which makes me take a hesitant step back. As if something has heard me. And then my shin bumps into something. Startled, I look down, trying to determine if I am hurt.

It's a stroller. A bulky baby stroller, like those used in the nineties, its bright colors are hidden under layers of dirt. The water ripples around it, each splash revealing rags and mud caught in its body. Some pale sphere draws my attention, and I take a step closer to take a look, in some morbid delirium. Is this a bowling ball?

Oh

My

God.

I stumble backward, my jaw dropping in a silent scream of terror. It's a skull.

A female skull, judging by the long strands of hair floating around it, mummified hands still clutching the stroller.

A place where people discard things... Cyrell warned me.

What kind of secrets do these tunnels hold? What kind of tragedies have these walls witnessed?

A freezing draft makes the hairs on my arms stand up. This unnatural silence, as if I'm in a vacuum bubble, suffocates me. Reeking mist pools at my feet. It ripples and climbs, covering the dreadful remains.

Something is wrong. I can't say how I know this, but it vibrates in every single cell of my body.

Run, a warning stirs my guts.

Save yourself, the draft beckons.

Yet I stand petrified, eyes wide in terror, watching a phantom rise from the murky water.

I have heard stories of vengeful spirits at sleepovers with friends, and I've seen my share of horror movies. I consider myself an expert in all things spooky. Yet this... this is something else.

And when a pale figure of a decaying, skinny woman rises just three feet away from me, her eyes black wells of unspeakable pain, dark blood oozing from the multiple stabs on her chest, I know I have to stay calm.

Yet primal fear grips me in its tarry tentacles, and I retreat.

"You cannot take my baby!" The jaw of the apparition opens, releasing a swarm of flies, and I retreat cautiously, the thick water deeper, swirling around my hips, the stream getting stronger, pulling me in.

"You cannot take her!" Her blood-curdling scream forces me to take a couple more steps into the deceiving water. I feel the bottom slipping underneath my bare feet, and the current pulls me into a black river, its raging waters thundering under the low ceiling.

"Give me back my *babyyyy!*" the howl borders on ultrasound, when I realize I must fight for my life. The current is dragging me into utter darkness. I struggle to keep my head over the thick, pungent water.

"Help!" I squeak, but the waves swallow it.

So this is how it ends, is my last thought, when my body is hurled against a metal grate. A flash of light is the last thing I see when my head hits the bars hard.

CELESTE – THE ANCHOR

I wake up to something warm and moist gently scraping my nose. Is there a giant dog licking me? When I open my eyes, I meet the concerned sapphire gaze of Diaphonus, removing the dirt from my face with a hot, wet towel. I'm wrapped in cozy blankets like a giant stinking burrito.

Some soothing vibration shakes me, a calming noise in the surrounding that tempts me to go back to sleep.

"Where am I?" I choke on a wave of vomit after I sense the terrible taste in my mouth. Visions of the horror in the sewers flood my mind.

"We're on our way to Cuba. We're taking you somewhere safe," Tarcyll explains briefly, peeking behind Diaphonus' broad back.

I blink a few times and look around. White leather seats, polished surfaces, clean lines, and bright sunshine behind the round windows. I'm in a private jet. Terror squeezes my throat.

"You can't take me to Cuba! My apartment... my job... my cat!"

"Jasmin is taking care of all that," Tarcyll croons soothingly, the rolled-up sleeves of the white shirt revealing his tattooed forearms. "Diaphonus called her. She fetched your purse from the nightclub and will care for the cat. For the rest: your boss knows you need some time off due to a family situation…"

The blond artist wipes my face, and I try to jerk away, only to realize the tight seatbelt holds me into place.

"Am I your captive? What is happening?" I demand, trying to figure out if I want to back away or lean into the warmth of his palm. Why is this man so devilishly handsome?

"You are not a captive, Celeste." Diaphonus´ attention is now on my neck, and he is scrubbing the dirt above my collarbone while I try to calm my breath, "but you must understand that you need our protection."

"I guess that tunnel dweller has probably told you already who we are and why you're so important to all Faëheim." Tarcyll's voice fades when he lifts the curtain at the bottom of the cabin and disappears into the galley. "You are the most powerful Anchor since the beginning of the Siphons´ invasion." He reappears with two glasses and hands me one. Whiskey. Perfect. I down it in one go and wave to him to pour me more.

"Anchor?" I mumble, my throat still burning from the drink.

"A human gifted with magic. A chosen among millions. You are the key to the salvation of our people, Celeste." I feel Diaphonus 'fingers on my collarbone and below, tauntingly close to my breasts. Goosebumps appear beneath his electrifying touch, and I pray he doesn't notice. "Me and Tarcyll agreed to... cooperate, to keep you safe, because you drew the attention of another, far more dangerous and ruthless Hunter."

I open my mouth to inquire how they have reached an agreement about my destiny without involving me in the process when the dark-haired man returns with another drink.

"You react to our magic in a compelling way, Celeste. Your response to the weakest spell is like a signal flare into the void, and that lured the Prince of the Underworld himself, the one we call the Dreadful One." I immediately think of the demonic figure that landed on top of my car and the creepy black mist in the parking lot. And the phantom in the sewers? Probably also him.

"I react to your magic?" I ask, still unable to understand. Diaphonus blushes and looks away at this question while his friend grins smugly.

"Or more like *his* magic." He points accusingly at the blond man, who looks back at me like a kid caught with his hand in the cookie jar.

"My friend glamoured you, Celeste." Tarcyll smiles smugly and hands me the drink. I sip the amber liquid, savoring the smoky taste.

"Glamoured me?" I blink. I think I'm a little slow today. Not a surprise after the recap of the day: a demon is after me, a white-haired weirdo with a Transformers dog kidnapped me, and the ghost of a dead mother tried to drown me.

"He put a spell on you that made him appear irresistibly attractive to you, attempting to put you in his power," Tarcyll finishes with a note of evil triumph.

I pant, outrage choking me. "You mean like the creeps spiking girls´ drinks in the bars?"

Diaphonus looks at me warily. His broad shoulders hang helplessly. I want to scream at him, yet simultaneously, I wonder why a man like him would use such a trick. He is gorgeous and I was ready to… never mind.

"I am sorry, Celeste, I should not have done that, yet it was the only way to interrupt them—"

"He was just jealous that your eyes were on me that night, Celeste," Tarcyll casually adds and sits next to me.

"Her eyes were not on you, you mutt, but on her friend, who was being defiled—" Diaphonus´ knuckles turn white. Here they go again.

"I'm sorry if what you saw was disturbing for your celibate High Priest eyes, yet I assure you it was consensual and that women enjoy my attentions—"

"Enough!" I shout, startling them. They immediately cease their bickering and look back at me.

"If you knew what the Dreadful One is capable of, Celeste, you would beg to stay with us," the blond man says soothingly. Wait, did Tarcyll call him a High Priest?

"At least until we figure out what to do," Tarcyll adds, his inked fingers turning the crystal whisky glass. "I have a safe house near Varadero. He will not be able to track us there unless we use magic. And it will take Cyrell a while to find us. So, rest now, and we will figure something out after."

"There was that... angry spirit in the sewers. She was asking about her baby. Was it a trick of this Dreadful One?" My voice still trembles when I remember the ghost.

Both Fae exchange looks, and I feel there is more to my question, something they don't wish to discuss.

"Since the Siphons attacked and we've started our hunt here, we have noticed that magic in your world grows more abundant. Paranormal activities are not as seldom as decades ago." I narrow my eyes in suspicion. Are they taking me for a fool?

"You mean that ghosts and the stuff of legends are becoming real?" Why am I so surprised? I saw what I saw.

"They've always been real, Celeste. There are just more of them now. Your world is changing. But we should all get some sleep now." Tarcyll wraps up the conversation.

I turn my face to the clouds, reflecting the sunlight like mother-of-pearl. With a demon after me and a mysterious sewer-dweller who wants to drain my magic by attaching me to an unknown torture device, the idea of flying to a tropical island for a spontaneous vacation with these two doesn't sound too bad.

The lights dim, and both men withdraw to the bottom of the cabin. I pull the window blind down and snuggle in the blankets. My tired mind is lulled into restless sleep by the alcohol and the monotonous roar of the engine.

The pull of the jet brakes wakes me up.

We climb into a massive SUV with dark windows that is expecting us on the tarmac. Tarcyll chivalrously covers my shoulders with his jacket, yet the hot concrete scorches my bare feet. It seems like an eternity since I last had shoes on.

The driver pauses for an instant when he sees me, but the sunglasses conceal his reaction. I can imagine his disapproving frown, but he doesn't ask questions and treats us respectfully.

He speeds up on poorly maintained streets surrounded by dusty tropical vegetation, and in a couple of hours, he pulls off onto an inconspicuous black road. The SUV halts before a concrete wall with an automatic portal.

The tall walls and the unblinking eyes of multiple cameras make it appear like a fortress. Or more like a prison.

Tarcyll's business must be running great, I conclude, admiring the colonial-style mansion hidden among a lush, well-maintained garden.

I get a room with a pool view and forget the mess I'm in for a few blissful minutes.

Dinner is served in the garden, next to the pool. I haven't seen any staff and wonder if my host is doing all the cooking and serving by himself.

Lanterns glow warmly among the fuchsia splendor of the bougainvillea branches, forming a canopy above my head.

Candlelight makes the red wine sparkle like ruby, and the piles of cheese, appetizers, fruits, and pastries glimmer in the tropical night like some Renaissance cornucopia.

The dancing shadows carve the angles of the Fae faces even sharper. Both men interrupt their muffled conversation and look up at me. Two sets of eyes that glimmer predatorily in the tropical twilight take in my white cotton dress. The wardrobe in my bedroom is full of designer clothes, all in a casual holiday style, and I try not to ponder whom they belong to.

Two sudden flashes of movement, and they loom over me, dwarfing me with their presence. Something savage glimmers in their eyes, and I lick my lips, fascinated and terrified.

Mouth-watering visions of Diaphonus clearing off the table with a single sweep while Tarcyll bends me over it flood my mind, and I feel a tug of desire between my legs. Have they just glamoured me again?

My dark-eyed host seems to notice it, too, as his nostrils flare, and he smirks, pulling a chair for me, "I hope everything is to your taste, Celeste."

That emphasis on "everything" is dubious and makes me steal another glimpse of their open shirts, displaying the rugged curves of their chests, the promising curls of their lips, and their muscular thighs as both retreat to their seats.

Diaphonus poorly conceals a grin and grabs an empty glass. "Wine?"

I spread the napkin over my knees, looking down to hide my blush. I can't shake the feeling that I'm an open book to these two, that they have somehow sensed my arousal.

"Do you have something stronger?" I blurt. I don't drink alcohol to relax or soothe my thoughts. Just like my mother, I drink to black out and escape. And vodka or tequila is the shortcut to getting wasted.

"Rum?" He raises a brow, and I nod.

They watch me fill my plate in silence. The soft bubbling of the pool pump and the orchestra of crickets are the only sounds in the warm night. We eat in silence.

Diaphonus clears his throat when I fill my second plate with Piccadillo. "Tarcyll and I have come to terms," he starts, and the latter nods in agreement, "to offer you a deal." He pauses, and both stare at me. I force myself to continue chewing, though the lump stuck in my throat makes swallowing difficult. A deal with Faeries? Isn't it what all fairy tales warn us about? I put the fork down hesitantly. "Oh, okay. Let's hear it, then."

"We will work together," he points at Tarcyll with his head, "to harvest your magic without harming you. We will find a way. Together. You will stay with us here, and we will protect you with our lives. And when we are done, you are free to go."

Wait a minute—

"We will not hurt you, Celeste," Diaphonus adds, lifting his wine glass and leaning back in the rattan chair. I quickly scold myself and avert my gaze from the gilded pecs peeking out of his casually unbuttoned linen shirt. Yet he catches me, and a faint smirk ripples his face. "But to find a safe way to draw this power from you and to help our dying world, we need your cooperation."

Wait a fucking minute—

"We will not use any spells on you or force you into anything that you don't agree to." Tarcyll crosses his arms in front of his sculpted chest. Images of unseen creatures and mysterious symbols twirl along his forearms, tempting me to speculate what the rest of his body looks like. "But we need time and your consent to pull this off."

I down the rum in one gulp and look back at them. Tarcyll's dark brow is arched, and he's playing with his tall glass, the ring on his finger catching my eye. An uninvited flashback of him and Jasmin hits me with the most miserable timing ever. Diaphonus´ muscles are tense as he watches me, his fingers rubbing the blond stubble on his cheek.

"So, the deal is that I help you find a way to extract my magic without hurting me and getting me killed in the process, and then I'm free to go?"

They nod simultaneously.

"And no more glamour?" Both confirm enthusiastically.

"What about your creepy white-haired friend with the steampunk dog and the demon you call the Dreadful One?" I ask, pouring myself another rum. I try to sound calm and keep my mind off what would happen if I had another episode without my medications.

Tarcyll crosses his massive arms behind his neck. The eerie creatures on his skin look like they're moving, "Without your magic, you're a mere mortal to them, and they will leave you alone. And so will we," he declares with convincing confidence.

Is it normal to feel a sting of disappointment after this revelation? What's wrong with me? Am I secretly enjoying being hunted by these powerful and gorgeous Fae males?

"I accept your deal!" I slam the empty rum glass on the table. The humid heat speeds up the intoxication, and the night garden spins around me. Terrified of losing control and probably doing something incredibly stupid, I stumble toward my room without further explanation.

I throw myself on the bed and listen to the serenade of crickets and the soft conversation both males hold in their enticing lilting language.

Each word holds power and charges the air around me, the melodic syllables caressing my skin, brushing my nipples, tickling my thighs.

Before I realize what I'm doing, my fingers push my lacy white panties aside and dip between my drenched folds. The muffled whispers become exploring hands, tongues hungry for a taste, and I climax quickly. The forbidden vision of Tarcyll and Diaphonus taking me simultaneously is so vivid that it fills the room. Then the rum drags me into the inky abyss of restless sleep.

TARCYLL – THE SPYMASTER

The night breeze wafts Celeste´s arousal as soon as she withdraws to her chambers. The priest senses it, too, his brow covered with sweat, and he excuses himself. Oh, I know the dark desires that taint his pristine soul; I know that he will please himself aggressively tonight, imagining taking her—claiming her in all possible ways.

I know because I do the same. And while I pump my rigid cock, visualizing rubbing it between her lavish breasts, I realize that this woman is the kindling to start a fire that could consume our entire world.

I find her swimming in the pool the following day. For some minutes, I just stand there and watch her frolic in the water, perplexed by her simple mortal joy of being. She savors the warm caress of the morning sun and the water's soothing touch. Her body is lean and glowing under the crystal surface, and she's wearing the revealing bikini I left in her room. This observation alone makes me hard.

I join her in the pool, unsure of my intentions. Our meeting with Diaphonus is after lunch. I feel her curious gaze on me when I dive and relish in the scent of her curiosity when I break the turquoise surface.

I'm aware of the effect my appearance has on human females. It's not only my imposing height and the mystery of the sacred tattoos covering my body but the otherness in my essence, that hint of barely leashed power under my skin.

She hurriedly leaves the pool, rewarding me with a delicious view of her backside, glittering water drops trickling down her curves. Will she touch herself again, thinking of me?

I need release before the meeting, as I cannot think straight. I head to the bathroom next to the pool, and visions of Celeste invade my mind. I barely contained myself not to rip that wretched bikini to reveal her center, pink and open, begging for me.

I find them both in the kitchen later. Celeste leans over an open book at the marble island, Diaphonus behind her, his arms encasing her, palms resting on the polished stone surface, his blond strands touching the top of her head. I notice how close his hips are to her rear. I bet she feels his heat through the airy fabric of her dress. He looks over his shoulder, and our eyes lock. I frown when I notice how the smug blond devil inhales the scent of her hair deeply before reluctantly pulling away.

Diaphonus the Fair. Countless Fae males and females lust after him. My own king summoned three youths bearing a striking resemblance to him to his harem. In my world, he is the closest thing to a sex symbol. High elves are just as promiscuous as all the Fae, known for their stamina in bed. Some priests take celibacy vows, and I speculate if that's his case. I have never seen him touch a woman since we've been in this realm, and he had plenty of opportunities. Yet his dilated pupils and the noticeable bulge in his pants are evidence of his carnal desires. Will the presence of our human guest make him rethink his abstinence from pleasures of the flesh?

Celeste notices me and smiles. My heart skips a beat.

The meeting kicks off with debates about the options we have. Diaphonus holds extensive lectures and explains to her how magic works. We chuckle more than once—so many things that are obvious to us and common knowledge for all Fae are new to our guest.

"Why do you call the humans with magic Anchors?" Celeste inquires, and I furrow my brow. Yet another chance for the priest to outshine me with some sophisticated rhetoric.

"Because people with such powers anchor your realm to the body of the Serpent. Without them, your world would float to the lower dimensions, and this is a place nobody wants to be," he concludes enigmatically, and I have the urge to slap the smirk from his beautiful face.

"What happened with the rest of these people, the other Anchors?" She shuffles nervously on the tall stool behind the kitchen island.

"The magical power in their veins drove most of them mad, many harmed themselves, and a couple fell victim to other Hunters."

"Do you mean Cyrell?" she asks, paling. So, the high elf has enlightened her about what our friend from the tunnels is and his experiments with human blood. Or she has guessed it herself.

"We would never do something that barbaric to you, Celeste," I reassure her, leaning on the cool stone. While I fully mean it, I don't know what options we have, as all of Diaphonus' research has not provided a solution yet. And time is precious. How long will the shifters´ armies of Verdant hold? The mighty wards etched in the centennial oaks of the Northern Forest failed, and the magic-devouring demons swarmed the sacred lands. My king, striding proudly in the form of a golden-furred mountain lion, led the knights to the tormented woodlands. I cannot fail. I cannot betray their trust.

Days pass, and all the priest's books, magic, our speculations, and lengthy debates have not brought any progress. The hope to save Faëheim without harming Celeste fades with each passing day, while the tension between us three becomes nearly palpable.

We distract ourselves at the pool to avoid the chilling recognition that we have no solution, that the majestic, deadly power locked in that tempting fragile body cannot be harnessed without destroying it.

Time is running short, and I notice Diaphonus getting impatient. I wonder if he is up to something.

We spend the morning swimming, and our frolicking in the water is so pure, so full of innocent joy, that I almost forget how hopeless the situation is.

Funny how fate has ways to change the course and sink the proudest, sturdiest ships.

I feel the heavy tentacles of the storm long before it appears, and yet I am too absorbed in our game with Celeste to warn her.

"If you come to Verdant when this is all over, I am afraid I'll have to compete with the king himself and all the knights of the court for your attention!" Mesmerized, I watch her freckles drown in a wave of scarlet when she blushes. I notice how her gaze brushes my inked stomach muscles, tempered by ages of swordplay and rigorous training. We are at our fourth margarita, and I feel my length painfully straining against my shorts. The idea of pouncing on her, pinning her tender body beneath mine, and capturing her lips suddenly seems completely sane. The beast beneath my skin craves release.

The rain saves me—the heavy drops surprisingly cool, and before we can seek shelter, it catches us in its gray net.

Anticipation tingles my spine. The change in the weather just a harbinger of other, far more lethal changes.

CELESTE – THE ANCHOR

The strands of my long hair are thoroughly soaked, and I'm sure my lips turn a funny shade of blue.

"We need to warm you up, Celeste. Follow me," Tarcyll declares, his eyes lingering on my pebbled nipples, which push against my bikini. I part my lips to object, but the chattering of my teeth says it all. He reaches out and wraps a fluffy towel around my shoulders. His scent and proximity hit me like the most potent shot I've ever had, the brush of his fingers over my bare shoulders, the heat of the massive bulge between his legs, I try to look away, but my eyes are drawn to his aggressive erection as if tied to an invisible thread.

I feel a familiar twitch at the apex of my thighs, and without thinking, I squeeze them tight to create some friction. God, I can come only by looking at him.

His beautiful lips curl in a roguish smile that makes me blush ferociously. He is a spymaster in a Fae court, Diaphonus mentioned before, an expert manipulator, skilled in reading his foes. To him, I am but an open book. Let's hope I'm an intriguing one.

"Do you know what a hammam is?" Tarcyll asks casually, his hands still on my shoulders, guiding me toward the house. His tattooed skin glistens, the hieroglyphs and creatures on his skin buzzing with power. His massive sapphire ring brushes my cheek. For some twisted reason, the memory of Jasmin's pussy devouring his finger all the way to the ring pops up. I squeeze my eyes shut.

"No," I squeak.

"It is a Turkish steam bath, perfect for warming up and relaxing. It is exactly what you need now," he rasps and licks his lips. He looks at me hungrily, his eyes darting between my lips and my breasts. The fact that he's not even trying to conceal his desire is so arousing that all my reason and sanity remain outside in the rain. Dear Lord.

I nod and let him guide me, pondering if I'm under a spell or tricked in some eerie Fae way. Power seeps through his fingers as they wrap around mine, yet I know he would not risk exposing our hideaway with magic. Whatever is about to happen, I have only my own stupidity to blame.

We cross the green marble foyer and descend the stairs leading down into the depths of this palace. Thick aromatic candles burn in niches along the walls, and incense smokes in bronze vessels on the polished, black, granite floor. It looks like this place has its own spa.

Tarcyll releases my hand. We have arrived. He pushes a massive glass door and disappears in the thick aromatic steam that fills the room. I follow, filling my lungs with the soothingly warm air. Water murmurs in the steam-filled depths.

A few hesitant steps in, and the warmth relaxes me completely. My head is spinning—perhaps all the margaritas combined with the sudden heat make me dizzy. I head to the stone benches lined along the walls. The colorful mosaic stones are all drenched from the steam. There's no sign of my companion, though the vapors are so thick that I can barely see my own hands. I stretch out on the bench, soaking up the blissful humidity, and let the towel slip from my shoulders.

My nipples are still hard, and I feel my center dripping wet, the juices of my arousal leaking onto the warm marble surface. I can't stop thinking of Jasmin's pink flesh clenching around Tarcyll's finger as he was penetrating her, the heaving of her bare breasts, begging him to grope them. He was teasing her entrance with his massive ring—that must have felt amazing—and my face flushes even more as I brush my hands over my straining nipples. The way he was looking at me when he was fingerfucking my friend, his eyes full of hunger and dark promises.

Without consulting my brain, my fingers travel down to my slit, and I slightly spread my legs. Pulling my thong aside, I create full access to my twitching folds. I bite my lips and slowly circle my clit, then my fingers trail down, disappearing in my aching opening. A fragment of my mind wonders if Tarcyll is still around and if he can see me. Then I realize that I want him to see me. I close my eyes, imagining him watching me, pleasing himself, his tattooed muscles straining in the effort, sweat beading on his high brow, his handsome face distorted by the urge of his need, his massive dick salivating.

My fingers are frenetic as I defile myself feverishly, legs shamelessly spread, my middle finger knuckle deep in my pussy.

All my life, I was in control. Compensating for an irresponsible alcoholic mother, I guess. Shedding this false sense of control over my fate and future now feels liberating. Trembling in the waves of the orgasm, I celebrate my new-found freedom by doing something preposterous and utterly stupid. I let go of control and the pressure it brought into my life.

And I smile.

My therapist would be so proud.

My smile freezes when I feel a steely grip around my ankles. Tarcyll lifts and places my feet on the bench, spreading me wide and exposing me completely.

He growls as his gaze travels over my throbbing open slit, my need inviting him to fill me. I gasp but don't attempt to hide as he stands before me, tall and magnificent, still in his swimming shorts, the outline of his enormous cock seductively accentuated by the wet fabric.

He leans in as if reading my mind, and his finger enters me without warning. He curves it inside me to hit that special spot, that wicked massive ring rubbing my entrance. I got my wish.

The warm, ribbed metal rubs me with each movement, sending jolts of pleasure to every cell of my body. I moan like a whore, and he smirks, his face veiled by the steam.

"So tight and wet—" his voice is husky, his digit gliding in and out of me, and I press myself onto his hand. I clench around his finger, feeling an earth-shattering orgasm build up.

"Our people believe," he rumbles while untying his shorts with his other hand, "that a human female would likely not survive mating with a Fae male. Our bodies are too powerful, and the magic within us too intense for you to handle." I swallow, wondering if that is reason enough to stop.

His heavy, blasphemously large cock is out, only inches away from my mouth, and honestly, I don't care about his warning. I want this so much that I'm willing to risk it. All I want is all my holes stretched by his hard length.

"Yet I had my share of pleasure with your people—" he continues, pleasing himself with firm strokes, "and there were no fatal endings yet. His dark smirk makes me whimper. "Quite the opposite; they seemed to enjoy it a lot."

Tarcyll withdraws his finger from my slit, and I hiss, disappointed, open, and needing.

He kneels before me, spreading my folds just in front of his face, and before I can react, he dips his tongue deep into my pussy without any warning, licking me on the inside. I squirm as he penetrates me in a way nobody has, his sharp white teeth grazing my clit, his hand pumping his cock.

Suddenly he withdraws his sinful mouth, and his eyes, so dark I see star clusters inside, delve into mine.

"I have wanted you since the moment I saw you," I take a sharp breath as his engorged, dripping head rubs at my entrance. A shameless moan escapes me at that promise of a really good stretch, "Since I felt your essence beckoning me. It is an irresistible call. One that very few Fae males could refuse."

He slowly enters me, his fingers pressing my thighs open, leaving marks on my wet flesh. My lips form an O as another inch penetrates me, and I feel my walls squeezing him. I wrap my arms around his toned neck, the mystical symbols on his bronzed skin twirling, enthralling me. I trade the frail illusion of control for the thrill of touching his sinewy muscles, the sensation of them rippling beneath my fingers, his magnificent cock filling me.

"Too long I have waited to have you," he whispers in my ear, "too great is my hunger for you, and too long it was unsatisfied," he sheaths himself almost to the hilt, and I squirm around him, afraid I cannot take any more, "so I am wholly famished now, and I plan to ravish you. I will take you like a beast, Celeste."

Without warning, his hips start pounding me madly, the sound of flesh meeting flesh reverberating in the steamy chamber, tangled with my hollering.

He has transformed into some mythical beast, a satire defiling a nymph, a tentacled monster bruising the pale flesh of the fisherman's wife, an Olympic god claiming a mortal virgin. His steely abs are tense, and the mystical hieroglyphs on his massive biceps swell. The stretch he gives me borders on pain, yet he mercilessly increases the tempo.

"Just remember this moment, sweet Celeste, my beautiful mortal siren; remember who your first Fae male was." He grabs a fistful of my wet strands and forces me to look him in the eye.

"I want to see your face when you ride that wave of pleasure," he demands, and I obey.

With a wicked twist of his hips, his steel hits that spot inside me, and his knuckles brush my swollen, aching nub. I arch my back and claw at his toned stomach, captured by his gaze as my climax washes over me. One final deep thrust, and he spills himself inside me with a roar. My eyes roll so far back I can see the inside of my head, yet I sense that something is off.

I notice that he withdraws himself from me alarmingly fast, leaving me open, empty, and missing him already.

I blink away the mist of the ecstasy, and my jaw drops. My brain refuses to process what is happening. I am enshrouded in a gentle, supernatural, cold glow—it appears as if a shimmering veil wraps me. I levitate an inch or two over the stone bench. An odd vibration crawls over my skin like invisible fingers tickling me.

"Celeste!" the troubled voice of Tarcyll anchors me back to reality, "You're casting a spell—"

My head is still blurry from the orgasm, and I struggle to grasp his words, I miss his warning shout.

Then a deafening, mind-numbing explosion hits us.

My ears are bleeding from the denotation, and countless shards of broken glass pierce my skin.

I'm tossed away from his arms, from the marble bench, and land headfirst on the floor. Then darkness consumes me.

CELESTE – THE ANCHOR

Birds chirping and the gentle caress of sunlight over my eyelids wake me up. I prop myself on an elbow and look around. The warm breeze plays with the silky white curtains, shaping them into fantastical figures.

The scent of blooming roses from the gardens of Taer Vallhen tickles my nose, and I sneeze, pain ripping through my body.

I push back the soft linen cover and shudder. Purple bruises and various-sized cuts cover my naked body, some still oozing blood.

"Cær ta'er?" I call in terror. Diaphonus appears from behind the curtain. He must have been in the garden.

"Yes, cær ta'il?" he asks, his cerulean eyes holding the promise of eons of bliss that await us. "Have you forgotten about your accident?" he asks, brow quirked when he notices my terror.

I strain my mind to remember. I seem to be so perplexed this morning. I cannot remember anything from the days past, only that I am here, with my beloved, in Taer Vallhen, my home.

"Seems like wine makes you do unwise things, like dancing on glass tables, cær ta'il."

I shake my head thoughtfully. Wine? That doesn't sound much like me. I prefer more potent liquor...

"Come with me," he extends his hand and assists me in sitting up, "the healing waters will help."

I'm not disturbed by his eyes scanning my bare curves. Being naked with my Cær ta'er is the most natural thing, a pleasure and a privilege. And how I long for his touch. His throat bobs when he takes me in. He's definitely taking his time today, indulging in the shameless display of my curves. I'm pleased to notice the massive strain under his white priest garments.

"I am always amazed at how beautiful you are, Cær ta'il," he purrs. His palm rests on my lower back as he guides me outside.

A crystal infinity pond stretches before my feet, and I enter the lukewarm water. The pain in my injured feet disappears when I step on the rounded pebbles at the bottom. I dive in, enjoying the caress of the sapphire water.

I reach the far edge of the pool and gasp at the shimmering abyss that lies beyond. The pool water splashes outside into the white clouds below, each drop turning into a tiny rainbow.

Crowned by a shimmering white city, an island floats at the horizon—Taer Vallhen. The temple of the Light shines bright as a diamond, the sacred ibises flying in swarms around its crystal dome.

Terraced gardens add freshness and color to the pearl of the high elves kingdom, airships float gracefully toward the main island, and a distant waft of the holy incense burning in the sacred halls reaches me.

The movement of water draws my attention, and I turn around to face a naked Diaphonus wading into the pool, approaching me. Diaphonus the Fair—the monicker beyond well-earned. High Priest of the Order of the First Light, my master and lover.

His long blond hair braided in a complex hairdo, tiny glistening drops snake between the muscles of his broad, golden-skinned chest and cascade down the slope of his rippling abs. The earrings gracing the tips of his pointy ears reflect the bright sunlight; the heavy golden strands and amulets around his neck and wrists—signs of his high rank—are almost blinding. All this beauty and splendor frames his warm smile like a halo.

The most powerful mage of the kingdom, the most devoted priest. My beloved, my Cær ta'er.

"Who are you, Cær ta'il?" he asks, cupping my nape and pulling me in, his eyes piercing mine, loaded with unspoken questions.

"What got into you, Cær ta'er?" I playfully slap his hand away, which greedily reaches to my breast. "I am your favorite concubine. I was gifted to you by my father—"

"And will you do everything that your master commands?" he asks, voice husky, lowering his face to me. I feel the heat of his lips and see his heavy cock rise in the clear water. I try to remember what he enjoys in bed, but my memory fails me again. Heavy oblivion covers everything before this morning.

"Your wish is my command, Cær ta'er," I murmur as his lips slam into mine.

DIAPHONUS – THE PRIEST

I have been dreaming of this moment since we met.

Celeste offers me her heavy breasts, and I am in a frenzy—cupping, kneading, squeezing the tender flesh, taking the hardened peaks in my mouth, tormenting them with my tongue. She is so exquisite, so deliciously different than the elven females I've had. The contrast of her lusty curves, tiny waist, and slender legs awakens a beast in me that I never suspected existed. I remember the ferocity with which Tarcyll was taking her in the steam bath, *like a beast*, he growled while I stood at the door, my cock harder than ever, my heart torn apart by envy and jealousy. I should have entered then. I know that the lusty spymaster wouldn't mind sharing this divine treat, that his dark appetites even sharpen when there are more than two involved in his games of passion. Oh, how tempted I was to barge in and fill her sinful mouth with my thick arousal, to make her scream my name.

My attention is drawn back to her lips, and I punish her for frolicking with the other Hunter. I suck and bite, caress her tongue with dominating strokes, until I notice she pulls away, whimpering and gasping for air.

Will she cast another spell when I make her climax? Or does it work only with Tarcyll? Possessiveness rears its head again, and I grab her hips under the water, pulling her in so she straddles my thigh. I don't need to guide her anymore, as she starts rubbing her throbbing folds against me in a frenzy and grabs my aching cock with her tiny hand. She can't even close her fingers around my girth, I realize with a smirk.

"Not yet, Cær ta'il," I command, and Celeste obeys, yet her hips still rock on my leg. The glamour I placed upon her is so strong that she would do anything I ask of her. I grab her hair and pull her back so that our eyes meet. Oh, what a bottomless, dark, and delicious Pandora's box I have opened by dragging her to my hideout!

I turn her around and bend her over the pool's edge; she faces the illusion of Taer Vallhen I have created, and the perfect rounding of her ass presses against the tip of my cock. One jerk and I would impale her, and she knows it. Now she stands completely still, and my brow furrows, noticing the bruises left by Tarcyll's fingers.

I am mesmerized by these two perfect spheres rubbing greedily along my length, and I contemplate how to have her. I remember my oath to my people, my promise to harvest the magic from the most potent Anchor ever, even if I have to strip the flesh off her bones and realize how wrong I am. I exhale with a hiss when she once again struggles against my grip and tries to skewer herself on my cock. She gives me a heavy-lidded look over her wet shoulder, wondering why I'm so reluctant. Her autumn-colored eyes are glassy from my spell.

And then I realize it.

I cannot have her against her will.

I want her to look at me with heat and plea, just like she looks at the spymaster.

"Not yet, Cær ta'il!" I whisper gently and reverse the glamour spell.

The magnificent Taer Vallhen dissolves. Dark nothingness and a belt of barren floating rocks replace the pearl of the elven kingdom. A chilly wind sweeps over us, powdering us with fine black dust. Distant starlight pierces the murky air around the massive hovering rock on which my hideout stands.

Without magic, the water quickly cools, and Celeste shudders. Covering her bare breasts, she turns to face me.

Her beautiful face freezes in confusion.

"Diaphonus, where are we? Tarcyll? What happened? What was that explosion?"

So, she remembers. Venom taints my veins when she mentions Tarcyll. A vision of her, panting, lips parted, as she watched the spymaster fondling her friend. He would have had the girl straight in the middle of the club and then move on to Celeste without blinking; I'd seen him do it before.

How can she still hunger for the lusty spy when she can have the fair and pure priest?

"It is a place between places, a moment frozen in time. My hideout between the realms. I shaped it to remind me of my home—".

"You glamoured me again, didn't you?" she snaps, and I feel my power over her crumble.

"Let me explain, Celeste."

"How did we get here?" She looks around in confusion, suddenly appearing small and helpless, and I gesture to invite her out of the water into my chambers, where I have warm blankets and a fire.

"I portaled us here." She lets me wrap my arm around her shoulders, and I gently guide her out of the pond.

"You used magic and disclosed our location to that monster chasing us!" the human hisses and struggles against me, yet I hold her tight until she relents like I would hold a tiny, wounded beast while healing it.

"The Dreadful One is not interested in harming us, the Hunters." I calm her while walking her into my bedroom. "And you are the one who cast a spell first, Celeste. When you... had your release with the spy—"

She freezes, looking around with eyes wide. I guess it's a lot to digest.

"I was... glowing," Celeste says softly as if speaking to herself, "and for a moment, it felt like... like I was levitating!" She looks at me questioningly, and I nod. "I was using my magic!"

We enter my hideout. The chamber hasn't changed much since she woke up inside. Just the deep sapphire of the skies over Taer Vallhen has melted into the darkness of the interdimensional void.

I wrap her in a blanket and seat her next to the crackling fire. She looks like a scared human child in the flickering light.

"Tarcyll is probably unharmed. When Fae withdrew from the human realm, all kingdoms agreed to keep our existence hidden and operate in your world in utter secrecy. No Hunter would risk a conflict with another unless there is no gain. And the Dreadful One is after you. You are safe here. He cannot enter this place. The wards protecting it are ancient and powerful, and it is hidden well among the cosmic chaos," I add, trying to cheer her up.

"Tarcyll is probably unharmed? And that's good enough for you?" Celeste is furious. So unusual for her reserved demeanor. Her eyes glitter with rage, and I suddenly feel like a monster. "I thought you were friends."

"More like competitors turned partners due to a common interest. And I am sure he would understand that I took you to this safe place to protect you. The arcane wave you released when you climaxed was noticed all over the Crystal Serpent," I answer, rubbing her shoulders and feel the already familiar sting of jealousy and possessiveness. I am treading dangerous ground here.

We sit in silence. I give Celeste time and space to adjust.

"What are you going to do with me now?" The flames reflect in her strange eyes, and I am again drawn to her in a way I have never felt in my long life. Was it a coincidence that I have crafted the illusion of us as cæer-ta'alm, souls bound to find each other in all planes of reality? Is this what I desire?

"Feed you, as a start." I gesture toward the dining room, where the table is already loaded with steaming plates. The mouth-watering aroma tickles her nose, and she stands up and follows me to the feast I have just created.

Moments later, the human dunks pieces of golden-crusted bread in the stew, chews flavorful tomatoes, and helps herself to large pieces of aged cheese, flushing them down with a strong mead. A drink she was cautious about at first but praised later.

Brows arched, I watch her eat and enjoy the sight. Humans and their short, hurried existence, fragile, like candles on a windowsill, beautiful and fleeting like shooting stars... What an irony to place the hope for our powerful kind in one of them.

"And what comes after?" the woman challenges behind the raised glass.

"You know what we are after, Celeste," my voice rumbles and startles her. "You have cast a spell. Powerful enough to draw the attention of the enemy."

She winces under the blanket, "You have saved me..." she mutters reluctantly.

I nod.

"I know how it works now, Celeste," I say softly and study her face. "I know how to reach out to that power locked inside you. And you know it, too."

She stands up abruptly, the blanket slipping from her shoulders and revealing her pale breasts, the smooth skin already healed. "Are you telling me some magical Fae dude has to fuck me and milk my magic?" Her pretty features distort in anger, and if it were not such a severe situation, I would have laughed at her comical expression.

"It seems like you didn't mind a Fae male fucking you just hours ago." I rise from my seat but halt when I see that she shudders in fear. I realize how menacing I look to her, much larger and more powerful than her, so I rein myself in and sit back, "Let us explore this, Celeste. Even when you are not mating with a Fae, I think your magic is raw and primal, locked in the same place where other raw and primal instincts are. Let me gain your trust and look into these theories."

She pushes her chair back, looking around for a way out. There is no way out from here.

"You want to keep me imprisoned here and fuck me until you find out how to harvest my magic?" she asks in disbelief, her eyes welling, and, by the Light, this is a sight I do not enjoy.

But by the Serpent, how I love the idea.

And how it hurts that she seems to be hating it.

"All I am asking you is to trust me, Celeste. Stay here as my guest. You are safe here. Together we can find another way to save my realm."

She considers my suggestion, when I snap my fingers, and the sleeping spell hits her. I catch her before she slumps on the floor and carry her to the bedroom.

Tucking her in, I feel a strange surge of warmth, and I lay next to her, letting dreams and hopes conquer the fears for the first time in a very long time.

CELESTE – THE ANCHOR

I wake up to a tray of freshly baked pastries and fluffy croissants. The aroma of hot espresso makes me sit up abruptly. It's still dark beyond the French windows. It seems like it's always dark here. A place between places, Diaphonus called it. A hidden corner somewhere in the Universe where the laws of physics and magic are different. I assume it is morning and wonder how the Fae doesn't lose track of time.

A simple but beautiful emerald gown is spread on the chair and invites me to slip in. I purr at the sensual touch of the luxurious fabric over my skin. The priest hasn't left any underwear. I guess sex hostages don't need that.

I wander the empty halls, as, given I will be spending God knows how much time here, it is better to look around.

The rooms are full of artwork and exquisite objects. Murals on the walls depict gravity-defying landscapes, similar to what I saw when I was under Diaphonus' spell.

There is a grand library, several sleeping chambers, the kitchen and dining room I already know, and the garden with the infinity pool that looks melancholic in the starlight.

My host, or rather my captor, is elusive.

I find him later in the library. His fingers weave threads of pure light, and I step into a shimmering three-dimensional landscape of a magnificent city floating over pale lavender clouds. Its beauty is so pristine and ephemeral that inexplicable longing squeezes my heart.

"This is my home," Diaphonus explains, watching me intently, though I don't need clarification. He looks exactly like someone descending from a magical city in the sky. "And this is the Kingdom of Verdant, where Tarcyll serves as a spymaster to the king."

The vision blurs, and dramatic emerald hills covered in millennial woods stretch around us. Tall towers strain to reach the mauve sky among the leviathan trees, and colorful treehouses sparkle like gems in the lavish sunlight, peeking out of the green canopy.

"And these are the Lower Lands." He snaps his graceful fingers, and our surroundings change again. Rows of stone houses carved into the bedrock bathe in the warm light of floating magical lanterns; strange machinery and mechanical creatures, reminding me of Cerberus, crowd the underground streets. The roofs' glazed tiles reflect the light of a massive glowing disk, resembling the sun, "The home of a certain vicious warlord you have already met. Cyrell's domain borders the Underworld, the dwelling of the

Dreadful One. I cannot show you any of what we call the Underworld, as no one has returned from it to tell us how it looks..."

Cold terror crawls up my spine. A forbidden underground kingdom, where no one returns from, ruled by a terrifying demon prince. Sounds familiar.

"Four realms, four Hunters hoping to save their homelands." Diaphonus spreads his arms to maintain the vision, yet his eyes rest on me, "This is how our world looks now."

I gasp at the apocalyptic visions of the floating cities lying in rubble on the ground, the lush forests of Verdant consumed by fires, the light fading from underground galleries, their floors covered in bones.

"The laws of nature rule your world, Celeste, but magic rules ours. And you see what happens when demons starved for magic find their way in."

Diaphanous lowers his hands, and the shimmering projections are instantly gone. He paces between the bookshelves, the skirts of his long white tunic sweeping the floor. Since we are here, he wears the High Priest garments, light fabrics that follow the hard lines of his body. The decadent golden jewelry makes him appear regal and exotic. I lick my lips while watching his graceful moves, his alien elegance. Testing the relation between my magic and my sexuality with him doesn´t seem like a bad idea right now. It seems like I must add Stockholm Syndrome to my ever-growing list of mental issues.

"Many suspect that the Dreadful One summoned the Siphons, following his twisted agenda..." he halts before me.

"Why would he put your whole world at risk?"

He resumes his pacing. "Because evil is in his nature. And hate. He is in a constant war with the Dark Elves. His Black Guardians raid the borders, killing everyone in sight."

"Without any provocation?" I cock an eyebrow. I'm not about to play the devil's advocate here, but it's doubtful that such a severe conflict continues without instigations from both sides. It seems like Fae are very similar to humans after all. When they are confused and angry, they only need a scapegoat, someone to blame.

He stops and crosses his arms at his chest; his broad back turned to me. "Some say that dark elves´ mining expeditions wander deep into his territory, as his lands are rich in metals and minerals. Most of them never come back, but... I forgive you for trying to justify his deeds because you are a stranger to our world, Celeste. If you were one of us, you would know that he is pure evil."

This is something worth looking into, I decide. There should be more information about this mysterious villain somewhere in all these books. And why is Diaphonus avoiding discussing it?

"Blessed be the Light, we found you. You will help us save and recover some of our homeland."

"And by some, you mean yours, Diaphonus," I declare softly and notice the muscles in his back tense up. Honestly, I'm surprised by my boldness. Maybe I should be more likable and meeker when I'm held captive in some enchanted interdimensional hideout and this male is holding the key.

"My people wield the strongest magic in Faëheim, Celeste. The High Priests of my order are the mightiest wizards in our realm, the only worthy opponents to the Siphons. The only challenge for the corrupted power of the Dreadful One. If there is hope for my world, it lies within the borders of my home." He turns to me, and his steely gaze softens. "Help me rebuild Taer Vallhen, strengthen the wards, and purge all the Siphons from my homeland, and my brethren and I will work tirelessly to free the rest of Faëheim."

Fae never lie, I'd heard. The heated confidence and the plea in his voice almost convince me.

Almost.

I cannot shake off the feeling that he is hiding something. Like an annoying fly, that buzzing feeling in the back of my head tells me something is wrong. I shrug helplessly. Right now, my only option is to cooperate.

"It is a special night tonight," Diaphonus declares over dinner, and I cock an eyebrow. "By some surreal whim of magic, the lights of the Crystal Serpent will be visible with bare eyes. A myriad of stars, shards of pure magic, will dance for us, Celeste. Do you wish to see it from the front row?"

I nod; every suggestion for entertainment is more than welcome. How many days have I been stuck here with this magnificent, strange, Fae male?

Too long, I guess. I have lost track of time. There is nothing else to do besides sleeping and wandering the empty rooms.

He stands up, and I catch myself checking him out; he's so regal and handsome in his high priest frock. The steep incline of his broad shoulders down to his narrow hips has probably broken many hearts over the centuries. He catches my stare, and his cornflower eyes beam.

The dark garden with the infinity pool is transformed into a night paradise. Nightingales sing from the rose bushes; heavy blossoms spread their intoxicating scent. Flower petals float on the surface of the inviting pool, the unknown constellations drawing mysterious marks on the water.

A deep mauve sky hangs over us, and comets pierce the shimmering clouds as stardust flickers around us. I never knew that starlight could have so many colors. Behind the flashing crossroads of shooting stars, a massive vein of diamonds stretches across the horizon. It resembles the curled body of a reptile.

"The Crystal Serpent," I whisper in awe. It feels like I am in a glass cabin of a spaceship, and at my feet are the dazzling depths of the Milky Way—an explorer setting foot in lands no mortal has ever seen.

"Are you coming in?" Diaphonus asks, wading waist-deep in the water to the pool's far end. His clothes are piled at my feet. My throat bobs. The delicate silver light makes him look like a statue of a sinful pagan god.

"Your swimming garments are in your bedroom," he declares with a timid smile and dives in with a merry splash.

I find a copy of the same designer bikini I wore in Cuba in the wardrobe. I slip in and rush to the night garden, curious about what this magical night has in store for me.

The water is pleasantly warm and soothingly swirls around my body. I swim toward the pond's edge and realize what the elf meant when he said, "from the first row."

I join him and take in the magnificent view, propping my chin at the pool's edge.

Minutes, or maybe hours, pass. Wrapped in a bubble of tranquility and timelessness, I pay no heed to time.

He turns to face me, his eyes the color of pristine water, glowing with the lights of the Serpent above us. His scent—of summer evenings, pinewood, and sweet promises—caresses my senses, and I feel myself trembling with unbidden excitement.

"What about you, Celeste?"

I blink at him, surprised.

"Since we have found you, it has always been about us. Our people, our realm, our salvation, our desires. What about you? How was your life before the Serpent brought us together? What do you like? What makes you laugh? When was the last time you cried?"

I stare at him for a moment, searching his beautiful features for any sign of mockery or deception. He looks at me intensely, and I realize he is genuinely interested in my story.

No man has ever asked me these questions. And I have never found myself worthy of this kind of attention. I can almost see my therapist nodding and explaining something about negligent parenting. After the occasional attempt to get into my pants, all communication with my boyfriends was limited to explanations of why it wouldn't work. Why I wasn't good enough, or there was always something more important than me in their lives. Dozens of pathetic "it's not you, it's me" variations.

And now I am here, with this powerful, magical being, who would make any male model turn green with envy, and all he wants to talk about... is me.

His body is facing mine, his face leaning in to hear me better.

A dam bursts.

I take a deep breath and start talking.

The comets above us seem to freeze mid-flight, listening to my account of an isolated childhood dominated by a narcissistic, addicted mother, an adulthood marked by anxiety and panic attacks, a mediocre love life with men who were always emotionally unavailable, "a tragic strategy to cope with childhood trauma" as my therapist explained; a string of insignificant draining jobs that I kept only to be able to continue my independent life in solitude... I talk and talk and do not notice when the tears come.

My last words drown in a choking sob, and my whole body convulses.

Without a word, he pulls me in. My cheek rests on his chiseled pec. He lets me cry until utter exhaustion, until each bad memory is confessed and purged.

Then he utters soothing words in his strange language, holding me tight, his long fingers gently stroking my hair. Nobody has ever touched me like this.

The warm brush of his skin on mine, the calming moves of his broad chest, the safety of his embrace—I feel protected and cherished.

And feeling his soft lips on mine is natural and welcome; so are the delicate, gentle moves of his tongue in my mouth. A fleeting kiss, and he pulls away, panting.

"I'm sorry, Celeste, I didn't mean to. "

I ball my hands into fists, disciplining myself not to throw myself at him, and look back at the sky.

The Serpent is still in its zenith. The mesmerizing comet nets are gone. Without a word, he gently scoops me up and steps out of the pool, murmuring something incomprehensible, and the exhaustion sweeps me into a dream where a handsome elven lord, a magical being wielding ancient power, chooses me over thousands. We rule together for an eternity before the Shadow rises. It's beautiful and terrifying.

I wake up next to him in the giant king's size bed, and memories of last night flood my mind. I feel cleansed, reborn, like I've just had the best therapy session ever. As if a skillful hand has applied soothing balm over the wounds of my soul.

The Fae head rests over his arm, and his serene features appear even younger and softer in his sleep. His chest is bare, and my gaze wanders down his defined pecs and abs—what a contrast to his beautiful and innocent face—and I criticize myself when it lingers over the linen sheet casually thrown over his loin. I bite my lip when I recognize the massive contour of his half-hard cock.

Hunger stirs in my center, and I feel the aching twitching of desire between my legs.

Am I half-naked in a bed with a priest, lusting after him?! Damn those Fae males. Why do they have to be so beautiful?

As if responding to my sinful thoughts, his length throbs and grows, swelling to proportions that make me gasp. I feel the nectar of my need pooling. My folds are swollen and throbbing, begging me to touch them. I look down at my body, still wearing the bikini from last night, the damp spot between my legs awkwardly visible on the pale fabric.

Diaphonus seems to be deep asleep, so I do something reckless. I slip the thong to my ankles, and my fingers travel down to my aching pussy. I'm thoroughly drenched; who wouldn't be with a naked Apollo sleeping next to them? My middle finger gently circles my clit before diving into my slit while I watch, enthralled, how his length rises to its full height under the sheet. I finger myself deliriously, my nipples piercing the soft fabric of the bikini top. My eyes are fixed on his full lips now. How would it feel to have these lips explore every rim of my drenched sex?

He suggested we explore that specific way of awakening my magic—the only one we know so far. Right now, this appears as a completely acceptable option. Right now, I'm aching for it.

All reason abandons me, and I carefully lift the light sheet, revealing this feast. My middle finger is buried deep in my hole, and I lick my lips at the magnificent sight of the elf. A thin trail of dark blond hair descends from his navel, expanding to a golden triangle between his powerful thighs. Straight and magnificent, his erection begs me to impale myself on it. He would fill me to the limit, and the veins beneath his sateen skin would rub all the right places inside me. The tiny opening on his engorged crown is salivating—a drop of crystal liquid gathers and drips down his length.

Some carnal urge seizes control over my body, and I lean down, flicking my tongue over the throbbing top. I softly whimper when I taste him.

Terror petrifies me when Diaphonus responds with a moan and a gentle thrust of his hips. His eyes are still closed, yet his broad chest is heaving. The move has shoved him into my mouth, filling me all the way to the throat, and I'm savoring his divine taste, needy for more. I move my head up and down, intoxicated by the sight of this powerful male at my disposal. He responds to my moves with short thrusts and muffled moans. His head thrashing, eyes still closed, probably having the wildest dream right now. Or he's pretending, I speculate.

And I don't care. That suffocating grip of iron self-control I've always had is gone, melted in the heat of the moment. My therapist would be so proud!

My middle and index finger are not enough to fill me, and I lift my head, his shaft escaping my suction with a pop, and look around, desperate for release. If I mount him now, I will orgasm immediately. The walls of my pussy are already spasming around my digits. With his involuntary assistance, I would probably start glowing, as it is already known that I start channeling my arcane power when I'm climaxing with a magical prick inside me. And his is the most magical of them all. I squirm at the embarrassing possibility of him waking up to me taking advantage of him. So I grab the massive handheld mirror discarded on the nightstand at my bedside. It has a thick metallic handle engraved with flowers and leaves that would provide excellent friction.

I slowly insert the cool silvery handle into my dripping opening, giving my pussy time to adjust to the hard, ribbed surface. I softly moan as I start gliding it in and out, my fingers gently stroking my nub. I catch a reflection of my spread pink flesh on the mirror's surface, and I watch, hypnotized, how I stretch around the metal. My movements are becoming more frantic, and I feel an apocalyptic climax building up.

Suddenly a hot spurt of liquid slaps my stomach and breasts. I look away from the mirror to see Diaphonus looming over me, his fist still pumping his enormous erection, the last drops of his seed dripping on the sheets.

"I'm glad you've started exploring my theories," he purrs and smiles smugly.

DIAPHONUS – THE PRIEST

Celeste is petrified, her face burning bright red in shame.

Her body is drenched in my seed. Her sex is shuddering around that mirror handle.

I've intervened at a pivotal point. And this is good, as I have better plans for this mouth-watering opening of hers.

I gently pull the mirror from her slit, finding her open and hungry. My nostrils flare, the scent of her arousal maddening. It's been centuries since I have felt a female's heat, and the ages of celibacy have only sharpened my appetite.

The beast inside me awakens, and I throw myself over her. My lips suck, lick, caress, and consume. I'm drunk on her exotic flavor. She's reluctant at first, but then my tongue finds her pearl, circles it, and slides down, trailing the outline of her opening. She thrashes under my ministrations, arching her back and grabbing my hair, making the cutest little noises I've ever heard. Pure music. Could Tarcyll make her squeal like that? I think not.

Then I slowly dip a finger to find her ready, thirsting for more. And I rise, looking down at her.

This is how I wanted her from the very beginning. Spread wide open for me, craving me, her eyes worshiping my cock, her body begging me to penetrate her. No glamour, no tricks.

And I oblige. I slowly sheath myself into her, giving her time to adjust to my thickness. I feel the wet velvet of her flesh stretch around me, and her eyes widen in fear.

"Diaphonus," the human whispers, and I cannot tell if it is a plea or an order as I lose control. Gone are the mighty mage and fair Priest of the Light. Only the beast remains.

I plunge until the sheath envelops me whole, and she squirms under me, powerless in the raw grip of my hands. I spot the purple marks of Tarcyll's fingers on her thighs, which drives me into a frenzy. I want to reclaim, punish, and conquer her only for myself. And so I do.

I am pounding into her with ferocity, my cock unable to get enough of her hot tightness. Her hands are on my stomach, and I cannot understand if she is trying to pull me in or push me away.

Then she cries a short warning, and I feel her squeezing my length. I deliver a series of fast and powerful trusts, and she is done for. I gently gather her in my arms as she falls apart, murmuring unintelligible words, and sheath myself fully, spilling myself with hot intense gushes inside her. Her twitches slowly die out, and I release her. Suddenly I feel the pull of raw magic distorting the reality around me, a wave of untamed power sweeping my hideout so violently that the walls shake. I'm still hazy from my release and don't react fast enough to capture this force, and it seeps through the world around us, lost to me forever.

Then I realize it: if I want to harvest all this arcane energy, we need another. Another male to please her so I can focus solely on absorbing and studying this power.

My body and mind react controversially to the thought of seeing her ravaged by Tarcyll again. My length gets heavier, and I lick my lips, anticipating the sight of her stretched wide while my friend brutally takes her. Yet jealousy stings my heart, and I decide to have her for myself a few more times before presenting to her my suggestion.

It is a long way to unlock all her potential, yet the first steps are taken. I cradle her in my arms and kiss her forehead.

"We did it, Celeste. You did it," I purr while I watch sleep claiming her.

The human agrees without hesitation to continue our "experiments." The mage inside me triumphs but so does the male, gone feral at the thought that she is only mine for a while. And she is quite devoted to the cause.

Her limbs are tied to my bedposts with silk scarves—this is how I desire to see her—naked, helpless, and at my mercy. Her seam glistens wet in the warm candlelight, and her nipples stiffen as she watches me approach her and slowly disrobe. Her soft eyes burn with anticipation while she stares at my torso and erect length. I lean down and roughly slide it into her mouth, savoring the sight of her teary eyes as she chokes on my cock. Then I kneel before her slit, smirking at how her pink flesh throbs, responding to the hot huffs of my breath. I have had her in many ways in the last days, and her body has learned to worship mine. I rub my dripping tip against her nub, taunting her, and she moans, her lavish breasts heaving. By the Serpent, I could do this forever.

"Look at me, Celeste," I demand, and her glazed eyes meet mine while she tries to impale herself on my thick cock. I deny her this pleasure and insist, "We have discovered the way to awaken your magic," she confirms with a distracted nod, her opening pulsating with desire. I enter her with just the crown of my manhood and feel the stretch of her silky walls welcoming me. She shudders and tries to take more of me, yet the ties hold her in place. I am fully in control.

"The primal pleasure you experience, combined with your reaction to Fae magic, hold the key to harnessing your power." The human writhes around me as another inch penetrates her. "Yet I find myself too... invested in the process to be able to harvest the magic you emit fully." She looks at me, her gaze hazy, unable to understand why we are discussing this now.

"That is why I have decided to ask an old friend for help. Tarcyll will join us in exploring this so I can focus on researching your... reactions..." Her lips part as if about to object, yet I sheath myself fully, filling her up, the spasms of bliss depriving her of the ability to speak.

"What do you think of another Fae male pleasing you, Celeste?" She clamps around me, desperate for friction, yet I remain firm and motionless. "How would you feel if the spymaster ravishes your mouth while I do this?" A moan escapes her when I slam my hips against her, "Or do you prefer him worshipping you as I do while I watch?"

Her climax is close, and I withdraw from her pussy, a cruel smile on my face. "Both of us feasting on the divine pleasure your body can provide simultaneously?"

"Diaphonus, please—"

"Yes, my little bird." I circle her soaked, shuddering slit lazily with the tip of my cock. "Would you want this?"

She tugs on the scarves restraining her wrists and ankles, panting.

"Tell me what you want," I command, slowly entering her.

"I want you—" she squirms, and I smile, "and him too..."

"You want us to do what to you, Celeste?" I insist and withdraw again, sweat dewing my brow at the effort to restrain myself.

"I want your cocks buried deep inside me... at the same time—"

The idea is so maddening that I fill her up with my seed after three deep pumps. I consume her mouth in a bruising kiss, feeling her clutching around me in aftershocks and curse myself for all that magic that showers around us, disappearing into nothingness.

Then I untie her and head to my study. It is time to see an old friend.

When, hours later, a surprised Tarcyll steps out of the portal, looking frighteningly beautiful in his immaculate suit, a bottle of tequila in his right hand, Celeste retreats a step. I cannot conceal my triumph—it is me she trusts the most.

Celeste is quiet over dinner, listening attentively to our conversation with the spymaster. He flashes his white fangs in a predatory smile when I reveal why I brought him here.

"You are forgiven, priest, for leaving me at the mercy of the Dreadful One, who, by the way, never appeared. Yet it is important that our human guest agrees to this arrangement."

He tucks a dark strand behind his pointy ear, and each move is a display of casual grace.

Celeste nods.

"I do. No glamour, no tricks. We get to the bottom of this, you drain me of that cursed magic, and I am free to go," she declares, encouraged by the tequila shots she had before dinner.

We move to the grand hall after dinner, and the air is charged. I feel the tension between us three drawing purple lines in the fabric of this dimension. And we all had one too many drinks.

Tarcyll notices it, too, and his straight nose greedily sniffs the air—he has just caught the scent of her heat.

Celeste sits on the sofa, wearing the white silk dress I gifted her. Fine golden jewelry clinks with her every move when she turns a page in the book, open in her lap. Probably a romance novel, I stacked up on these reads, hoping to excite her. And it seems that it's working.

"Lift your skirt," Tarcyll's voice suddenly breaks the silence, and I freeze. Would such a demeanor work on our human or put her off? Her scent gets thicker and heavier, and I feel my cock straining against my robe. The ache becomes unbearable as I watch her hesitate yet follow his order, obediently putting her book aside and raising her dress. She holds her knees together, yet I can glimpse her glistening rim.

"Open your legs and show us this pussy, Celeste," Tarcyll demands, unzipping his designer pants. His hard cock spills out, and the human stares at it, hypnotized, like a doe before a hunter, yet she obeys. My erection is at its full stretch when the spymaster starts stroking his length.

"Touch yourself." His rough demand whips the air. Without hesitation, her slender finger descends to her folds and starts rubbing her most sensitive spot. Tarcyll is stroking his cock roughly, pearls of desire dripping from his massive, engorged head.

"Spread yourself wide for us, Celeste. Show us what we are about to have."

Celeste's caresses are getting more intense; it seems like his game turns her on. Her delicate fingers stretch her labia wide, and I can see her pink, pulsating opening, the nectar of her desire spilling onto the couch. I have never been so close to madness.

"I will have you now," Tarcyll declares, and the woman dips her finger deeply into her slit. "I will try all your holes," she winces at these words and adds a second finger, sliding them in and out in a frenzy. I cannot resist this temptation and lower my robe, releasing my throbbing member. I please myself slowly when I watch the other male pounce at the human, tall and imposing in his perfectly tailored navy suit with just a few buttons open to show off his fit, tattooed chest.

He gently trails his finger along her jaw, lifting her face. Their eyes meet, and I savagely rub my cock as I watch him shove his massive erection into her mouth. Oh, how I crave that sensation again, her wet hotness giving in to my brutal thrusts—

Celeste chokes on his length, saliva trickling down her chin and onto the floor. The spy grabs her nape, controlling her movements, and I'm growling, crazed by the view of her luscious lips around his thickness, jealous of the pleasure he is experiencing right now. I stand up and stride toward them, Tarcyll noticing me and inviting me with a mischievous smirk.

"Join me at this divine feast, priest," he rasps.

I kneel before the couch and pull her tiny hand away from her folds. Her fingers are dripping, and I lick them, a low rumble of pleasure coming from my chest, before turning my attention to her heat. I drool when I take her precious pearl between my lips, sucking on it while pumping my cock with my fist. Celeste freezes, startled by my ministrations, but Tarcyll doesn't halt his assault on her mouth. I suck and graze her pink bundle of nerves, and my finger spreads her folds and sinks into her tense, hot slit. I can feel the other Hunter brutally defiling her, her whole body shaking with his mighty shoves. A rip of fabric startles me, and I lift my eyes from my feast to see her heavy breasts bouncing above me. Tarcyll has torn her gown open and is now filling his greedy hands with her supple flesh.

I can't resist this temptation and rise to take a nipple in my mouth, teasing the tender skin with my fangs while the spy roughly gropes the other, his cock still shoved deep in Celeste's throat. I grab and knead the tempting flesh and moan at the feeling of her heavy sphere in my large palm.

I meet the corner of her gaze, and there is a plea in her teary eyes. I know exactly what she needs and rub my dripping tip over her folds. A deep moan confirms that I am right, and I slowly enter her, my eyes devouring the sight of her pink glistening flesh stretching around my cock.

So wet and so tight. Tarcyll ceases his onslaught and takes a step back to enjoy the view, her saliva dripping from his massive manhood. His eyes appear black in the candlelight; feral hunger has dilated his pupils.

For a moment I am afraid that he will morph into his bloodthirsty beast form, and I speculate if he will defile her with his enormous cock or tear her apart. Or both. But the spy keeps himself in check, and I turn my attention back to Celeste.

I wrap my arms around her thighs and lift her, capturing her swollen lips in a kiss. She hangs on to me as I lay down on the sofa, my shaft still buried deep inside her, placing her on top of me.

Celeste purrs, enjoying this new position that gives her more control, and impales herself on my cock frantically, her jolting breasts an offering to my hungry mouth. I violate her nipples with my tongue, my arms groping the firmness of her backside, spreading it wide.

Tarcyll, the villain, has snuck behind her, biting his lower lip while savoring how my blade pierces her.

"Oh, brother, you should see this," he hisses, "how greedy our little human is!" then stalks toward Celeste's backside.

"I promised you I would have all your holes," he rumbles and bends over her, and I feel her stiffen.

"So wet," the male murmurs in her ear, "so tight. Now open up for me, Celeste. Let me in."

I can feel him pushing inside her other opening as suddenly, her hole gets impossibly tight, and I sense the pressure of his relentless cock behind the thin layer of flesh. Celeste releases a moan that drives us both crazy, and we resume our movements, finding some savage harmony between our thrusts. This is bliss I have never thought possible.

I feel her clenching around my steel, her moaning more intense, her nipples pebbled and shoved into my face. I know that her climax is nearing. I quickly withdraw from her, leaving her hissing in disappointment. I gesture to Tarcyll, and he pulls out, too. Swiftly, I lift her body, her limbs hanging helplessly like a rag doll, exhausted from our rough ministrations, and lay her flat on her back. Without wasting any time, I shove my length between her lips, losing myself to the feeling of having her that way, too.

"Now I will try this sweet tight cunt of yours," the spy rasps, and I explode when I see his firm cock slowly disappear between her swollen pink petals. My seed fills Celeste's mouth and runs down her face, and she tries to pull away, yet I bury myself even deeper, pinning her down to the red velvet of the couch, sensing the resistance of her throat against my tip. Oh, I would gladly trade all eternity for the feeling of my aching balls pressed against her silky face.

I'm panting, my knees are weak from my soul-draining climax, and I withdraw and watch her flesh bounce while Tarcyll savagely pounds into her. He shoves himself all the way in, murmuring words in our language that make me blush ferociously. Our human shudders, convulsing. Then the miracle happens again. Her skin starts glowing.

Tarcyll notices it, too, and tries to prolong Celeste's pleasure, brushing his calloused knuckles over her nub. Barely recovered from my climax, I quickly utter a spell.

I absorb all the arcane energy this time, and no drop is wasted. That sensation of power roaring in my veins is as intoxicating as our games with the human. She shimmers faintly, and her eyes close, my seed still dripping from her half-open lips, when the other Hunter growls and fills Celeste up with one final, brutal thrust. Then he leans over her and places a soft kiss on her breast.

"It worked," I mutter as I stumble away to find something to clean the mess up.

Tarcyll gently places her in the aromatic bath I have drawn for her. The soothing scent relaxes her, and my friend takes a towel and carefully cleans her face. I raise a brow, stunned. Never have I expected such tenderness from a ruffian like him. I join in his efforts and cast some mild restoration spells. Our human must be sore. I see how the furrow between her brows smooths, and I head to the kitchen to prepare her favorite tea.

I find them in the bedroom when I return. Celeste is sound asleep, spooned against Tarcyll's large frame. I put the steaming cup on the nightstand and lay down, too, and when I feel her arm over my chest, I surrender to the sweet fatigue.

CELESTE- THE ANCHOR

I wake up to the smell of fresh coffee and waffles. Memories of last night flood my brain, and I bury my face under the fluffy pillow. How would I look these males in the eye again? Yet hunger gets the best of me, and I sneak into the kitchen. I'm grateful to find it deserted and throw myself over the steaming pile of food.

After washing the last waffle down with coffee, I head to the library.

There, I spot the athletic silhouette of Tarcyll, bent over a book. His short, dark hair is messy, with some longer strands framing his defined jawline. His thick brows are furrowed, and he appears deeply invested in his lecture. My memories of last night are still fresh, so I retreat a step, blushing.

Yet it is too late. The spy whips his head, and his gaze softens when he sees me.

"Good morning, beautiful. I hope you liked my breakfast." He smiles and invites me to the chair opposite with a gesture.

"Where is Diaphonus?" I mumble, sinking into the soft embrace of the chair.

His brow arches at my question, and I wonder if I see a spark of jealousy. "Out somewhere, doing weird high-priestly stuff. What brings you here? Maybe I can help you, too." The mischief in his tone heats my core, but I discipline myself. It's so rare to speak to him alone. Maybe I could get some helpful information. Or see if Diaphonus is hiding something.

"I was hoping to learn more about your world," I blurt. Tarcyll's gaze lights up. It seems like I have found the soft spot of the roguish spymaster.

He disappears into the depths of the bookshelf labyrinth that fades into the gloom. *How big is this room, actually?* I ponder. And is space determinable when you dwell in an illusion floating somewhere between the realms?

Tarcyll emerges, holding a heavy tome bound in soft white leather. He slams it on the reading table, and I pull my chair closer, peeking over his shoulder curiously.

The old paper cracks under his slender, tattooed fingers. Artfully drawn maps grace the pages, followed by text passages in an unknown language. I roll my eyes in frustration. How can I investigate other possibilities to defeat the Siphons when I can't even read Fae language?

He shows me pictures and explanations about each of the four realms, yet just like Diaphonus, he hastily flips the scarce pages dedicated to the Underworld. Is the Kingdom of the Dreadful One so despicable? Is the Dark Prince so terrifying that they avoid the topic even in books?

"What do you know about the Underworld and the Dreadful One?" I ask, and he curiously cocks his head.

"Well, this is an odd question. Why are you suddenly interested in that?" He shuts the tome and leans back in his chair.

"All I hear about the Dreadful One is that he is, well, dreadful, yet nobody seems to know anything about him or his kingdom. He hasn't harmed any of you Hunters, though he could have done it countless times. What if he wants to share something? What if he has some information we don't? Something that could help us save all Faëheim, not just parts of it..." The last words slipped out too fast. He tenses up. My speculation has set him off.

"I forgive you for saying this, Celeste, as you are a stranger to our world. He is a beast. A demon. The most powerful sorcerer in our world, yet using his god-like magic only to kill and destroy. He is the one who brought this evil upon us. And the only reason he is after you is, I am afraid, utterly selfish."

His knuckles are white, and a vein throbs across his forehead. I have struck a sensitive nerve. He and Diaphonus are obviously not entertained by the idea of involving other Fae in our arrangement.

"And yet he has never hurt anyone, though he had the chance twice—at the nightclub and in Cuba," I insist, for a reason I cannot comprehend. Am I defending an otherworldly demon? That deeply-rooted sense of justice inside me got me in trouble at school and work often. It's what Jasmin admires about me, yet I would gladly trade it for more practical qualities.

"Only a human can be so naïve and look for goodwill where there is none." He rises and heads to the door, "You, me, and the priest—we have a good plan, Celeste. Diaphonus is getting stronger with each…" he grins as he searches for the right word, "session. I believe you are not suffering, either. When we are powerful enough, we will return to Faëheim and retake our homeland." His tone suddenly darkens, "Please do not fail us now." Then he abruptly leaves, slamming the door behind his back, his words hanging ominously in the air, and I suddenly realize I am a prisoner.

The bookshelves spin around me and tighten like cage bars, and I start hyperventilating. I haven't had an episode in a while, which my therapist would chalk it up to abandoning my obsession to control everything and shifting the focus from my mother's poor parenting and years of bullying at school to my actual life.

I have no time to lose and no medication in my pocket, so I open the heavy book he left on the table, desperately trying to distract myself.

The Underworld. My eyes cross when I struggle to decipher the thin lines of strange letters. It is impossible, so I focus on the scarce maps and pictures instead. They are painted with incredible detail, sparkling in beautiful colors, outlined with golden ink.

I leaf through cryptic maps that cannot tell me much, but a vivid painting follows, stretching over two pages. It shows the Underworld as a lush, green woodland, where thick vines intertwine and strive toward the arches of the rock vaults, piercing them and heading to the surface. Magical lights dance among the thick green leaves, clusters of crystals, and eerie glowing vegetation, making the landscape appear mysterious yet somehow dreamy. My finger traces the vines´ deep roots digging through the rocky soil, reaching down like bony fingers to an unseen light source.

What lies below the Underworld?

This sounds like a question for a certain High elf priest.

I find him in the pool. Tarcyll is nowhere to be seen. I strip down to my bikini and dive into the lukewarm water.

Diaphonus follows my moves with a dreamy smile, and I cannot help but admire how the angles of his body reflect the meager starlight. The tail of the Crystal Serpent shimmers above us as I join him at the edge of the pool, overlooking the cosmic abyss.

"I heard you were asking some rather odd questions—" the elf starts, and I roll my eyes. It's enough that they are keeping secrets from me and probably wouldn't let me go like they promised. They don't have to act like parents.

"I'm just trying to learn more about your world." I try to smoothen the tension between us. He nods in approval; I know he is the better one to press for information. The spy is short-fused and dangerous, too suspicious to manipulate into talking.

"I have learned much about your lands, yet you barely mentioned the Underworld. And I need to know more about our common enemy if I am to face him again," I explain with a straight face, ignoring that he approaches me and his fingers gently brush my collarbone.

"I saw a picture of a strange forest down there, the roots of the jungle going deep," I casually chirp, disregarding how he looks at me and how my nipples acknowledge his imposing presence.

"The vines of the Underworld are nothing but a myth." He pulls me in and places a chaste kiss on my forehead. "Nobody has seen them for real." The second kiss is on my neck and is not that modest. I feel the train of my thought taking an unpredicted turn.

"What are they?" I murmur, feeling certain parts of me twitch with desire. I'm running on borrowed time here.

"Just an old legend, Celeste." He flicks his tongue against my earlobe, and my toes curl. It's just a question of mere seconds for me to give in. Subtly yet decisively, I pull away, "What legend?" I insist.

He growls in disappointment, his fingers resting on my lower back. I bet Diaphonus the Fair thinks I'm taunting him to sharpen his desire for me.

"Ancient Fae believed that the Underworld was a subterranean paradise before we—the High elves—exiled our most powerful sorceress there. They say that, enraged by her downfall, she burned everything down. Some argue that the vines were destroyed by the Siphons. Who knows? The witch lost herself and surrendered to the darkness. Her son survived, and you have briefly met him at that parking lot..." he roughly pulls me in and takes my mouth.

It takes sheer willpower to move away and continue, "And what is below the roots of the vines? It looked like a pool of lights…"

He frowns, annoyed by my stubbornness. "It's the lifeblood of our world. Pure magic. Some claim that the vines were the blood vessels transporting the magic to the surface. But all these are just tales."

"And you don't think it's worth investigating?" I ask incredulously.

"And how are we to investigate this? Ask the Dark Prince for assistance?" His hand curls around my nape, pulling me in for a kiss.

"I think we are to consider every theory—"

I try to reason, but his lips silence my voice. There is no escaping him now.

He doesn't respond. The magnificent high elf seems determined to have me only for himself. And I gladly surrender.

I reason weakly that he would not be able to reap the arcane power when it's only two of us, yet he snuffs out my words with bruising kisses I simply cannot resist. His hands are on my breasts, greedily cupping them, pinching my peaks. His need is making him vicious. I moan in his mouth, and he loses his restraint. His graceful fingers dive between my thighs, pulling aside my bikini. I immediately feel the stretch of his massive cock at my entrance. The priest doesn't waste time in foreplay this time but aggressively penetrates me.

He cups my backside in his large hands, the water supporting my weight, and punishes me with his thick, veiny cock. A move behind his shoulder catches my eye, and I notice Tarcyll, naked and gorgeous, the mystical tattoos on his bulky arms and chest telling fantastic stories, his erect length tempting me to grab it. As if reading my mind, he enters the pool, the turquoise water rippling around his sculpted abs and the V-shaped lines deeper. In an instant, I feel his warmth behind my back.

"Celeste was quite curious about the Underworld," the blond priest says breathily while stretching me to my limits.

"Mhm, quite curious indeed," inked fingers close around my throat, and the spymaster tilts my head, covering my jaw in kisses. Then his hungry gaze focuses on my wet breasts, bouncing with each of Diaphonus´ trusts. "Some questions are better left unanswered, Celeste," he rumbles, and the hard curves of his muscled torso press against my back. Something else presses too. I gasp and arch into him. It will never cease to amaze me how large these Fae are.

"We work perfectly together, Celeste. Let's stick to our plan..." the elf purrs, grazing my neck with his fangs. His wet hair clings to his high priest jewelry and bronzed skin, and I thread my fingers through it. Heavenly soft, unlike the rest of him.

Tarcyll cups my breasts roughly, and his hot hardness settles between my ass cheeks. I feel the need to be stretched by both of them, to have my holes filled by these exquisite males, to explore these gray lands between bliss and pain, to make them lose control by the pleasures my body can provide. I want to see them in a frenzy, their beautiful features distorted by primal, carnal desire to conquer me.

"You better focus on what matters, Celeste," the spymaster breathes in my ear and slowly enters my rear. I arch again, serving my stiff nipples to the hungry, relentless mouth of Diaphonus, who latches onto my right breast, sucking so hard that I'm sure it'll leave a mark.

"Be a good girl for us, Celeste, and let us harvest your rare gift," Tarcyll commands hoarsely, and his tone fans the flames of my lust. I adapt to the strange and sweet feeling of being completely filled, stretched, and moan like a whore when they move inside me at a shattering, unforgiving pace.

Diaphonus angles his hips and finds the sweet spot inside me, his clear summer-sky eyes delving into mine. "Do you like that, Celeste?" he breathes, and his lips brush mine, but before I can utter a warning, my skin starts glowing, and my eyes roll back. Darkness engulfs me while all my nerve endings wiggle at the pleasure, my pussy and ass twitching in a mad, soul-crushing orgasm, and I hear the muffled curses of Tarcyll behind my back. I feel both men spilling themselves inside me simultaneously, the intense spurts of hot liquid prolonging the wave of ecstasy I'm riding.

We remain like this for a few moments, melded into each other's arm. I tremble in their embrace until I come to my senses. Tarcyll's fingers gently trace the line of my shoulders while the elf leans his forehead against mine. Then the spymaster cautiously scoops me up and carries me to the pool's edge, where his friend awaits me with a soft towel.

"It was an amazing explosion of energy, Celeste," the elf's cobalt eyes glow with pride, "I managed to store it all! So much power! If we continue like this, soon we can travel back home and liberate half of Faëheim!"

The spy chuckles and pats his friend's back.

I nod, snuggling in the fluffy towel, but my busy mind struggles with the word "half."

The seeds of doubt are already sprouting in my mind. Why is the Underworld such a taboo? And why not unite forces with the most powerful sorcerer and at least try to liberate their whole world? What if the key to saving their home is somewhere there, among the vines that reach down to the magical core?

TARCYLL – THE SPYMASTER

I have always been a sucker for female charms. I'm known for it at the golden court of Verdant. The pleasures were always shared, the ladies desiring me equally in my man and beast form. My favorite pastime was frolicking with nymphs and dryads in the perennial forests or savoring the exquisite charms of the Elven and Fae ladies in waiting of the king, sharing some of the willing ones with His Majesty himself. Yet I have never sought out a female again after receiving satisfaction. I have never craved her presence or hungered for her after the deed was done. Until now.

Is it the magic inside Celeste that hums to the beast inside me? Is it the throbbing, hypnotic pulse of the Crystal Serpent pulling me toward her, or is it her otherness, her human nature?

Since being inside Celeste for the first time, I find it hard to focus on something else. My other form threatens to come out, ravish her, force himself upon her, consume her. It's getting harder to hold the beast back. I'm grateful for Diaphonus´ presence, not only for the mouth-watering sight of her being taken by the beautiful priest but also for his soothing nature. He senses when the beast starts distorting the constraints of my body and calms it with a spell.

With each release, I'm getting stronger. Diaphonus is getting mightier, too; a strange afterglow lingers in his gaze for hours after. An unsettling one. Is it hunger? Or greed? Something tells me that I need to be alert, and I follow him like the shadow I am, never leaving him alone with Celeste.

I should have known that the blissful Idyll we've lived in the last few days was doomed. I am a spy, a blade lurking in the shadows, an assassin whose survival depends on his gut feeling.

Yet my instincts were too busy getting high on her scent, seeing her break in my arms when I fuck her, drinking on the gentle magic she spills around her when she climaxes.

The disaster comes shortly just a few days after my arrival. Me and the priest watch helplessly how Celeste struggles to breathe, her delicate face distorted by panic and pain. I have never felt so helpless in my life.

She has mentioned her odd sickness before but never appeared ill to me. When her crisis strikes, the priest and I watch her terrified. The high elf shakes his head, explaining it is a sickness of the mind caused by anxiety and stress, and he can't do much.

The woman explains that there s medicine for it in her realm; she just needs to buy it at a pharmacy. She adds that she is missing her sick mother and cat, which probably triggered the panic attack.

The priest and I exchange looks. The decision is quick. We will portal to her world and move away quickly.

Surely our arrival will draw the attention of the Dreadful One, so we have to be prepared.

Traveling between realms is easy now. The elf's magic is fully restored, he announces, and all the chunks of his powers he has spent battling the Siphons and defending his home are replenished. I am relieved. He is the mightiest mage of Faëheim, second only to the Dark Prince, and the best ally to have.

Celeste suggests a spot close to her work, stating that the place is crowded in the day, and the chances of the Dreadful One risking an open attack are slim.

A simple in-and-out operation, she calls it.

Diaphonus opens the gate, and we step out into a narrow side alley littered with trash and discarded boxes. The smell of the human realm hits me like a fist. One week in the priest's hideout, and I have almost forgotten the reek of garbage, the toxic vapors of their machinery, the odor of their otherness.

We leave the back street hastily, and Celeste leads us to the subway. The escalator takes us deep into the bowels of the city. It's the fastest and safest route, she declares.

I cannot look away from her enticing lips as she explains that this is her daily route to work when her boss summons her to her working place. The late afternoon commute is full on, and we let Celeste lead the way to the train that will take us to her house. She navigates through the crowd, and we do our best to keep up. We reach the platform when the train halts and get carried away by the stream of people disembarking. Celeste goes to the last cart and gestures for us to get in. The crowd thins, almost everyone who wanted on is already aboard, and we hop on the train from the second to last door. Celeste moves as if to follow us, heading to the last entry, but hesitates. I rush toward the platform to drag her in, yet too late. The doors close in my face with a hiss, and the train accelerates.

My last glimpse of her is disappearing into the darkness of the tunnel behind, and I curse loudly while Diaphonus demands that someone stops the train.

CELESTE – THE ANCHOR

Tormenting flashbacks of how I almost died on these tracks invade my mind, but I focus on the task ahead.

"Cyrell!" my voice echoes into the tunnel, red light glowing like evil eyes. Squinting my eyes, I stare into the blackness ahead, trying to make out the tall frame of a certain white-haired dark elf and his metallic companion.

I do not debate if this is a good idea. My sanity has withdrawn to a quiet corner since this whole mess began. Or is this my messed-up sense of fighting injustice again?

I know that something is eluding me, that the charming duo who did everything they could to please and keep me happy in the last days is withholding information.

And I happen to know someone who might help me uncover it.

A chill runs down my spine when I take a hesitant step into the darkness, remembering the phantom who got me nearly drowned.

A couple of weeks ago, my biggest problem was an aggressive customer or Sandra's request to work from the office.

Now I'm compromising my safety to uncover some—most likely imaginary—secret that could help me save a world I'm not even sure exists.

Yet there is something else—some twisted thrill that I have never experienced. I have never been keen on taking risks. Growing up with an alcoholic mother, I was always the pragmatic cool head, the mature, self-controlled kid, always warning the others when they were up to something stupid. Oh, how the tables have turned, how the last days have changed me. Here I am, walking in an off-limits area, expecting to be arrested or kidnapped by a mythical creature with dark plans about my destiny.

I just hope he gives me the chance to speak before hooking me up to his wretched extractor.

With another step into the darkness, unfamiliar scents and distant scratching raise the hairs on my forearms. I hope my gamble was right.

CYRELL – THE WARRIOR

Tracking enemies in complete darkness is my element. Cerberus´ senses also extend beyond the sophisticated mechanics of his body. He was defeated and damaged by the other Hunters when they attacked my den, but I managed to patch him up. The scent of Celeste's fear left a bright trail for me to follow. I ran the gloomy tunnels, calling her name, and realized she was gone when I reached the corner where the vengeful fantom lingers.

The spy and the priest were faster than me.

My fangs extended, and I punched the wall, craving the pain to sober me up from the dangerous frustration brewing, threatening to swallow the last pieces of sanity.

For days I feared they might have already taken the Anchor to Faëheim. Yet the other Hunters would not risk delivering such a powerful weapon straight to the Siphons without tapping into her magic first.

So, I decided to wait and kept an eye on her house. Maybe she would return to pick something up? I saw her friend dropping by daily, probably feeding her cat, yet no sign of Celeste's bright presence.

I stalked her friend, watched her, studied her routine, and looked her up in the realm they call cyberspace.

The messengers of human communication—those white doves darting between different virtual locations—are so easy to intercept. Jasmin was receiving messages from Cuba, pictures of Celeste in a pool with the other two Hunters, looking happy and relaxed.

Relief soothed the poisonous sting of jealousy. Celeste was still within my reach! They took her to the safe house of Tarcyll.

Tapping into the all-seeing eyes of the video surveillance system took me a while. And then I watched those wretched Fae around the human, day and night, drooling like starving wolves around a lamb, competing for her attention. My punches cracked the table.

The priest was up to something. When Celeste entered the steam bath with the spy, I could see the sparks of powerful magic. Something happened inside, something disturbing enough for Diaphonus to take our valuable human somewhere else—to another safe place.

I watched the desperate and betrayed Tarcyll destroy most of the house in the following days and drank himself into a stupor. Oh, how well I knew this feeling of failure and desperation.

Then, a week later, the elven priest suddenly reappeared, looking serene and radiant, and portaled them both elsewhere. It should be a place the elf feels utterly safe if he is risking drawing the attention of the Dreadful One or even the Siphons by using magic. Picking up a trail like this—finding someone across plains of reality and realms—would be a challenge even for an Elder.

Days pass, and my hopes fade.

I have failed my people.

My sister and nephews will perish in the suffocating darkness. Countless innocents will pay with their lives when the Council of the Elders starts sacrifices to appease the Siphons.

I pace the room, swinging my lance and replaying the events from the last weeks repeatedly in my mind. A blade has always calmed my racing thoughts. Cerberus' glowing eyes critically follow my every move.

I halt in front of a pile of disemboweled appliances, kicking an old cell phone.

Should I return to the Council empty-handed? Should I confess that the spy and the priest have outsmarted me? And what would kill me first when the Elders´ vile magic tentacles dig into my memories? Their just rage at my failure or my shame?

There must be another way.

Maybe my loyal friend can pick up the trail of her magic across the realms, maybe—

"Cyrell!"

Cerberus cocks his massive bronze head, hearkening. He might be large as a chariot, yet he has the soul of a puppy. Am I hallucinating?

"Cyrell? It's me, Celeste! We need to talk!"

She is far, yet distance in the underground darkness is nothing to a dark elf warrior. We follow the sweet poison of her voice and find her close to the tunnel where we first met.

The relief of finding her is snuffed by white-hot rage. Who does she think she is, defying me, collaborating with the other Hunters?

"I see you have finally come to your senses!" I bark, roughly grabbing her arm. I pull her behind me down the tunnel, probably leaving bruises on her tender skin.

I catch her scent. Good. She's not under a spell, nor is she intoxicated. The trap I have feared is not there. Yet there is something else—

By the Serpent! The Anchor reeks of them. I bare my teeth. She is pumped full of their seed.

They had her in all ways possible.

I growl. If the human has survived mating with a shifter and the most powerful elf of Faëheim, then she would survive me. I see red at the thought.

All the frustration and the dark desires that stole my sleep erupt and sweep my common sense away.

"Guard the entrance," I yell at Cerberus while I drag her and tie her to the table.

I want to taste her before the Extractor does.

"Cyrell," the woman cries, her eyes wide. The leather bonds sling around her slender ankles and wrists, stretching her on the wooden surface. I'm panting when I tighten the leash around her neck, and I feel my throbbing cock straining against my pants.

"Cyrell, I came here of my own will, risking everything—"

Her heavy breasts press against the silk of her dress. Her breathing is fast and shallow, and her pupils dilate—is it fear or thrill I see?

I am the most feared warlord in the Lower Lands. Legions kneel at the sound of my voice. And this human has defied me, escaped me, made a fool of me, and given herself to the other Hunters. She must learn to fear me—

"I need your help," she breathes. My hands freeze in mid-air. I trust my sharpened senses, suggesting that I need to hear her out.

Is this a trick by the other Hunters? Some dark plan to lure me out of the shadows and destroy me?

"I know how to tap into my magic, Cyrell."

It's clearly a trick. The location of my hideout is compromised; probably, the priest and the spy are on their way. I have to hook her up to the Extractor quickly.

She should not have come here. It could only end one way for her.

"I have some questions about the Underworld and the Dreadful One." Her voice almost breaks when I reach for the cables.

So, he, the Dark Lord, sent her to lure me to my demise. It all makes sense now. He has always been the archenemy of my people. He probably found a way to take her away from the other Hunters, break her, bend her to his will, then send her back to me to aid him with his evil plan.

"I need your help, Cyrell. Diaphonus and Tarcyll have learned how to unlock my magic but plan to use it to protect their lands only. And I believe the Underworld is the key to saving all Faëheim."

I drop the cables and slowly turn to face her. She is pale and shaking, visibly terrified, and I turn away, hiding all the emotions sweeping my resolve away. What have I become? The protector of the Lower Lands who has never hurt an innocent but is now set to brutalize this magnificent female. I remind myself that the fate of all my people is at stake, yet doubt has crept into my heart. My heart of a warrior, of a protector, cannot just doom this life to a painful and agonizing end.

She takes short, pained breaths, beads of sweat forming on her forehead.

"Experiencing pleasure while making love to a magic-gifted being, to a Fae, unlocks my magic—" she blurts out, and I have to steady myself, leaning on the table she's tied to.

The human is telling the truth, I can smell it, and the realization sets me ablaze. Deadly sharp, my fangs elongate; my chest heaves at the thought of all the endless possibilities to test her claim. I am so aroused that I almost attack her in an instant, like a mindless beast. Yet I withdraw my greedy fingers and cock an eyebrow.

"How... how does it work?" I rasp. Curiosity will get me killed one day.

"When I am pleased by a Fae, I release a wave of arcane energy."

My pheromones set off before I can rein myself in. I have desired her for so long, fantasized about having her in many ways, dominating her, worshipping her, punishing her.

Centuries of discipline and stoicism are swept away by the need of my powerful body, a need I can no longer deny.

My fingers brush her cheek and dive lower, down between her breasts.

Her nostrils flare, and she looks me straight in the eye. Her pupils are so dilated that her irises appear as black and hopeless as the darkness of the deepest tunnels back home.

"We should not do this, Cyrell, or he will find us," her voice breaks.

She tugs on the restraints, her lean body arching, leaning into my caress, and I grind my teeth. I need all my willpower to steady myself not to pounce on her, feast on her blood, and consume her flesh while mindlessly tearing her apart with my cock.

A low growl escapes me.

"Who is he?" I ask, distracted. The still functioning part of my brain strains to hatch a plan. If what she says is accurate, and all my being believes it, I can create a massive output of arcane energy and capture it with the Extractor without risking her life. I will please her, store her magic in the device, and make her mine.

"The Dreadful One, Cyrell," she breathes, gasping when my calloused fingers roughly squeeze her breast.

"Do not worry, Celeste," I whisper in her ear before tracing the intoxicating curve of her lips with my tongue and diving deep into her mouth, "I will capture your magic with my machine," Our breaths entwine. "You are safe with me..."

The human responds eagerly to my kiss, her tongue flicking over the razor-sharp blades of my canines. "Do you trust me, Celeste," my voice is deep, enthralling, and I know its effect on the females well, "do you want this?"

She nods, and I slowly lift her dress to find the white lace of her undergarment already soaked. I pull the fabric aside and indulge in the sight of her pink, quivering flesh. My finger casually traces her slit, and she struggles against the restraints, eager to impale herself on it. A smirk dances on my lips when I settle between her wide-spread legs.

"Are you ready for my cock, Celeste?" I ask, my eyes locked on hers. Oh, I will take my time with this treat.

"I am," she whispers. I refuse to believe it's only my pheromones working her up like this, needing me, begging me to take her.

The universal law is that magic is drawn to magic, and with her powers awakened by the other hunters, she craves me as much as I desire her.

My face is buried between her legs, and I scrutinize the pink throbbing flesh. She speaks the truth. The human is ready for me. My tongue trails each fold, explores every rim, and my rumble almost makes her come. I'm taking my time, and the moisture of her need pools on the table when I tongue-fuck her, the blades of my extended fangs grazing her opening. She writhes underneath me, and I feel her velvet walls clenching around my tongue. She needs more. If she speaks true, I must build up much tension before capturing the power she will release. I withdraw and smirk at her disappointed hiss.

I move to the opposite part of the table and loom over her head, pulling the tight leash at her neck to make her face me. She obeys, and I tighten it, the struggle for breath making her open her lips. Just in time to shove my massive cock as deep as I can into her throat. My fangs dig deep into my lips, and blood drips onto my shirt. I savor the resistance of her throat, the suction of her muscles when she tries to draw breath, the plea in her eyes. I'm drunk on that feeling of dominance and control. Pulling back slightly, I let her take a deep breath. The relief is only temporary as I penetrate her again, driven completely mad by the sight of her luscious lips around my fat length, and I lose myself, mercilessly pounding her. My claws are out now, and I rip her dress open, releasing her heavy breasts.

They jolt with each of my violent thrusts, and my human whimpers when my claw circles her perky pink nipples. The blades at my fingertips leave a red mark, but she seems to enjoy it as her hips rise and her juices drip on the worn-out wood. It looks like she likes it rough.

I wonder if the other Fae have treated her the same way, and visions of them taking her erase the last remains of control I have. I dive deep into her, feeling how she stiffens, and spill myself with a deep rumble, my seed spurting around her lips and trickling down her cheeks.

I withdraw quickly to give her a chance to recover. She spits and coughs as tears run down her cheeks, and I am ready to give her what she needs.

With a few deft moves, I attach the thick cables of the Extractor to her limbs and forehead and tighten the leashes, restraining her movements. Her eyes are all glazed, but she follows my actions, and I feel the thick aroma of her arousal linger.

Before slowly circling the table and climbing on, I let Celeste see me the way I am—the monster I am now.

My fangs crave her blood, and my dagger-sharp claws can instantly shred her tender flesh to ribbons.

"Are you ready, Celeste?" I position myself between her legs, feeling her soaking wet core press against my cock. I'm immediately hard again. She slowly rubs her clit up and down my length, and I throb in anticipation. That's all the answer I need. I try to be gentle when I graze her neck and tease her nipples, yet the darkness inside me is more potent than me. Trails of ruby drops follow my caresses. My pulsating crown presses at her hot opening, and she writhes under me, trying to get more of me, yet I freeze in anticipation of this sweet torture.

"Tell me how they fucked you," I demand, and she looks at me in disbelief, "answer me!" A pull of the leash on her neck reminds her that she owes me an answer.

"Were they gentle?" Her breathing hitches and she writhes beneath my weight, her pebbled nipples pressed against my chest, and I slowly enter her, "Or were they rough?"

Celeste gasps and lifts her hips, taking more of me than I anticipated.

"They were..." she looks me in the eye, taunting me. Devilish woman. "They were magical."

"Did they at least have the decency to take turns? Or were you pleasuring them simultaneously?" I'm not sure which answer I would prefer. By the Serpent, I find both options maddening. She struggles to say something, and I smile darkly. "Both at the same time then. Human females are more resilient than I thought."

Blood trickles from the scratches along her breasts, and it mixes with mine when my injured lips cover her in kisses.

She moans when I start moving, then screams when my hips slap against the silky skin of her thighs. The scent of her is so overpowering, so mouthwatering—

"Mine... mine..." is the only thought left inside my head when I sink my teeth into the tender flesh of her left breast and taste her blood. Her screams are a crescendo now; her writhing beneath me sober me up. I reign my bloodlust in.

I've marked her... I have claimed her. I have tasted her. Her essence was the sweetest symphony of longing and promises I have ever had. All the dark elves will treat her as mine, which will be great if my plan works and she survives the Extractor.

I withdraw from her bleeding breast but continue thrusting into her with a punishing force. I can feel her clenching around my cock, and I know that her release is impending, and it will be a cataclysmic one.

I hope the Extractor will be able to contain all that energy. Slamming deep into her, I reach out and turn the device on.

Celeste writhes underneath me, only the white of her eyes visible. My cum still drips from her lips, mixed with her tears. Another deep plunge and she clamps around me, her hot, wet tightness squeezing my cock, and I climax with a roar. The mighty jets of my hot seed push her over the edge, and she shatters around me with a whimper.

I watch in reverence how her skin starts glowing. Is this something all human females do, or is it the magic finding its way to the surface? Then I feel the powerful sweep of arcane energy, and the Extractor vibrates.

Electric sparks shoot from the apparatus, and a thin line of smoke follows. Still unable to peel myself from Celeste, I watch it catch fire. I force myself to pull away and leap toward the flames.

What have I done?

I stifle the flames with a blanket.

The only chance of saving my home is gone, destroyed by my lust.

My frantic gaze lands back on Celeste—she's still hazy but survived my rough mating. Her long lashes cast shadows over her cheeks, and she looks serene and beautiful. Regal and powerful in her vulnerability. A queen without a throne.

Mine.

She is mine.

I have claimed her. And she survived. With her powers, I might be able to find another way to build a future for my kind, for us. I'm respected and admired by many—an influential warlord. Maybe...

Her skin isn't glowing anymore, and I step toward the table.

And then, palpable darkness pools at the center of the room, consuming all the lights around.

A massive black figure rises and steps out of the murky haze. Another one follows. And another one.

I grab the first blade within my reach and whistle for Cerberus. He sneaks into the room, ears pulled back, growling.

Black Guardians. The faceless, phantom guards of the Dreadful One.

They are here for the Anchor. And I will defend what is mine.

CELESTE – THE ANCHOR

What happened to me? What did these three Fae males, these Hunters, do to me? My conservative, timid approach to sex is swept away, baring a starved and brave new me.

I felt liberation for the first time I gave in to their temptations. A sensation of power followed. Ancient, lingering power, soft but persistent, like the water eating up the biggest rocks and shaping them to its will.

Was it the magic pulsing deep within me or the gentle power of the female over a male? I cannot tell.

All my fears—would I look slutty or ridiculous if I followed my desires, what would happen if I lost control—all my doubts are wiped out by the life-changing events of the last weeks. And honestly, I like the new me.

When Cyrell finds me in the subway tunnel, I feel no fear. I relish the dark desire in his eyes, and his hunger for me, my flesh, and my essence ignites my bones. I can drive this male into a frenzy with just a few words or a swing of my hips.

Our union is violent. He bites me and drinks from me, and his blood drips into my mouth. It tastes like underground decadence and ancient secrets, like loneliness among golden tunnels filled with machinery and despair. My senses sharpen; my eyes pierce the shadows easily, and my nostrils catch the faintest scents.

And when he pulls away from me, I know I have given, but I have also taken something in return.

Then a dark presence fills his hideout, and four terrifying phantoms made of shadows swirl out of the black haze.

The Dreadful One is here.

Still sprawled on the table, I watch helplessly how Cyrell leaps onto them. His otherworldly agility and speed are so fascinating to watch. Caught in the momentum, his silver hair flashes, and then he flies across the room, swept aside as if he's not a six-foot six-inch warrior but a mere fly.

The sound of immaculately oiled transmissions follows the rumble of broken objects, and Cerberus leaps at the first black figure, aiming for its throat.

Metallic canines clack, the air densifies, then explodes, and the giant dog ends up in the far corner of the room in a shower of sparks, his hind legs bent in unnatural angles.

It's painful to watch Cyrell's companion struggle to rise, even more painful than seeing his master flying across the cramped room, crashing into the piles of machinery lying around. He stands up, bleeding, long talons protruding from his knuckles, and swings to slice the throats of the mysterious intruders. Yet the blades pierce only shadows. Three of them are fighting him. Or keeping him away from me, I realize.

The fourth shadow suddenly looms over me, and I shudder when I feel ice-cold fingers fondle the leash on my neck. I look up to the face of the abomination and freeze in terror. Warping shades of black stare back at me, and I know that I cannot expect mercy or empathy from a creature like this, that it would die and come back only to do its master's bidding.

Oh my God, what did I get myself into?

I feel my restraints loosen, and rough hands sit me up. It presses me against its chest and drags me toward the center of the room, and I can sense its disturbing scent of thunderclouds and barren rocks.

Cyrell rises again, a wound gaping on his right cheekbone, his white hair loose and matted with blood. Arcane force flickers around his hands as he tries to cast a spell, yet a powerful kick to his chest sends him flying. A sickening crunch is the last thing I hear when the dark figure pulls me into a whirlpool of pain.

I wake up confused, covered in caked blood and Cyrell's dried cum. A barren landscape in all shades of gray stretches to the misty horizon. The thin air scrapes my throat. My fingers dig into fine black sand, reflecting some distant cool light.

I blink and look around.

The monotony of this dark wasteland is disturbed by leviathan dead tree trunks. They strain to reach the invisible vaults above, fading into the heavy black sky above our heads. Light orbs dance between the withered branches and shriveled gray leaves.

I recognize the place, though it was a lush green paradise in Diaphonus' book.

The Underworld.

Four black figures stare down at me. When they see me coming to my senses, the tallest one—the leader, gestures for me to follow.

I nod and slowly rise, my bones and muscles screaming in agony.

Sharp pain pierces my chest, and my breathing becomes shallow and fast. I recognize the symptoms immediately.

No. I cannot let it happen now. I need all my strength and wits to survive. So much has happened, and I have managed to avoid this, except for when I faked it to escape the priest´s hideout.

I can do this. This was my goal, after all—to search for other options to get rid of the cursed magic inside me. And my hope lies within this mysterious domain. I harness all my willpower to believe this.

The effort to slow down my breathing is physically exhausting. But it works. I wipe the sweat off my brow and follow the phantom figures, patiently waiting for my crisis to pass.

Each step raises a cloud of black shimmering dust, and soon my white, lacy, ballerina slippers turn entirely gray.

Where are they taking me?

The four tall specters are wrapped in darkness and move in complete silence and creepy synchrony. I cannot hear them breathe. Are they physical, or are they spirits bound to the wicked will of the Dreadful One? They pace ahead, not bothering to look back to see if I follow. Indeed, where would I go if I decided to flee? Nothing here can offer shelter or any means of survival.

Does the key to saving Faëheim lie here, deep in the Underworld? What sort of unimaginable terrors do my captors plot for me?

The eerie forest gets thicker; black leaves the size of a car stick from the petrified tree trunks. Indeed, it looks like this place flourished before, and some unknown plague destroyed it. Was it the madness of the Dark Prince's mother?

We follow a barely noticeable path meandering among the mummified vegetation. The sand under my feet is replaced by white pebbles.

A landscape just like out of a Halloween school play stretches at my feet. Even my guards pause for an instant to acknowledge its haunting beauty.

The vines before us intertwine, building a gargantuan canopy over a filigree Gothic castle. The vegetation sparkles in a deep green shade, and dark flowers peep from the tall grass. The white pebbled road mouths to a deserted courtyard littered with the remains of what once was a magnificent garden. The chipped rings of dry fountains, broken marble statues, and stumps of ancient trees are all that remains now, yet decadent splendor wafts from the building and its surroundings.

Slender towers scrape the inky mists above, and tracery windows trickle warm light into the eternal twilight around. Faerie lights twirl everywhere, their timid glow smoothening the darkness and making it appear almost welcoming. A place like this would inspire countless stories of haunted palaces, cursed princes, and evil witches.

We ascend the imposing black granite stairs to the main building. I feel dwarfed by the symphony of stained-glass walls, arches, and gargoyles that look disturbingly alive.

A black veil of shadows covers the guardians´ faces, yet I can bet they wonder if I appreciate the dark grandeur of the palace. They urge me to enter, and I comply.

As soon as I set foot inside, they shut the heavy, wrought iron gates behind my back, and the sharp echo climbs the miles-high arches.

Distant candlelight dances on the polished black marble floor at my feet, making it look like dark water. I take a cautious step, afraid the shimmering surface might swallow me. The millennial silence greedily swallows the soft sound of my steps, and I wonder if this castle is deserted. I walk along a colonnade, peer into the impenetrable shadows that linger beyond it, and cold chills crawl up my spine.

I feel watched.

The deserted entrance hall leads me to a door, its tall, bronze wings covered in artful bas-reliefs of fantastic plants and unknown beasts. It's open, and I step in.

The burning incense makes the darkness palpable. Fairy lights float around vine-covered pillars lined along the walls, and the checkered floor stretches toward a tall dais crowned by a throne.

My heart skips a beat, and my feet refuse to take me further.

There is someone on that throne.

Each haunted castle has its cursed prince.

The shadows thicken, weaving an imposing figure sitting on it.

So, this is my mysterious stalker, the fourth Fae Hunter.

The Dreadful One.

My first instinct is to turn around and run, yet unseen hands grab me, squeezing the air out of my lungs, and hurl me toward the dais.

I roll on the cold floor and come to a halt at its feet, my joints pierced by sharp pain. Pulling my ruined dress down, I try to scramble myself up. If I am to die, I will do it standing, looking my tormentor in the eye. My doom is already upon me. Slow, heavy steps slice the silence, and long, gloved fingers lift my chin.

Once again, I steady my breath.

What kind of monstrosity has earned himself the name the Dreadful One? Is he a Fae or some apparition, like his guards? His powers deem him almost god-like, his evil will breaking everyone who sought refuge in those cursed lands.

I finally gather enough courage to look up, and I gasp. I catch the glimmer of turquoise eyes under long, thick, black eyelashes. Full lips are quirked in a roguish smile, playfully displaying the dangerous tip of a fang.

"My, my, look at what the cat dragged in!"

His voice is deep but soft, and the notes hang heavily in the air when he circles me. I follow the feline moves of his impossibly tall frame, shadows trailing behind him. At first I think it's a richly draped cloak, complimenting the finely-tailored midnight-colored suit he's wearing. When I look closer, I realize that those are wings. Wings, made of condensed shadow. He must be a terrifying sight when he spreads them. No wonder all Fae are terrified of him. A feared warlord and powerful mage.

In other words... an Archdemon.

His circle around me is complete, and I try to cover myself up, mortified under the scrutiny of these otherworldly glowing eyes. I still wear the ragged dress, stained by blood and... other body fluids, my breasts almost fully on display. I cross my arms defiantly as he clicks his tongue.

"I think you need a bath to wash all these males from you," he suggests, his dark, velvet voice covering a blade.

"I've always been curious about your kind," the shadow of his mighty wings frames his broad shoulders when he approaches me, "you are so fragile yet persistent. Against all odds, you are still there! While we are about to perish. Is it because you breed like a pest?" He looks down at me, head cocked, shoulder-length ebony lock falling over a razor-sharp jawline. I know better than to answer to his provocation. "Your weakness turned out to be your salvation. Your insignificance your biggest perk. At the same time, our power brought us our doom. There is some bitter justice in that, don't you think?" I swallow dryly and notice the first signs of hyperventilation. *Not now*, I grit my teeth, *not when I have to negotiate my fate.*

His half-lidded gaze shifts to my exposed, heaving breast, and he smirks devilishly.

"I have noticed that you and the Anchor Hunters have found a very… creative way to tap into your magic." Perfectly shaped dark eyebrows furrow with distaste over a straight, regal nose. All Fae males are beyond handsome, but this one has the lethal beauty of a jeweled blade in a dark alley, of a siren´s call luring seafarers to their doom. Nature has created him to be the perfect predator, a deadly trap for naïve souls like me. I am enthralled, unable to move, like a rabbit in the headlights. "Yet I would love to run a few experiments myself, Celeste, and for that, I need you to follow me to the dungeon".

Experiments? Oh my...

The panic strikes without warning; I'm hyperventilating uncontrollably, and pain pierces my chest.

"So fragile—" is the last thing I hear. Then the Dreadful One casts a spell, and I drop at his feet.

I wake up in a cell that looks like something out of the D&D universe but is disturbingly real. The humid walls reflect the light of the single candle glued to the rough stone floor, and the stench of mold is overwhelming. A bucket of relatively clean water is placed next to me, and I drink, then wash up as much as I can.

The echo of water dripping far away suggests I'm in a larger underground hall.

Suddenly I sense the gravity of an intense gaze and jump, pulling my ruined dress over my chest in a pathetic attempt to cover up.

The heavy metal bars of the door creak open, and the tall shadow of my captor swallows the meager light. Without a single word, he grabs my arm and drags me out to a wide corridor.

Dark openings gape left and right, and a glimpse of a skeletal hand still clutching a bar makes me pull back and put up a pathetic fight, thinking I might end up like the unfortunate there. Or maybe a worse fate awaits me?

Resisting is useless. The Fae is ridiculously tall, and there is that disturbing aura around him, that sensation of barely leashed power. He could snap my neck with a single move.

His fingers feel like steel under the soft leather gloves, and he hurls me into a wider hall.

I press my hands to my lips to suppress a scream. We are in a medieval torture chamber.

Chains and ropes decorate the stained masonry of the walls, and rows of terrifying tools glitter in the flickering light of the sconces. I almost faint when I notice an iron maiden and a spiked chair.

"All of these are inspired by your people, Celeste," the Dreadful One whispers in my ear, guiding me to a wooden pillory. I try to resist and yank my arm free, yet his grip is relentless. "My kind would never think of harming each other in such clever ways. Yet my mother found these devices fascinating." His voice is dripping with threat. The heavy frame of the pillory locks over my neck and wrists.

The Hunters were right. This male is a monster.

I am bent forward, exposed, and helpless. The Fae latches the device and moves to face me. His fingers lift my chin so our eyes meet.

Once again, I am hypnotized by the cold, cruel beauty of his gaze, and see my death sentence among those blue-green flames. He bites his lip in something that looks a lot like anticipation and disappears from my view.

I can hear him shuffling behind me. Oh my God, what kind of terrible torture instrument is he holding...

"You know, Celeste, deep in your soul, there is a raw, untouched corner where all primal emotions lie. Pain, aggression, lust, and pleasure have not changed much since you were nothing but beasts. Primal magic lingers among these primal drives. Concealed well, untouchable. That is why the Siphons never came for you. Yet my brethren discovered something that my mother had suspected long ago. If you stimulate these primal emotions in the magically gifted few—the Anchors—you will tap into their magic. Brace yourself, human. It's time for my first experiment."

I stiffen, feeling my dress travel up above my waist. I shake the pillory, trying to pull my hands out of the holes and free myself, but I know my attempts are futile. I hear the male take a sharp breath with a hiss, probably noticing my ruined lacy panties.

And then I hear the crack of a whip.

I bite my lips when the first lash lands on my exposed backside. I feel the sting across my right cheek, yet it is not as painful as expected from a six-foot eight-inch demon with a warrior build. He's holding back, probably testing how much I can take before unleashing himself upon me. The second lash makes me squirm helplessly. A short, sharp scream escapes my lips, and the third lash catches me unprepared. The onslaught continues, and my tears wet the ancient stone floor.

"Embrace the pain, Celeste, let it lead you to the sanctuary where your magic lingers," the demon suddenly stands before me, tucking a dark strand behind his ear, its pointy tip adorned with a stunning black earring. He leans down and studies me up close. A forked tongue darts over his full lips, and he smirks. My eyes follow the casual grace of his moves, and I notice a blatant bulge between his legs. Is he aroused?

Another crack, but I have no strength left to scream. I feel the lower part of my body hanging helplessly in the merciless chokehold of the torture device. My feet slip, and I slump, all my body weight supported by my wrists and neck. The pressure on my nape becomes too intense. Chaotic lights float around, and the ground below my feet spins. My tormentor senses it, too, and ceases his assault. Steely arms wrap around my waist, and the click of the devilish mechanism announces my release.

His experiment has failed, what will be my punishment? A shower of magical sparks and fatigue crushes over me. The sleeping spell hits me, and I rest my face against the soft velvet of his jacket, trailing off in dreamless sleep.

I wake up in the cell, sprawled on a rough, straw-stuffed mattress. It rustles when I move, and a rich, thick blanket is thrown over me, preventing the cold from seeping into my bones. I wrap it around my shoulders and risk a look around. More candles burn on the floor now; their waxy tears trickle between the rocks. I pull away from the tiny flames, terrified by the possibility of starting a fire while locked behind the massive bars. Prisoners' safety was obviously not a concern when they built the place.

I can make out a bowl full of some unknown berries and a piece of fresh-looking bread. The bucket of cold water is refilled, and I crawl toward it, numb pain in my backside reminding me of my humiliation earlier. I splash my face, then grab the food and withdraw to the farthest corner of the cell.

A dark figure watches me from the gloom, announcing the arrival of new terrors. His aquamarine orbs shimmer coldly, and his black wings are spread. Oh, God, how massive he looks.

His hauntingly perfect features remain impassive while he watches me eat. The lock clicks open when I take my last bite, and he enters, magnificent and terrifying, and I fully understand why they call him the Dreadful One.

The air around him vibrates with power, and he doesn't need words to make my body obey him. I leap onto my feet and follow him through a maze of sconce-lit tunnels, deeper into the dungeons.

The Dreadful One halts before a massive wooden door, a rusty chain with an ancient lock drops to the stone floor after he barks a command.

Then he turns to me, the flickering light making his face appear more angular. A cruel smile curls his full lips, displaying elegant yet feral-looking canines.

"What is beyond that door?" My voice is hoarse, and I'm surprised by my bravado. He seems impressed, too, and he quirks a brow, amused.

"Those who passed beyond are not to be disturbed, Celeste. Even your primitive people know that. My mother had committed many crimes," I search his phosphorescent eyes for any sign of emotion, yet he is so alien, so unreadable, "but raising the dead to do her bidding was one of the worst. They all came back changed. Mindless beasts, lost in bloodlust." I take a hesitant step back, yet his will holds me in place. He hands me a vicious-looking curved sword, and I almost drop it. The steel's cold weight feels so unusual in my hand.

"I want to see you desperate and terrified, fighting for your life. I want to see you aggressive and mindless, slicing throats, spilling guts. How fascinating it would be to watch how fear and self-preservation instincts tear down the glaze that culture and civilization have forced upon you." His turquoise gaze glows with excitement, and I feel my knees shaking. "My theory is that a life and death situation will make your magic shine like a lighthouse over a stormy sea!" he triumphantly declares and pushes the heavy door open, inviting me in with a dramatic gesture.

"You have no idea how far I am willing to go to make this right, Celeste," his voice is dangerously low behind my back, "to liberate my world. Now get in there and hand me over the power you received by some divine error!"

The change in his tone is strange, but I have other problems at hand. My feet follow his command, and a terrible stench makes me choke on my vomit. A snap of his fingers sends a couple of light wisps in. They hover high above the surface as if scared and repelled by the stench, just like me.

The door behind me closes, and the ominous sound lingers too long, reverberating against the stone walls of a rotund chamber.

Eyes are on me—cold, unblinking, dead eyes.

"The resilience of your species is one of the most fascinating mysteries of the Serpent, Celeste," I hear the muffled voice of my captor beyond the door, and I suddenly see red. That bastard!

Shuffling and dragging footsteps pin my attention back to the reeking gloom of the empty hall. I squeeze the sword with both hands, my head whipping left and right.

How many walking corpses are in here with me? My blade raised, I am determined to skewer anything within my reach.

I'm pretty fit, and all the running and exercise are paying off, yet I have zero experience with swords or any martial arts. But how difficult could it be? You just have to stick the pointy end into those trying to harm you.

What I am not prepared for is their speed. And strength. And their sneaky attack from behind.

My shoulder blade explodes in a cacophony of pain when long claws dig into my skin. I fly toward the rough stone floor and hit it hard, instinctively softening the fall with my hands. It sends my blade flying, and it lands with a clang at least two feet away.

The stench and the agony from my torn skin fill my eyes with tears that I blink away.

It's on my back. Oh my God, I feel its deadweight hanging on me, sharp teeth sinking deeper into my flesh. I wiggle in the ice-cold bony grip of the creature, turn around, and kick at its lower torso with all the strength of my legs. The maneuver makes me face it for a split second before my kick tumbles it off me. I waste no time pondering if what I have just seen in the cold fairy light is real or some twisted, *Walking Dead* requisition brought to life by evil spellwork.

Its eyes are milky white, its flesh peeling in ribbons, displaying bones and dark innards. Rags hang from its sinewy limbs, and unnaturally long hair strands hint that long ago, it was female. Surprisingly fast, though, it's back on its feet, preparing to leap on me again. My blood pools on the masonry of the ancient floor, driving the creature into a frenzy. The wound already feels hot, pulsating with some terrible infection.

It pounces at me, claws out, just at the instant I roll to the left, and my fingers close around the soothing coolness of the sword handle.

"Mindless beasts lost in bloodlust," I remember the Dreadful One's words. Indeed, the abomination is crawling, licking my blood from the stone tiles; its smacking mixes with the repulsive sniffing of the two holes on its rotting face.

Soundlessly, I leap to my feet and sneak toward the massive pillars holding the dome. I shudder at the thought that more might lurk in the gloom beyond. My retreat catches the attention of the monstrosity, and it turns to face me. I press my back against the cold stone of the pillar and lower my blade. With my left hand, I smear some of the blood trickling from my back over my face and chest.

A menacing rumble escapes the beast, and it bares its black, rotten incisors in something resembling a smile. Frenzied by the blood all over me, it leaps toward me, confident that I have nowhere to escape.

Timing is key.

I raise my blade and point it at its heart at the exact moment before it reaches me. A sickening crunch and a moist whoosh confirm that I got it. Its jaws click powerlessly just an inch from my face, and I kick the convulsing body with disgust. It lands on the floor, pulling itself free from the sword. I lift the heavy blade, smeared with thick black ichor, and aim for its throat. My cry of terror and triumph lingers in the vault when I severe the zombie's head, dark blood and reeking viscera splashing over the stone floor. Then I drop the sword, and the adrenaline rush subsides. The pain from my torn skin burns me, and rivulets of scarlet run down my legs. No magical explosions, no warm, glowing skin. My captor's theory was wrong. Fear doesn't unleash my powers.

I lose balance and stumble into a firm, but warm embrace.

"Still no trace of your magic," he murmurs, and the pain fades.

I wake up on that dreaded straw mattress, perceiving his presence beyond the metal bars.

How long has he been watching me? My injuries are gone as if they were never there. Has the Dreadful One tended to my wounds? Or was it all just an illusion, some twisted nightmare? I throw myself over the flavorful cheese and fresh bread that await me, leaving these questions for later.

The rusty hinges creak, and there he is, his presence crowding my cell. The shadow of his powerful wings contours his sharp profile when he looks down at me. My tormentor is cruel and unpredictable, but he looks... annoyingly perfect.

"I must admit I'm impressed, Celeste," he says softly, handing me folded fabric.

It's a clean cotton dress, simple but practical.

"This human resilience, the way you clutch to life, it never ceases to amaze me. Put it on. It's time for our next experiment."

I blink at him incredulously. Does he expect me to change before him? I stare at him, furious, and he gets the hint. Yet he crosses his arms stubbornly and looks down at me. Fine. He's seen all of it anyway.

I slip out of my dress's tattered, stained remains and stand before the fern flicker of his eyes. His jawline tightens, and his massive arms tense up as if he's keeping himself in check. I throw the fresh dress over my head, wondering the reason for the sudden heat between my thighs.

He's at the door when my face emerges from the neck opening.

"Follow me, Celeste. We have work to do."

I blink twice to make sure my eyes aren't deceiving me. On his knees in the throne room, wrists bound behind his back, is Cyrell. His shirt is torn and bloodied, exposing the swell of his mighty pecs. A wound gapes on his cheekbone. He doesn't look defeated but stares the Dreadful One defiantly in the eye.

The demon prince studies my reaction, a predatory spark in the sage green depths of his gaze. I retreat a step, only to feel his rough grip on my forearm. He suddenly produces a long dagger, its curved tip reflecting the cool glow of the floating wisps.

"Kill him," he commands.

I hold the blade, its weight straining my wrists.

Cyrell's lips are drawn into a thin line, his eyes glued on our tormentor, full of hatred.

"What else to expect from the Prince of Filth..." the dark elf spits on the floor, and I freeze. Challenging this demon right now might not be the wisest thing to do.

The prince ignores the insult and nods to me, "Kill him, Celeste. I know that you care for him. Let me see if the jets of hot blood will awaken your power—"

"No."

Terrified, I drop the dagger. He cannot force me to participate in this twisted experiment. Whipping me and abusing me is one thing, but murder...

His black eyebrows narrow, and my stomach sinks.

He is suddenly at me, the cruel blade in his hand, pointing at my neck.

"You dare to disobey?" he hisses.

"I cannot kill an innocent." My voice trembles, but I don't flinch.

"It seems you don´t understand, Celeste. It´s either his life or yours. He is a trespasser. This is already a crime punishable by death."

"So, this is what happened to all the dark elves who disappeared in your lands? You executed them. The other Hunters were right. You are a heartless monster." Rage slices Cyrell´s voice.

"You mean the slaves who escaped your tyrannic Elders and sought refuge here?" Sparks gather and dance around the clenched fists of the prince. "I reassure you they are far better off here, under my protection."

Wait a minute.

"Slaves?" I ask in disbelief.

We stare at each other in silence, the air between us charged and crackling with static electricity. With magic.

Cyrell squares his shoulders, as much as the restraints allow it.

"I am not responsible for the decisions of the Elders' Council, and I do not approve of some of our traditions, either. You dare accuse my people of crimes, Prince? When the dead bodies on the pyres of Thaíl Vah´tlin are still smoking? When even the children—well, only the children who survived, still remember the carnage when your hordes of Risen found an entrance to our city..." I shudder, unable to imagine the scale of the atrocities from centuries of war. His tone drops to a plea now, "If you think that I deserve death for what my people have done, go ahead and deliver my sentence, but keep her out of this." I blink away tears. Cyrell's protectiveness is such a stark contrast to the Dreadful One's cruelty that it's heartbreaking.

"I am here of my own free will. I came here for her, not to discuss politics or the dark elves' ways with you, Dairell." He cocks his head in my direction. "I am not a spy sent by the Elders. Just like you, I'm looking for salvation for my people. And I think we all know how her powers work."

Both males stare at each other, and my nape hairs stand up, charged by the tension of this invisible clash.

Cold shivers ripple down my spine when my captor retrieves the dagger from the floor. Yet I manage the courage to look straight into his sparkling aquamarine eyes.

"Is this your final decision, human?" he sneers dangerously. I struggle to steady my breath, standing my ground, something I´ve never been good at. Until there is no other choice. I doubt he'll kill me, my gift is precious, valuable to him. Chills run down my spine at the thought of the punishment that awaits me for defying him.

"I will not kill him," I manage.

He strides to Cyrell's back, raises the blade... and cuts his wrists free.

"You are not experienced in the ways of magic, dark elf. The energy Celeste releases when she climaxes is not enough to change much in our world. We are still missing something, but I am about to find it." He lowers his voice as if speaking to himself. "Yet it seems you care for this human," the Dreadful One mocks. "Well, she's mine now. Let's try something else then," he casually suggests, circling his prisoner. A wave of his hand, and Cyrell's eyes glaze.

"Dark elf," he purrs in his ear, and the glowing eyes of both males land on me, "you've managed to unleash her powers before," A morbid realization dawns at me, "do it again while I watch. Show me how deep you can tap into this magic well, blessed by the Serpent!"

He gracefully climbs up to the tall throne, the shadow of his wings trailing behind him like a dark velvet train.

DAIRELL – THE PRINCE

My mother did everything she could to shape me into a lethal blade that would help her conquer this world. Cruel and terrible as she was, I still have some endearing memories of her before she lost herself to the darkness.

All these were related to her expeditions to the human realm. The stories she told me, the artifacts she brought back. How many evenings we spent laughing heartily over the narrow-mindedness of that clumsy kind? The shenanigans she had orchestrated. Oh, how I begged her to take me on these trips, yet she had always refused, which led me to believe that I was dear to her in some way, that my life was worth something to her... until she did the unspeakable.

Yet something about them, their perseverance, their will to fight and survive, their mad passion for life—it was all so different and fascinating to my young mind.

Seeing the fragile female who has never wielded a weapon in her life slice the head off a Risen without blinking an eye got my pulse racing. How brave and desperate she was, her triumph mixed up with her tears of terror! I have never seen anything more beautiful and intense in my long life.

It was when she refused to kill Cyrell that I saw her for what she really was. Trading someone else's life for your own is an easy decision for all Fae. It´s natural for my kind. Everyone would slit the prisoner's throat, hoping to save their own skin.

But not her.

Fragile and mortal, she dared defy the order of the mightiest mage in all Faëheim.

She is precious to me, not only because she is the most powerful magical artifact of her world. Humming with a power she is unaware of, her eyes are haunted by distant pain. There is sharpness in her, that fascinating resilience so typical for her people, but more intense. She is wrapped in secrets, and I am curious.

I feel alive. Infected by the human, primitive passion for life, all my senses are on painful alert as if I haven't slept for nights, and my mind cannot tell reality from hallucination anymore.

I dwell in the deserted halls in an odd state of daydreaming, and somehow my scattered thoughts always return to her.

The fascination and awe I feel shouldn't hinder my quest to save my lands. So, I did what was expected of a Prince of the Underworld. I tried to pry her shell open to study her abilities.

Oh, the bitter irony of the Serpent, to place the might to destroy and remake whole worlds in the tender body of a beautiful female. When she was bent over before me, locked in that pillory, her backside exposed, I had to strain all my self-control to resist the temptation, to not succumb to the longing born of ages of loneliness. That tender pink flesh, inviting me to bury myself in it! Dark desires took possession of me, and I had to interrupt the experiment for her and my sake.

My mother told me that no human could survive mating with a Fae. I believe this perpetuated lie serves only to discourage our males from hunting human females into extinction. This little one has endured many matings, with more than one of us, and from what I perceive, she has enjoyed it. It has made her stronger, smoothened that inexplicable sadness in her otherworldly eyes.

So, I sit back on my throne and indulge in the spectacle, ready to step in as soon as I feel a shift in the arcane vibration around her. I am prepared to protect her should the dark elf gets some bad ideas.

Cyrell instinctively emits his pheromones, enthralled by my spell, and I am mesmerized by her body's response. The dark elf wraps himself around her, aligning his massive warrior frame with her back. She looks so tiny in his arms. His right hand tightens around her neck, and he brushes his lips along the sateen skin of her jaw. I'm already panting, and when his extended claws slice her dress open and her heavy breasts spill out, I need to adjust myself. My length is pressing painfully against my leggings.

Celeste initially seems perplexed and scared, and then the pheromones kick in. I lick my lips, and my fingers dig in the carved armrests of my throne. His hands are full of her breasts, his clawed fingers digging into the supple flesh, leaving tiny ruby drops behind. He hungrily grinds his hips against her rear.

Celeste leans into him, responding to his slow thrusts. The fangs of the dark elf warrior extend when his fingers disappear between her legs. The scents of their need intertwine and intoxicate me. I stalk toward them.

The chemistry between them hypnotizes me; their heat hits me like a matured wine, and I justify my actions with the necessity to get closer to sense any magic.

Cyrell releases his thick shaft and rubs it against her perfectly rounded backside. I'm close now and see his dangerous claws trail her soaked folds, my nostrils flaring, catching her delicious flavor. I ignore the desire to kneel and feast on her. Instead, I watch, feeling the throbbing ache of my longing. The elven warrior grabs her left thigh and lifts it, leaving her drenched sex bare and open before me. I curse softly; there is only so much a male can take.

I wave my hand, and they freeze, my spell warping time around the couple. Like that, I can explore this exquisite otherness.

Now I can succumb to my dark curiosity, and I bend a knee, inspecting her pussy from up close. Her pink, dewy flesh is open, swollen, begging for a touch, her opening glistening, promising divine delights. I slowly plunge my finger into her, and despite the glove and the time-warping spell, I feel her clench around my digit, pulling it in. So wet, so tight, so tempting. Her pulsating nub catches my attention. I'm salivating, and against my better judgment, my lips close around it. I gently suck on the sensitive flesh, savoring her earthy, eerie flavor—unlike anything I have tasted before.

I open my breeches and release my heavy cock, and I start pleasing myself with rough, slow strokes while exploring her folds with my tongue. Eager to try more, to discover another taste, I loosen my grip on time and watch closely as Cyrell's cock slowly plunges into her, his thick, massive erection disappearing in her soft, pink, welcoming flesh.

The frantic moves of the elf appear slow and deliberate to me, and I pump my length aggressively—this is all too much to take.

I've had my share of pleasures of the flesh. My mother believed that every young prince should be experienced, so she gave me a harem, which I disbanded after she got lost in the dark. Yet this mortal heat, eagerness and passion, and this rounded, mouth-watering flesh is an experience I have never had before.

And novelty is a rare treat valued above all when you have lived for several centuries.

I feel the sting of jealousy at the pleasure the dark elf experiences while he takes her, his cock buried to the hilt now, and I jump to my feet.

What is this bitter-sweet pain ripping through my chest? Is this just desire? Can someone destined to an eternity of loneliness among the darkness of the Underworld feel something like this? Or is this confusion caused by the way she is? So fragile yet powerful. So simple yet surprisingly hard to figure out. I see her squirm in the strong arms of Cyrell; I sense her release building up.

"Enough!" I roar, and a flick of my wrist sends him flying across the hall, and he crashes against a pillar with a painful gasp. I catch her slender frame before she slumps to the floor, her mind hazy, her eyes black pits of need. Gravity presses her against me: her luscious breasts to my chest, her sex against my aching arousal. I feel her pulsating nub sliding along my length, and spasms shake her body. The sight of her coming apart, the feeling of her against my cock—it's all too much. I climax, and powerful jets of my seed spill against her. She mumbles something, and her eyes roll back.

A shattering wave of arcane energy sweeps the hall, whirling the dust in the farthest corners of my palace. She shudders, and I still hold her, my arms wrapped tightly around her, unsure what to do. I revel in her warmth and the stolen intimacy of the moment, yet wince at the realization that I have let someone that close to me.

My hesitation lingers only momentarily; I remember my duty as a prince of these lands.

"Come here!" I growl and grab her by the hair. Then I drag her to the stairs at the eastern side of the hall, and I can swear my heart has never been darker and emptier.

My caress brings only suffering. My touch eternal curse. Until I figure out how to deal with these disturbing emotions stirring inside me, until I sort myself out, the woman should remain hidden, safely locked away, but not in that wretched dungeon.

An exquisite treat like her should be treated with care. A divine body like hers should sleep in the softest sheets.

A smirk curls my lips while I drag her up the stairs. I have many ideas about my future experiments.

CELESTE – THE ANCHOR

Whatever happened at the foot of the black throne worked out well for me because I wake up in a gothic princess boudoir. Heavy brocade fabrics drape the windows and the chairs, and a king-size canopy bed beckons me to lose myself between sheets of black satin. Candles flicker to life as soon as I open my eyes. A cozy fire crackles in the cast iron fireplace. A silk screen conceals the entrance to another room. It's definitely an upgrade from the cold dungeon floor.

For a moment, it feels like I'm not held captive by a twisted monster on another plane of reality but a star in some dark and exciting movie.

My mind still drifts back to my tiny apartment, and nostalgia is as powerful as at the beginning of that mess. Yet I do not allow myself to succumb to sadness. I am the main character of my life now; not my miserable upbringing, regrets, or fear of the outside world and losing control. It's me who makes decisions now, not the circumstances of my past.

It turns out, thrill and risks are not as deadly as I thought. I chuckle at the thought that I was nervous to email my boss just a month ago and that yesterday, I defeated a bloodthirsty undead monster, chopping off its head as if it were a routine task.

I stretch on the satin sheets with a smile. The realization of that hidden power, of strength and resilience I have never suspected I possess, fills me with confidence.

Come what may, I'm ready to face it.

Fate responds to my challenge immediately. I hear a knock on my door.

Before I can react, a tall, winged figure stands in the doorway, leaning casually against the frame.

Did Cyrell call him by his real name?

"Dairell?" A fleeting smile curls his lips when he hears his name. He's wearing all black today, the tailored suit diving from his broad chest and shoulders to his narrow hips. Soft breeches hug his muscled thighs. My eyes wander back up to his face and find him grinning, dark strands that escaped his casual man bun framing the hard lines of his jaw. I avert my gaze quickly, but it's too late. He seems pleased with my attention.

"We will have dinner in the hall. You have ten minutes to get ready." This is not a request but an order; I know better than to challenge him.

To my horror, he strolls in and makes himself comfortable in the velvet chair beside the fireplace. Face leaned on his palm, he watches my struggle with amusement.

"It's already nine minutes, Celeste. When your time is up, I will drag you to the dining hall, dressed or not." His deep voice rumbles a warning, and I know he will do it.

I know I am dressed in rags, so I wrap the silky sheet around me and slip into the chamber behind the screen. It is a bathroom, as expected, and I'm grateful to find it similar to those in our world. There's a shower built into the flawless marble walls, and I gratefully rub myself with the sweetly scented oils I find.

My hair is still dripping when I sit at the vanity table loaded with hairbrushes and flasks. I don't waste time wondering whom they belong to, as Dairell announces, "Four minutes!"

I quickly brush my hair and slip into a soft, green, strapped dress that flows to the floor. Twirling in front of the mirror, I scrutinize my reflection. It's not bad for someone held captive by a demon prince, someone who was tortured and killed a zombie.

Something in his eyes changes when I emerge from behind the silk screen. Yet he blinks it away, and that spark of warmth is gone so fast that I think I imagined it.

The prince rises to his feet and turns to the door lazily, the shadows of his wings swallowing the flickering reflections of the fireplace, "Follow me, Celeste."

Strolling through scarcely lit stairways and mazes of passageways, we reach a door covered in peeling gold varnish.

Heavy chandeliers shed warm light over the crystal glasses and delicate china dishes loaded with unfamiliar fruits, cheese, and pastries. The aroma of freshly roasted meat tickles my nose, and I drool. When was the last time I had a proper meal? And who prepared all this, as I haven't seen anyone here except Dairell and the Black Guardians.

He gestures to me to sit, and I sink into the heavy chair, the tapestry brocade scratching through the fine fabric of my dress. The table stretches into an endless decadent hall, only our corner blessed with light.

A crystal decanter levitates toward me as if held by invisible hands. The prince fills his plate, oblivious to the floating flask that gracefully pours amber liquid into my glass.

"I know that you prefer more intense liquor," he declares smugly from his seat ten feet away. I struggle to appear unimpressed and focus on my food, ignoring how various objects gain a mind of their own and float over the table, rushing to assist him.

"Salt," he commands, and an ivory-colored salt shaker takes off before me and lands into his outstretched hand.

I mimic his move and softly request water, hoping he won't hear me. A heavy pitcher clumsily rises and hurries my way, spilling some of its contents over the roast. Dark, glossy strands veil Dairell´s face, and I cannot see his reaction, but I hear a muffled chuckle.

A few more experiments with levitating cutlery among the awkward silences, and the dinner is over. The prince looms over me, then escorts me to my room without saying a word.

I follow him through the dark labyrinth, heart pounding wildly. Will he try to… tap into my powers? Or is he planning another horrible experiment?

Am I looking forward to that?

I squeeze my thighs, remembering the bliss I've experienced in the arms of Tarcyll and Diaphonus, the mad desire of the rough mating with Cyrell.

Would it be different with the most powerful male in Faëheim?

Heat streams to my core at this thought. Tracing the rugged outlines of Dairell's powerful back and massive arms and the menacing whisper of his wings, I cannot help but wonder how it would be with him. Would he take me slowly, exploring the sensation with scientific interest, or would he be raw and demanding? The twitching between my legs gets distracting and, mortified, I see him tense up instantly.

We enter my chambers, and he lingers, his presence filling the space, the hum of his power rippling through the velvety gloom. And something deep inside me responds to his call.

He studies me; his head cocked, his defined eyebrows curiously raised, a dangerously sharp fang biting his lower lip. Is he having the same thoughts as me?

I was about to major in psychology before dropping out, so I'm fully aware of what Stockholm syndrome means, yet I vow to do some extensive research once I get back home.

A flash of darkness, and he is onto me, his gloved fingers raising my chin. I'm torn between the primal instinct to run and a scorching dose of lusty curiosity. Heavy-lidded, he scans my face as if searching for something, and then his lips crash into mine.

His firm grip pulls me into the kiss, his tongue intruding, demanding, inquiring. This is not an exchange of affection. This is a brutal interrogation. He dives deep inside me, drinks my essence, samples my flavor, and reaches into my mind. His forked tongue is firm and silky, and I wonder how it would feel to—

Wrapped in the relentless embrace of his massive arms and wings, I'm getting high on his scent of midnight herbs blooming in secret gardens, dewy moss, and mountain glaciers. My fists land roughly on his wide chest, shoving him, fighting him to get another breath. Finally, he releases me, stepping back, panting, his eyes completely black.

Then he turns on his heel and leaves my room, soundless as a shadow.

I throw myself on the bed, feeling something I have never felt before. Loneliness. I have always sought voluntary solitude. I have always been content in my own company, yet now I'm close to begging my captor to stay.

Frustration and longing simmer beneath my skin, and my hand snakes between my legs. By touching myself, I find some meager release. When my fingers sink inside me, I bite my lips, imagining how having him do it instead would feel.

Dining together becomes routine, the awkwardness melting away. I get much better with making cutlery fly, and the prince opens up and answers my many questions. Yes, there are servants in the castle and a fantastic cook; they work here voluntarily and get paid well. Yes, there are villages and even cities in his lands, where locals and exiles from other kingdoms dwell, and many escaped slaves from the dark elf-dominated Lower Lands. Yes, it was all peaceful and prosperous until the Siphons arrived. No, the Black Guardians are not Undead but warriors, bound to this realm and the realm of the spirits, and yes, they have willingly chosen their fate.

Then, I finally gather the courage to ask about Cyrell. The shift in the atmosphere of the dining hall is palpable.

"Do not dare to ask me about him again, human." A wrinkle appears between his finely shaped brows.

"You ordered me to murder him. I am worried about his whereabouts," I start and cannot finish because his tall shadow suddenly looms over me, eyes narrowed in frustration.

"Does he mean a lot to you?" Dairell inquires softly, but I can perceive the concealed threat in his tone, "Cause I will erase him from your memory, just like the other two."

The chair beside me squeaks under his weight, and his hand shoots up to my forearm and pulls me into his lap. Face down.

I fight back, aware of how futile it is to try and free myself of the steel grip of a winged male twice my size. He slings me over his knee and bares my behind. I'm more mortified than scared.

"I will make your body forget them," he rumbles and raises a hand. It lands on my bare behind with a smack, and I bite my lips to stifle a scream of humiliation and pain. His massive rings surely have bruised me.

Another smack, and I squirm. My breasts are pressing against his muscled thigh, and I feel—oh God, the intoxicating mix of triumph and terror—an enormous erection pushing into my stomach. No wonder Fae claim that not all humans survive mating with them.

"Let me explain to you a few things about Fae males, Celeste," the slap echoes among the hall, "They might have done their best to appear nice and civilized to you," his hand lingers on my sensitive skin and against my better judgment I press myself into his cool touch. The prince notices it instantly and roughly squeezes my ass, drawing a surprised moan. "But they would rip you apart, consume you if you were not that important to us, and then fuck your cold corpse."

Mortified, I sense my nipples pebble, and his fingers brush against the strip of my thong. I take a deep breath with a hiss, stiffening. I'm sure I'm soaking wet.

"Because this is in our nature, Celeste." He pulls the string aside, and I struggle to escape, but his left hand on my back keeps me steady." I will not sugarcoat it for you; I will not pretend I'm any different than them," his brutal assault continues, a heavy slap landing on my ass cheek, "but I will never glamour you, confuse you with pheromones, or use any other trick to get you in my bed. But by the Serpent, I do enjoy the view!"

His voice is husky, and his rock-hard arousal is bruising my ribs.

His hand kneads the reddened flesh of my rear, and I feel dampness spread between my thighs. Before I know what's happening, I slightly open my legs, taunting him. The onslaught on my backside continues, yet his fingers linger longer on my flesh, his fingertips casually tracing my soaked folds.

"You have to beg me if you want me the way you had the others," his thumb presses gently against my opening, and I arch my back against his palm, still firmly planted on my shoulder blades.

"Oh, the symphony of pleasure and pain we could create together would light you up like a beacon of magic!"

I can feel his magnificent cock straining underneath me, and my inner whore is about to get on her knees and take it in my mouth.

As if reading my thoughts, the tip of his thumb enters me, and then he withdraws it and smacks my reddened cheeks again. I squirm, unable to tell if I want him to stop or continue, if I want to impale myself on this massive length or lock myself in my room and cry.

Sharp pain and pleasure followed by more pain and more pleasure. The need builds up inside me, and I don't even bother to hide it anymore. I'm all drenched; pretty sure it stains his pants. I can hear him breathing heavily, his digit entering me deeper after each slap, then withdrawing to leave me gaping, aching for more. The toxic cocktail of extremes intensifies, and I desperately need friction; need to be penetrated and stretched. An approving growl confirms that he senses it, too, his hand greedily groping my cheek, spreading my backside open for his viewing pleasure.

"Do you like that, little human plaything? Do you want me to make you come?" I nod warily, shuddering.

"Then ask politely!" the prince hisses, a cruel smile rippling his lips.

"Please," I mumble, all common sense buried under lust and shame, "please make me come!"

He doesn't hesitate and roughly plunges two fingers, knuckles deep, inside me. It sends me immediately over the edge, blinding white light blurring my vision while he pumps my pussy with his hand. I whimper weakly, my walls clamping around him. Time shifts, the tide of my orgasm slowly floods my whole being, and I almost faint.

It seems like it lasted... minutes? Or hours? I can't tell. My whole existence has shrunk to my greedy, starved flesh, clutching around his two fingers. He glides them slowly, in and out, cold and terrifying in his self-control and discipline. His glowing eyes never leave mine while I fall apart.

A release of such colossal proportions would surely draw all Siphons to his doorstep.

He gives me time to recover, then helps me up, and I sit on his lap, blinking sheepishly. His arms cradle me for support. I still struggle to breathe when he steadies me.

The prince looks surprised, and distant warmth sparkles in his seafoam gaze. Or is this a self-deception to justify my surrender to him?

Without a word, he lifts me and carries me to my room. He carefully lays me on the bed and heads to the door. Standing. at the doorway, he turns around again, and there it is, without a doubt: awe and longing.

DAIRELL – THE PRINCE

I return to my chambers, aching, and please myself like a madman over and over again. My sheets are soaked with my seed, yet I'm not even close to satisfaction. Visions of her, open and dripping, my fingers buried deep into her slit, steal the sleep from my tired eyes.

The energy and the life pulsing beneath her skin are much more intense than any immortal. Feeling that desperate passion for life, that savage pursuit of pleasure is simply addictive. I was wrong. Humans are not cursed by the Serpent. They are truly blessed, because the eternal pulse of the universal energy beats wildly in their veins, making their short lives and insignificant experiences much more intense than our millennia of lingering existence.

This tiny body harbors so much raw power, I cannot comprehend how it is not tearing her apart.

I can barely wait for the morning to knock on her door, eager to solve the riddle she is.

When you roam the Underworld for ages and wield supreme magical powers, there are not many mysteries left for you. And this one is so rare and delicious that I feel the strangest thing: a thrill.

The breeze of my wings disturbs the light wisps of the ancient corridors when I rush to her room.

Celeste sits at the window, contemplating the eternal twilight outside. The tray with her breakfast is still on the table.

"How do flowers grow without sunlight?" she asks, and this oddly logical question takes me aback.

"Those are night irises," I join her at the window, and we stare at the garden of midnight velvet blossoms, "this is their home."

"They don't miss the sun rays?" Her eyes are still glued to the flower bed outside, and I cannot help but notice that this conversation has a deeper meaning.

"They grow only here. Sunlight will kill them." My eyes dart to the tray. Has she eaten? I have to remind myself that humans must be constantly sustained to survive. I remember my mother's stories. They need food, sleep, movement, and more... fresh air?

"Would you like to see them up close?" The question slips so fast that I don't have time to ponder why I would suggest such a thing.

"How do you know it's day?" Celeste breaks the awkward silence while we stroll in the ruined garden, her fingers brushing the deep purple blossoms of the night irises.

I raise my hand, and myriad light wisps that dwell near the invisible rock vaults above swarm us. Their cool light blinds my sensitive eyes, but Celeste smiles and reaches to touch them.

"The surface world has sunlight, and the Underworld has abundant magic. Both move with the pulse of the Crystal Serpent, ebb in the day, and recharge at night. The magic here is stronger than above, as we are close to the beating heart of our world." I struggle to compress the complexity of magical fluctuations into simple words.

Her brow furrows, and she appears deep in thought.

"I saw a picture in one of Diaphonus´ books," her gaze lingers on the horizon, fingers twirling a black blossom, "the roots of the vines run deep, reaching some place of light—is this what you mean by the beating heart of your world?"

I nod. "Our realm is alive. Its lifeblood is magic. And its largest deposit is deep below, out of our reach. The vines were transporting this life-giving essence to the Underworld and the surface. That's why we are dying after the Siphons' attacks. It's not only about casting spells or having the conveniences that magic grants. It's about what we are."

"Is there a place where we can get close to that source?" Celeste asks thoughtfully. I look carefully into her eyes. She's up to something. This human proves more surprising with each day.

"The roots of the Sentinel—the oldest magical tree—run straight to the core. Yet it is dead, its magic consumed by the Siphons. Now it is nothing but a husk, a painful memory of times gone—"

"What if we bring it back to life?" the woman interrupts, and I am stunned by her boldness, "You said there is a beating heart below our feet. In my world, we have a way to bring back to life a heart that has stopped beating, it's something we call defibrillation," my eyes narrow, now I am the one lost.

"Defibrillation?" I ask, though I do not like to confess my ignorance.

"Yes, if you apply a well-aimed and measured shock of electricity, you can restart the heart."

Silently, I lay a hand on her shoulder to interrupt her blabbering. She understands.

"Well, it's kind of a magic, too. What I mean is that we can kick-start the system with the power I hold, right?"

I scratch my chin and start pacing among the silky dark blossoms.

"You think a powerful enough eruption of your magic can revive the Sentinel." What a daring and fascinating theory. The little human seems to have many talents besides playing with my most sinister passions.

She nods.

I halt in front of her, rubbing my chin thoughtfully.

"It's risky," I scan the mists above us, "the lands around the castle and our major cities are safe, yet my protection doesn't stretch over the whole Underworld. We can run into a Siphon." I expect her to be terrified. To my surprise, she is still determined. Naïve little human, she has the advantage of never experiencing these horrors firsthand.

"I still think it's worth the risk. Will I be free to go home if it works?" the human asks softly, and I see through her agenda. Bitter disappointment spears my heart. She didn't agree to help out of altruism. It was her faint hope of freedom. I clench my jaw. A vision flashes before me: of endless gray centuries ahead, dwelling alone in these dark halls, with the echo of her moans lingering in the corners to remind me of what I have lost.

Coldness grips my chest, yet I nod in agreement. I might be cold and cruel but not that kind of monster. "If your theory is right and you help me restore the power of the vines and vanquish the Siphons, you will be free to go."

Her shoulders relax, and she smiles, a ray of golden light piercing the cursed darkness of these lands.

"Which way then?" Celeste urges.

I take another step toward her, dwarfing her tiny figure, and grab her in my arms, careful not to crush her.

"Up," I whisper and shoot up toward the gray clouds.

CELESTE – THE ANCHOR

I have been on a roller coaster only once in my life. Not only because I grew up with an alcoholic mother who ignored all family activities and basically deprived me of childhood, but also because after thirty minutes of throwing up, I insisted on never going back to the fair. At least I got spared another panic attack.

I feel the same acceleration, the air draining from my lungs, the fear when the stable ground below my feet fades. Dairell is holding me against his chest, which seems to be carved of solid rock. His face is mere inches away from mine, his eyes focused ahead. I hang on his neck; maybe I squeeze too tight, but I don't care. He should have warned me. My hair whips his face, and his gaze shifts to meet mine. Amusement ripples his angular features. He's probably finding my terror entertaining.

His mighty wings of shadow carry us just below the murky haze, where light wisps swarm. He deftly navigates between vines that pierce the clouds on their way up to the surface.

"Don't look down," the prince warns me, and I turn to face him. He's the most stunning man I have ever encountered, but seeing him now, in his element, dark wings spread wide and whipping the air with mighty strokes, he looks god-like.

Now, when I faintly hope to leave this mess and go home soon, I allow myself to ogle him. We fly fast, and he avoids the vine stems appearing from the mist by mere inches.

His chiseled pecs contract with each powerful swing of his wings, his stomach hard against my hip, and his arms cradle me. Warmth crawls through me and turns into a wildfire when I remember how my magic is summoned.

He will touch me again. Or maybe even more? I lick my lips as thrill mixes with anticipation, brewing a dangerous cocktail. Reminding myself how sharp all Fae senses are, I look down to distract myself before he catches the scent of my excitement. The endless black jungle of vines below our feet gets thicker, and he flies lower. Dairell scans the surroundings and suddenly dives, tying my stomach into a knot.

We softly land on the scorched forest floor. The vegetation around us appears charred and brittle.

A leviathan tree stretches its bony arms, frozen in eternal agony, toward the black sky. Light wisps dance among its mummified branches and clusters of faintly glowing mushrooms cascade like ghostly waterfalls down its bark. It appears ancient, a silent obelisk of times long past, a witness of the fall of the Underworld, a sentinel whose watch has ended.

Sadness seeps into my heart, seeing this devastation. This place must have looked breathtaking before. Probably lush green canopies stretched here, crystal creeks meandered between the mossy hills, and critters ran in the tall grass, carried away in their little-troubled lives.

It is now when Dairell releases me from his steely embrace. I stumble away, missing the hard warmth of his body. My palms rest on the uneven bark of the tree, and a distant sigh echoes among the dry leaves above as if the Sentinel greets me.

Dairell's squints; his aquamarine eyes scan the surroundings, and then he slowly stalks me.

A dark smirk curls the right corner of his lip. "Are you ready for one more experiment, Celeste?" he asks, his voice dripping promises of dark pleasures.

The moment I have anxiously expected and feared has arrived. I nod, blushing viciously.

He's on me instantly, his body aligned with my back, mercilessly pressing me against the tree bark. The rough surface scratches my face and teases my hardened nipples. Dairell nuzzles my neck curve, murmurs, "Should it be pleasure or pain?" and then closes his gloved hand around my throat.

The barely leashed power humming beneath his smooth, bronzed skin rings alarm bells, and I tense up for flight or fight. This power made my ancestors leave offerings at stone altars, cross themselves and spit when strange shapes twirled the darkness; put tiny bowls of milk and cookies at their doorsteps.

The concoction of terror and arousal is so intoxicating that I'm grateful for the firm tree trunk he presses me against.

I arch my back into him, my ass shamelessly rubbing against his hips. This male is the sweetest, deadliest poison I have ever tasted.

"I say let's try a little bit of both," the prince hisses and bites my earlobe. His hand travels below my navel to my panties, which are already embarrassingly soaked.

The feeling of the soft leather covering his fingers, spreading my folds, blurs all my senses. The world ceases to exist except for this aching, mind-numbing need that almost makes me howl. I'm starved for his touch, I realize, in an unnatural, feral way. Is it the magic in my blood responding to his power? Or is it his imposing presence, sculpted body, and face of a fallen angel?

Tantalizingly slow, his finger circles my nub, and I take sharp, ragged breaths, his hand still around my throat.

His attention shifts to my slit now, his digits lazily tracing it. I shudder in his hold, feeling his brutal arousal pressing against my backside. Sweet Lord, how big is this male?

"Tell me what you want, Celeste," Dairell whispers, his hot breath sending jolts of electricity along my spine. I grind against him, hoping that this will answer his question. The mind-blowing teasing continues, and I know I will scream if he doesn't penetrate me soon.

"Which part of me do you want inside you?" His hand squeezes my neck, and I part my lips. He stares at them under thick black lashes, "Can you take my tongue?" Before I can confirm, his mouth consumes me. It is a deep, ravishing kiss, his forked tongue whipping and twisting around mine. I squirm in his firm grip, and he finally releases me. A low growl of pleasure reverberates from his chest and vibrates down my spine.

"Who would have thought that humans are so delicious..."

The enthralling circles around my slit continue, and I angle my hips, struggling against him, trying to impale myself on his digit.

Dairell smirks, "Do you want more of me, Celeste?" the tip of his finger is inside me, and I cannot help but think how soaked his glove is right now, "How much exactly can you take?" he murmurs, and he's knuckle-deep inside me, drawing moans from me with each stroke. Then he suddenly removes himself and spins me around. My body protests at his retreat, and my legs almost buckle.

A swift move, a rip of cloth, and I feel the cool air on my nipples. The prince stares at my bare breasts; his eyes appear almost black in the eerie light of the wisps floating above us, hungry.

Something feral flashes across his face as he lowers his head and roughly gropes my breast. He squeezes it painfully, my flesh red from his grip, and I sense his hot, forked tongue circle my pebbled nipple. He pushes me against the tree, kicks my legs apart, and dips two fingers in my aching opening. This is more than I can take. The glide of his silky tongue over my sensitive flesh, his rhythmic movements stroking me on the inside. I'm about to fall apart, and he notices it. His turquoise gaze flashes predatorily, shaded by his black eyelashes.

"Not so greedy, little doll, not so fast, "He releases me and takes a step back, drinking in the sight of me naked, his fragile human toy, ready to submit to him.

"Now you will do exactly as I say," he commands, his voice low and dangerous. I nod eagerly. Do I have a choice? Do I want to have a choice?

"I want to see you open and aching for me, begging me to have you." Something in his tone makes my hairs rise, just like the rustling in the prehistoric night alerted my predecessors. Dairell grabs a fist of my hair and forces me to my knees, his other hand fumbling with the straps of his pants. I gasp when his aggressive erection is just an inch away from my face, and he strokes his massive member with his gloved hand. His cock, almost the size of my forearm, dripping, silky skin stretched over thick, bulging veins, inches closer to my lips. Gloved fingers wrap around my throat and squeeze.

"Open your mouth, Celeste, I know you want a taste. I've seen how you look at me." I obey, and he brutally enters me, making me choke.

"Now you will take it deep, like a good girl," Dairell rumbles while he mercilessly fucks my mouth. Then he suddenly releases me, and the tip of his boot nudges me to the ground. The dried leaves crunch beneath my weight, and I squirm when he commands, "Open your legs."

I obey. My open labia and dripping pink entrance are at his mercy. God help me, will I survive this?

He lets out a hissing breath, his broad chest heaving, his muscles tense for a leap. So, this is what an antelope sees before it gets its throat ripped out.

"They will tear you apart, consume you, and then fuck your cold corpse," I remember his warning, and his blood-chilling reminder that he is no different.

My thoughts are interrupted by a flash of white fangs. Suddenly I feel his weight against my thighs. His forked tongue is at my clit, encircling it, squeezing it into a maddening caress, then snaking down, feasting on each curve of my open folds. He tastes every rim before dipping inside me, and I arch my back, my mouth open in a wordless plea.

Can you die from too much pleasure? *Probably, I might burst a blood vessel, or get an aneurysm, or—*

This is the old Celeste speaking. The neglected, bullied, frightened girl, who has always made herself small to avoid attention. The new Celeste is full of magic and surprises. She can drive into a frenzy the most powerful Fae and gladly trades power for pleasure.

The prince lifts his head and smirks, "That's how I wanted you, Celeste, open and ready for me. What do you want me to do now?"

I try to gather my thoughts and answer, but sharp pain causes me to freeze—he has slapped my most sensitive spot, "Answer when I ask you, Celeste, what do you want me to do to you now?" the second of hesitation earns me another slap.

"I want you..." I mumble, unable to form a coherent sentence.

"Yes?" Dairell inquires, black brows dangerously furrowed. His mighty wings hover over us like a magical canopy.

"I want you inside me."

"Beg," the Prince of the Underworld commands and stands up, looming intimidatingly above me. It´s something he does exceptionally well. I lay naked and vulnerable at his feet, the tips of his leather boots mere inches away. For a moment, I wonder if he will fuck me or kick me unconscious.

"Please," I start, trembling with terror and arousal.

"Please what?" he rasps, his hand pumping his terrifyingly large cock.

"Please fuck me," I plead.

This is what this wretched demon wants to hear, because he unleashes himself upon me the very moment I finish the sentence.

He sheathes himself inside me without warning, and I clench around it in spasms, shattered by the brutal stretch and terrified that I cannot take more than half of this magnificent piece.

He starts working me with powerful thrusts, his gaze obsessively fixed on me, ensuring he won't miss anything from my reactions.

His fingers tease my nipples, and his gloved hands occasionally slap my bouncing flesh.

The sensations of stinging pain and otherworldly pleasure are mind-blowing.

Our eyes are locked, and I can see the bliss on his cruel, beautiful face, the ripple of his mighty pecs beneath the open shirt.

"You are so delicious, Celeste," he growls while brutally delivering a series of deep plunges, "I understand why the other Hunters are betraying and killing each other over this..." he bites his sensual lip, "otherworldly pleasure." His fingers gently rub my clit, then pinch it, and I moan.

"I can fuck you until you pass out," his gloved hands torment my body with punishing slaps, followed by tender caresses, "but your kind is so fragile."

A wicked twist of his gloved fingers over my clit, and I fall apart. A flash of blinding light and the world around me shatters into flickering pieces. The muscles of my pussy spasm around him, and he spills inside me with one final savage slam. A soft magical glow bathes the Sentinel and the dead vines around us.

I still shiver with aftershocks when he withdraws, leaving me empty and panting.

Perfectly composed, the prince stands up and watches changes in the forest around us, his eyes wide in marvel.

Half-lidded, I focus on his tall silhouette near me, already wholly serene. The bastard didn't even remove his gloves!

"Did it work?" I prop myself up on my elbow.

Some faint glimmer draws my attention to the dry grass on the forest floor. A tiny glimmering blossom, reminding me of a crocus, rears its crown among the leaves.

"It did." He whispers reverently, "The silverbells are blooming. Life returns to the Sentinel and the grounds around it. But this is not enough to replenish the magic of the vines, Celeste. We need more power." He bends down, picks up a tiny glowing flower, and twirls it between his fingers.

I watch him in silence. The regal lines of his profile are so mesmerizing against the silvery darkness of the awakening forest, that my heart bleeds. Am I falling for this beast who tortured me and tried to feed me to a zombie?

"Should we get—" my voice breaks, "the other Hunters, then?"

Dairell looks at me, some eerie melancholy clouding his gaze.

"We need them all to unleash your magic, Celeste." He gathers me cautiously in his arms, as if afraid that I might break, and shoots for the sky.

CELESTE – THE ANCHOR

"Tonight is special, Celeste," Dairell declares, settling in his usual seat at the cast iron fireplace. The warm reflections of the flames gild the firm outlines of his powerful body.

"Why?" I ask, changing into the beautiful black lace dress behind the silk screen of my room.

"Because tomorrow, everything changes. So, let's make tonight count!"

I follow him without pressing for more information, hoping he will reveal more over dinner.

To my surprise, he leads me outside, and we navigate a narrow gravel path that snakes between the toppled marble statues and the night iris flowerbeds. I startle when he grabs my hand and leads me between the vines, away from the castle. Light wisps dance over our heads, luring us deeper into the forest.

"Where are you taking me?" I try to hide the hesitation in my voice.

"To my secret garden, Celeste." The boyish grin on his handsome face is so infectious, that suddenly, we are two kids up to some mischief in the woods.

My jaw hits the floor when we reach a clearing. It's not too far from the castle, because the decay, which has destroyed the vines in this realm, hasn't reached it. I am relieved we are in the safe perimeter of the protective wards.

Shimmering night lilies climb the ruins of an ancient palace. Filigree arches glow in the ghostly light of the Underworld; delicate murals and crumbling mosaic floors tell a story of splendor long gone.

A table, loaded with steaming plates and drinks, drenched in candlelight, stretches before us. This almost looks like a date.

"What is this place?" I turn to Dairell and catch him watching my reaction carefully.

"It was my father's home, a favorite place when I was young." He lets go of my hand and pulls a chair. "Join me, Celeste."

We fill our plates. Bottles float across the table to our empty glasses. Crickets and some eerie night birds serenade us.

"So, your father is from around here?" I'm allergic to small talk; I always avoid the shallow and forced exchange of irrelevant information. So, my interest is genuine.

He carefully arranges his wings and leans back in the tall, carved chair, a glass of wine in his hand. Seeing him in his inky open shirt in the warm candlelight makes me salivate.

"My father was a Fae from the Underworld, the closest our people had to a King. We look slightly different than the Fae from the surface," he twitches a wing. "When my mother, a high elf sorceress, was exiled here, it was love at first sight." His gaze drifts into the distance. "A beautiful love story until my mother's lust for power took over. She consumed him. Destroyed him." I sip my drink quietly, realizing the prince is not the beautiful, heartless monster I believed him to be.

"My last conversation with my mother was here." He looks around, sadness darkening his features. "I tried to bring her to her senses. What a young, naïve fool I was. She died at my hands, Celeste," his voice breaks, and I dig my fingers into the wooden armrest; so heartbreaking his pain, and so frightening the revelation, "but the damage was done. She had summoned the Siphons. Death was upon all Faëheim."

His sage eyes delve into mine, studying my reaction.

I act impulsively, walking over to him and pulling him in. His head rests on my breasts, and I run my fingers through his soft hair.

"I failed, and I have lived with this guilt for decades, Celeste. It was all my fault. I couldn't stop her." His hot tears wet my skin under the black lacy dress. How does it feel to live with such a secret for so long?

"That's why I will do my best to make it right. And you know what's funny? That the first one who hears my story is human. That my only ally is human. My only hope is human." He looks up to me, and my heart shatters. Seeing the cruel Fae, the most feared mage, the mighty prince suffer like any of us. And there is nothing I can do to ease his pain.

"Thank you for sharing this, Dairell," I whisper, kissing his head softly. Oh, this maddening scent of night herbs and secrets! "I might be just a mortal, but I will try to help,"

"Just a mortal?" He shoots up to his feet and towers over me, cradling my face in his large hands. "You are the one who didn't give up on saving all Faëheim while the Hunters schemed to use you to protect their own lands! You refused to kill a captured Fae, even when your life was at stake! And you are here with me, helping me purge this evil from this world!" Fire burns in his irises, and now I know. I am more than a weapon and a depot of magical energy to him. My eyes well up. Before I can ruin the moment with some stupid comment, his lips crash into mine.

This kiss is not a struggle for domination; it's tender and pure, a confession and a cautious invitation.

It deepens, and he lifts me, wrapping my legs around his waist and carrying me to the soft grass. He lays me down gently and covers me with tiny kisses. I relish the weight of his body, the hard curve of his chest, the ripple of his stomach muscles under his silk shirt.

He takes me roughly, desperately, hastily, craving oblivion and forgiveness. When my magic pierces the forest's darkness, I scream his name.

Our limbs tangled, we lie on the grass carpet.

"Do you miss your home, Celeste?" the prince suddenly asks. I nod, and with a wave of his hand, he creates the perfect illusion of the starry sky above us. I can even recognize the constellations. The Great Bear, the Northern Star...

I chuckle and playfully kiss his shoulder.

"Why did you say that tomorrow everything changes, Dairell?" I ask him when we return to our dinner.

"Because we need allies to pull this off, Celeste." He smirks cryptically.

Indeed, the palace feels more crowded than usual the following day.

Black Guardians march perfectly aligned, and delegations of dark elves make themselves at home. Winged Fae resembling Dairell in stature and appearance roam the halls, and I guess these are his people—the secretive staff who take care of the prince's modest household.

I find Dairell and a familiar white-haired, broad-shouldered silhouette in the throne room. A wave of relief flushes over me. Cyrell is pretty much alive, carried away in a muffled conversation with the prince.

I note that he isn't bound or restrained in any way, quite the opposite: he's dressed in lavish burgundy clothes, and his glossy white hair cascades down his shoulders.

The throne room is crowded with Fae from different races, yet all conversations die out when they hear my steps.

Eyes of all colors and shapes land on me. Dairell invites me with a gesture to join him on the dais. I climb the tall steps toward the throne, feeling the scorching gaze of Cyrell on my back. A surprised gasp escapes me when the prince pulls me onto his lap, his glowing sage eyes fixed on the dark elf below us.

I pull my too-revealing dress to cover up, not out of modesty, but to avoid fueling the brewing conflict.

Dairell pulls my hand away.

"Do not hide this beauty," he murmurs, loud enough for the dark elf at our feet to hear, and his fingers travel along my thigh, lifting my skirt.

I swear I can hear Cyrell swallow hard. Even from the height of the throne, I can see how he clenches his fists so hard that his knuckles turn white.

"Track the other Hunters and bring them here." Dairell commands, his fingers distractedly trailing the outline of my inner thigh.

"I will do anything for the chance to purge the Siphons." Cyrell nods curtly, obviously regaining his composure, yet defiance flickers in his feline eyes, "but wouldn't it be wise to meet in more neutral territory, considering the history our allies have with your kingdom?"

Dairell's casual ministrations continue as if he's stroking a cat. What's the point he is trying to prove here?

"This is a good idea, elf. A gathering on neutral ground," the prince repeats thoughtfully.

"Better than a gathering. A ball where we can present our idea openly and get the nobles onboard. Each sword and each mage's staff counts."

"I like that," he rumbles, his middle finger descending between my legs.

Cyrell's face pales.

"Is it disturbing you—to watch me touch her?" Dairell demands, his tone sharp. The dark elf doesn't respond; he shifts his weight as if preparing to take a blow. I stiffen.

"Do you want her?" the prince continues teasing, a cruel smile curling his beautiful lips. "Remember this, elf, you can have her during the ritual, but she is mine. Mine to do with whatever I please." I open my mouth to object, yet I see the warning in his eyes. He releases me and sends me away with a gesture, and I quietly descend from the dais. Gasps follow my withdrawal. I guess the Court of the Underworld has a new star. Before disappearing into the shadows, I risk looking back. My eyes lock with Cyrell's, and there is so much longing and desperation in his gaze that my heart sinks.

Later that night, the prince bursts into my room, yanks my blanket away, and pulls me toward the edge of the bed. I try to struggle, when he tears my nightgown, grabs a handful of my hair, and forces my mouth open with his thumb. I spit and squirm while he violently fucks my mouth, my lips sore and wet around his thick shaft, his balls roughly smacking my chin. While choking on his seed, I realize it was all a power struggle. A way to humiliate his enemy, temporarily turned ally. The adrenaline rush of the situation probably got the better of him, and here he is, looking for a release. Maybe I'm nothing more than a pawn to him after all.

His slender fingers gently brush my face, his thumb smearing the tears and seed. I lean into his touch; oh, how I wish he'd stopped sending me these conflicting messages!

"Get ready for a journey, Celeste. Tomorrow, you will accompany me to the Lower Lands, where we will present our plan to the people of Faëheim," he announces breathily while closing his pants. Then he turns and leaves the room, tall, cold, and regal, leaving me alone with my thoughts.

I throw myself on the black sheets. Soon, this mess will be over, and I will go home. We plan to revive the Sentinel and the magical vines, and soon we will have allies. Seeing the door close behind Dairell's powerful wings, I feel sudden emptiness. And for the first time, I doubt that going home is what I really want.

The following morning, a carriage pulled by four enormous horses awaits us in the courtyard. Black Guardians swarm around us. Winged servants load heavy boxes on top of the vehicle. The clamor dies out when Dairell gives last orders, then gallantly helps me climb into the carriage, handing me a large picnic basket. It's full of food, judging by the aroma that tickles my nose and the merry clinking of bottles. He stands at the carriage door, inquiring if I have everything I need for the long trip. I nod, stunned by his thoughtfulness, by the flash of warmth in his aquamarine gaze. Then I remind myself of his rough manhandling, how he used me to hurt Cyrell, and close the plush-draped door with a frown.

I settle in the padded seat and watch the melancholic landscape fly by.

We travel fast, accompanied by a small army of Black Guardians and other Fae. I wonder if they are escaped slaves whom Dairell granted refuge.

Cyrell is nowhere to be seen, and I guess he left earlier to prepare our welcome.

The prince rides a massive mother-of-pearl-colored stud, which seems to glow in the twilight.

The road meanders among the trunks of the dead vines, the trip's monotony lulls me into sleep.

Shouts and a change in the carriage speed wake me up. The tall, black, iron gates of Thuar Haín, the capital of the Lower Lands, rise before us.

From here on, we continue on foot, led through the crowded streets by an escort of dark elves. Dairell strides next to me, drawing gasps and exclamations from the bystanders. I just now notice the thin silvery crown resting on his blackberry-hued tresses.

Soldiers line up on both sides of the broad, paved street, carved directly into the solid rock. Curious faces peek behind their gilded armor. All of them are albino-like, with pale skin and even paler hair, but sporting bright, colorful clothes, the females wearing extravagant jewelry and complex hairdos.

Gloomy passageways stuffed with machinery gape behind the crowds, endless bronze pipes stretch above us, and mysterious cogs the size of watermill wheels turn in the background. We walk among a surreal steampunk fantasy. Large mechanical creatures in different shapes, similar to Cerberus, glare at us with glowing red eyes, some of them mounted by elves. The constant buzz of machines fills the air, and I wonder what clever optical system delivers light to this subterranean world, as it is much brighter here than in Dairell's domain.

The prince's beautiful features are impassive, his gaze fixed ahead. His dark wings and imposing posture make him appear much taller than everyone. I notice a telltale tension in his sharp jawline. He's on alert. His muscles under the flowing silk tunic the color of a starless night are tensed, the natural reflex of a seasoned warrior.

I wince, surprised, as he grabs my hand, feeling the warmth of his fingers through the soft leather of his gloves. This gesture raises many eyebrows. Is this a warning to everyone that the Anchor is in his possession? Or is this the claim of a male who feels protective when rivals are around?

Then I see the reason: right in front of us, at the grand staircase which leads up to the palace stands Cyrell, dressed in a luxurious gold-threaded tunic. His shoulders are squared and brows furrowed; his glowing eyes follow our progress.

Four hooded figures wearing long crimson robes surround him. The Council of the Elders members are hard to miss or to confuse with simple nobles. The Lower Lands have no king. Their last ruler was abolished, and the council governs the nation. Its four members are elected by the nobles and are usually powerful mages. To avoid corruption, they rule for a maximum of one hundred years.

No muscle moves on Cyrell's face when he welcomes us; his voice remains loud and solemn, and I wonder if he feels something. The memory of the pain twisting his stoic features when the prince was touching me in the throne room is still vivid, and my eyes linger on him longer than they should.

Dairell squeezes my fingers, and an angry vein appears below his crown. A reminder to whom I belong. I shrug and try to ignore the annoyance simmering inside me.

As thrilling as these dark power games among the Fae are, I'm getting sick of feeling like a pawn. So, I yank my hand from his grip, smile encouragingly in Cyrell's direction, and vow to seek other ways to defy him. Standing my ground and not turning into his property is the only way I can fight for the chance to get back home when all of this is over.

The stairs, covered in gilded ceramic tiles, take us to a vast courtyard. The Palace of the People reminds me of Eastern European brutalism with its straight gray lines and minimalism. It's such a contrast to the artful and filigreed palace of Dairell.

The crimson-hooded figures bow, and we follow them into the mastodon structure. Every corner is teeming with dark elves and soldiers, many reluctant to welcome the Dreadful One. The Black Guardians surround us, their ghostly appearance and fearsome reputation cooling the crowds off.

We enter a meeting room the size of a concert hall, a glass dome arching over a massive round table. An excited clamor arises when we take our seats. Bronze mechanical creatures serve us refreshments, the sound of their heavy steps and oiled joints swallowed by the loud conversations.

The discussions thin out when they spot us, and soon, complete silence reins. My eyes sweep over the numerous attendees—dark elf lords, ladies, and some odd, short creatures with unhealthy grayish skin. My heart skips a beat when I notice Diaphonus, shining like the sun behind the clouds, clad in his pristine, white priest's garments. He holds my gaze and smiles, and I shuffle uncomfortably, remembering my trick to escape him. Next to him, sporting a casually elegant Brioni suit sits Tarcyll. His dark eyes glow up when he sees me, and he bites his lower lip with a fang, like a predator who has just spotted his dinner.

Everyone's attention is drawn to a councilmember who presents our plan in the lilting language of the Fae.

"Dairell Dunadhainne," the last two words hang in the air, which thickened after the mention of the Dreadful One's name.

And when the prince rises, regal and magnificent, his gloomy wings weaving nets of shadows, his presence electrifying the room, many cringe in their seats or look away from this dark splendor.

"Humans have always fascinated me," Dairell's voice slices the dense silence like a blood-soaked blade, "and I thought I knew their kind well. Yet I was surprised. Taken aback by the strength and power in their delicate mortal shell." He pauses and looks at me, and I tremble under the intensity of his peacock-blue gaze.

Everyone is glaring at me, and my palms start sweating. My breathing pattern changes. No. Not now. I will not allow it.

"I can confirm that," Tarcyll raises opposite us, "Celeste harbors the purest and wildest power of the Serpent."

"I support my brethren," Diaphonus confirms, flicking a blond braid back. "The Light had mercy on us and sent us the most precious gift. With Celeste on our side, we have hope to prevail and purge the Siphons from Faëheim."

Clamor rises in the room, and I distinctively hear the word "extractor" many times. Cyrell's lips are pressed into a thin line when he rises.

"An Extractor, honorable Elders, cannot contain the power our mortal ally wields," he politely addresses the crimson figures, yet his hands ball into fists at his sides. "I strongly suggest we proceed with the plan suggested by Dairell Dunadhainne. We—the four Hunters—will gather at the feet of the Sentinel and awaken Celeste's magic in the only possible way."

The idea that everyone in this room knows how my magic works and what the four Hunters are about to do to me is cringy. But I have learned that sexuality and magic are serious matters in this realm, and nobody makes indecent comments.

Some nod in agreement with his words. Cyrell has a certain influence over the nobles gathered here.

"We need to stand together to purge the Siphons from our lands. Even if this means allying with our oldest enemy," the dark elven warlord concludes.

Deafening protests shake the glass dome before the last syllable has sounded off. I can imagine how scandalous it is to disagree with the Elders.

My breathing gets shallow, my chest heaving. I'm so tired of this. I'm tired of having decisions taken away from me, of being powerless in situations that matter, of hiding, avoiding, and popping pills. White hot rage boils inside me, and I decide I've had "Enough!"

I slam my fist on the dark wood, unleashing all the anger that has been festering within me all my life, and my eyes widen when the ten-inch-thick wood cracks, and a blinding magical explosion shakes the room, knocking some odd gadgets from the table. In the sudden silence, I can hear glass cracking above my head.

"I have enough power to revive the vines of the Underworld!" My voice is different now, shaking the bronze-plated walls like a rumble of thunder. "Tarcyll, Cyrell, Diaphonus, and, "I pause to look at him and notice, amazed, that he is the only one in the room grinning, "Dairell will help me release and tame that force. And it will be enough," I roar, slamming the ruined table again, this time only sending sparks across the hall, "enough for all Faëheim."

I am panting, looking around challengingly. I feel so mad, so righteous in my rage that I could tear the whole place apart.

A soothing caress on my back cools me off. Dairell's wing is so soft when he brushes it against my skin.

"I stand by Celeste and will support her with all my power," his voice is loud and clear, the voice of a ruler, "If you dare stand in our way, you will face me and all the power of my kingdom."

Nervous shuffling and murmurs break the tense silence.

"As a representative of the High Elves of Thaer Vallhen, I stand by Celeste," Diaphonus joins us, drawing a wave of exclamations.

"And so do I, the right hand of the Shifters' King of Verdant," Tarcyll smirks roguishly and gives me a wink.

My gaze seeks Cyrell, yet he is gone. The councilmembers debate heatedly in their melodious tongue, and chaos returns to the meeting.

"The Council has reached an agreement!" someone exclaims, and all attention shifts to the mysterious hooded silhouettes.

"We believe that only by working together can we purge the Siphons from all Faëheim. And, as we have few options so far and not much to lose, we will put our trust in the human's abilities."

Dairell walks with me to my room; his arm slung protectively around my waist. I guess he aims to discourage anyone who still has ideas of harvesting my magic via an Extractor or using me for selfish goals.

He spends minutes carefully searching my bedroom, looking in every corner, checking the locks of the stained windows overlooking the city, and even kneeling to see if someone is hiding under the massive four-poster bed.

He sighs with relief and prepares to leave.

"What comes next?" I ask. I am the driving force behind the plan, yet all the discussions for the rest of the meeting were in that strange language, and nobody bothered to enlighten me.

"All the kingdoms of Faëheim will align on a counterattack strategy in the coming days. We will be ready to strike back at the Siphons when the vines start spreading pure magic again." He smirks and takes a step toward me yet keeps his distance, "You were so... convincing tonight," he declares, and I ponder if this is a compliment or a mockery. "Good night, Celeste."

The door clicks closed behind the twilight of his wings, and I sink into a chair next to the window, unable to grasp the emotions this male stirs inside me.

My eyes wander over the colorful lights of the subterranean elven metropolis—bustling with life, so different than the decaying, tragic beauty of Dairell's realm.

The buzzing of unseen mechanisms is everywhere, so my mind has quickly adapted to ignore it. Yet I register a distinctive click, and the hairs on my nape stand on alert.

I know I am not alone in my room.

I scan my surroundings. Everything is the way it was—the inviting blankets strewn on the bed, the eerie painting of a metallic monstrosity hanging over the stove, the bag with my belongings thrown on the black, plush ottoman.

My jaw drops when I witness a dark square form and soundlessly sink into the wall opposite me. A hidden door? What the...

Broad shoulders and a white mane emerge from the darkness beyond. Cyrell wears a casual black tunic accentuating his warrior frame and tight-fitting leggings, his long hair tied up in a low knot at his nape.

"Celeste," he calls me softly, his cat-like eyes burning. There is a flash of movement, and I feel his cool fingers on my face, brushing away the stray strands that escaped my messy ponytail. Not sure how to react, I retreat a step warily, yet my body craves his proximity, his touch. My hand absentmindedly feels the spot on my chest where he bit me. His slit pupils dilate as he registers my move, and I notice his broad chest rising.

"Seeing you scared of me breaks my heart, Celeste." He murmurs, looming over me.

"You tried to kill me, Cyrell. More than once. What do you expect?"

"I didn't know there is... another way, Celeste." He cups my cheek, and I lean into his touch without realizing what I am doing. "And you cannot deny the moment we had."

I remain silent, and he retreats to the gaping passage.

"Dairell is handling you like property, so I figured out the only way I can show you my city is by sneaking you out through this secret passage," he grins and appears even more attractive. I have never seen him smile before.

I open my mouth to object, then reconsider. A dangerous desire to defy the prince and prove I still have my freedom rears its head.

"Cerberus awaits us outside," he says over his shoulder, disappearing into the passage. And just like that, I follow.

He helps me mount the mechanical creature as we sneak out of the hidden door in the palace's walls.

Cerberus navigates the maze of streets, and I'm grateful that we don't see a soul. Low-hanging cables brush my hair, unseen cogs rattle, and valves hiss steam into our faces—as if the city is a living and breathing leviathan, machinery buzzing deep in its invisible depths.

Cyrell is unusually talkative, pointing at different gadgets; explaining the complex coexistence of magic and engineering that make the barren underground tunnels inhabitable.

I feel the rugged outline of his muscled chest, the vibration of his deep voice against my back, and heat floods my guts. I doubt he has sneaked me out just for sightseeing. Flashbacks of our brutal mating make me grind against

Cerberus' saddle. Cyrell's grip on my waist tightens, and he takes a breath with a hiss. My arousal is evident to this male with senses sharpened by ages of warfare in the darkness.

The mechanical mount climbs up a rocky hill with a magnificent view over the city. It reminds me of a typical spot where teenagers go to make out. Seems like men and Fae are not that different after all.

He helps me hop off Cerberus' back and leads me to a stone bench, his firm hand lingering on my waist.

I expect him to leap onto me with that ferocity I experienced in the sewers, yet he produces a water skin out of his pocket, takes a generous gulp, and hands it to me.

The scent of strong liquor hits my nose, and I can't conceal the grin tugging on my lips.

"What is it made of?" The fiery taste of the booze makes me choke.

"Deep worms and mushrooms," he shrugs, and I spit.

"Why am I actually here, Cyrell?" I finally ask the question hanging between us.

He takes the water skin and turns to me. I wince at the longing and anxiety in his glimmering eyes.

"The plan will not work, Celeste. The Sentinel and the vine forest were destroyed long ago. Even if you revive them,

I don't know if the magic will be enough to defeat all the Siphons that will swarm you."

I frown and take another sip against my better judgment. The care in the elf's voice gets to me.

"I trust you and the others; I believe in Dairell's judgment," I mumble, trying to digest the information, but haze shrouds my mind. The booze is more potent than I thought.

"Maybe you shouldn't. Never trust a Fae, Celeste." Cyrell looks at me, tucking a loose white strand behind his pointy ear. "There is no magic in this world strong enough to revive the vines, Celeste. It's what Dairell keeps from you. Your theory is nothing but a theory and puts everything at stake." His calloused fingers close around mine and squeeze with unexpected warmth. "Siphons will overwhelm you as soon as you perform the... ritual at the Sentinel tree. They will devour you, rip you apart." Pain distorts his fine features. "He throws away our last hope, gambles with your life, and the council is playing along..."

"I want to do anything possible to get rid of that cursed magic within me. It's the only way to get my old life back," I whisper, feeling a chill stiffen my limbs.

"There is another way, Celeste," he leans in closer, and I can see the dark outline of his lips, contrasting to his pale skin, so warm and tempting and close, "I am a respected leader. Many, tired of the Elders´ tyranny, will follow me anywhere. With your power, we can secure the Lower Lands and lead my people to an era of peace and safety!" His breathing is erratic, and I feel his palm sweating.

"I thought you didn't believe in my powers, Cyrell," I state coldly.

"But I do, Celeste! I just know that it's not enough to save the whole of Faëheim! Yet we can scavenge what is left, save as many as possible!"

"You are offering me to betray the other Hunters, to participate in a coup against your Council, and remain here with you if it works?!" I ask in disbelief, yanking my hand from his fingers.

"I'm offering you a choice, Celeste. Something the others didn't bother to do. I have claimed you, and the Lower Lands could be your home. However, I won't stop you if you wish to return to your old life. All I'm asking for is a chance. Together, we can save my home. We can overthrow the corrupt Council and lead my people. I will show you the wonders of the golden tunnels and convince you to stay here, with me, as my queen. If you could just trust me—"

He speaks fast, delirious; his eyes are burning, his broad chest heaving. What have I done? Nobody knows I'm here with him. How could I be so stupid and trust him again?

"You are the one who told me never to trust a Fae, Cyrell."

I rise to my feet and walk toward the mechanical dog. Its glowing red pupils scan me, and it cocks its massive metal head.

"Don't walk away, Celeste! Don't throw your life away!" I ignore Cyrell's pleas, but the desperation in his tone stings. I climb Cerberus, wondering if he will let me walk away just like that.

"Remember, I was the only one who gave you a choice!"

"Take me back to the palace," I whisper in the creature's ear. It turns its massive bronze head to its master as if expecting a confirmation.

The dark elf nods, and the mechanical beast carries me away. I look back only once, and my heart sinks when I see his shrinking silhouette, alone on the barren hill, his shoulders hanging. Pain is written across his beautiful face, yet something disturbing gleams in his predatory eyes.

CELESTE – THE ANCHOR

Cyrell is nowhere to be seen in the following days.

Dairell, Diaphonus, Tarcyll, and the Council hold multiple meetings, aligning strategy and battle plans for the counterattack. I lack the knowledge and the patience for all these things. Magical warfare is not something you learn at school.

I spend the time in my room, contemplating the movement of the artificial sun and moon in the vaults of the cavern, pondering Cyrell's words.

I have claimed you; the Lower Lands could be your home.

Can I grow to love the glowing crystal-covered spheres which move across the artificial sky more than the sun and the moon?

Something has changed inside me after the mating with Cyrell. Not only did my senses sharpen, but I got faster, too. After all, I managed to take down the undead horror in Dairell's basement. But the strangest thing is that I've started finding the Underworld... fascinating. The darkness is more welcoming, the tons of rock above my head—reassuring.

Dairell visits me occasionally, and I see Tarcyll and Diaphonus in the crowded banquet hall where we take our meals.

The days drag monotonously, and the ball approaches. The event fills me with anxiety and a thrill.

The old me, the one making herself small and invisible in order to not catch the attention of the cruel kids at school, would pop pill after pill and look for excuses not to attend. The new me, who cracks tables made of massive wood, wields magic, and entices Fae lords, wonders which color to wear.

Countless dresses lie on my bed, and I'm leaving the tub, where two silent dark elf maids have washed, scrubbed, plucked, and tormented me for something that felt like hours, making me feel like I haven't had a bath in months.

Without a word, they seat me before a massive vanity and proceed to the torture's next stage—getting me to look presentable for the nobles at the ball.

All the hair-pulling, curling, and trying on dresses worthy of an Oscar gala is worth it because the conversations in the Grand Hall mute when I enter.

An imposing winged figure stands in the eye of the storm and strides toward me, offering me his arm. A mechanical servant, looking disturbingly like an ancient version of 3PO, offers me a glass of bubbly wine, but Dairell pushes it away.

"Celeste will try the rhi'govanna." The stronger stuff, I guess, the one made of bugs and worms. We stroll among dark elf lords with glowing eyes, long white tresses, broad shoulders, and warriors' arms holding crystal glasses. Noble ladies in striking colors and exquisite makeup mingle. Some couples are dancing to a melancholic melody.

I receive my rhi'govanna, and it is as I feared, yet pleasant warmth spreads in my bones.

I notice Diaphonus among a group of stunning white-clad people, most likely the rest of the high elf delegation. All of them are breathtakingly handsome, yet he stands out. His monicker, the Fair, proves to be spot on.

A group of extravagant, white-haired ladies has Tarcyll cornered, and he seems to be enjoying the attention. Dressed in an immaculate suit in human fashion, he frequently runs his fingers through his short hair and stares in my direction.

We are not spared the social interaction. Three members of the Council start a conversation with Dairell, and I look around, distracted, taking in the decadent grandeur of the hall.

Many try to catch my eye; many males smile invitingly, and dangerous fangs flash behind ruby lips. *They would rip you apart, consume you if you were not that important to us, and then fuck your cold corpse.* The warning fits the atmosphere of danger perfectly, heated with curiosity and dark desires.

A tall, slender dark elf approaches me, asking for a dance. The prince, too consumed in discussion with the Elders, doesn't even notice that I accept, and the elf lord gracefully swirls me across the dance floor, the black silk chiffon of my skirts drawing enchanting symbols over the colorful mosaic floor.

I feel the heat and the tension in my dance partner's body, and he seems disappointed when he hands me to the next guest. I dance until my surroundings become blurry, a helpful hand refilling my glass with the strong bug liquor. The music is getting more intense, the dance moves heat up, and the touches of handsome elf males more daring. They all look at me as if I am an exquisite meal, and I wonder if the magic inside me tempts them or my otherness. Or my star status of a potential savior of their world.

Suddenly, I land in familiar arms.

"Celeste," Diaphonus's hot breath tickles my ear, sending heat ripples to a particular sensitive spot, "I am so grateful you are alive and well. We were so worried." I look around in the whirlpool of faces to understand who he means by "we." And there he is, hands in his pockets, the sleeves of his white shirt rolled up to display his athletic, tattooed forearms, smiling smugly. Tarcyll winks, and his dark eyes undress me. Before I realize what I'm doing, I press myself against the hard outlines of the priest's body, grateful that he's holding me tight; otherwise, my knees might give in.

"I need to see you alone, Celeste," he purrs in my ear, and my nipples stiffen, rubbing against his white tunic. I know he can feel them because he responds by squeezing my lower back. "Follow me," he whispers.

The obsessive need to do something reckless, to defy Dairell's claim over me, and last but not least—to have some time alone with the beautiful high elf, destroy all remnants of common sense. We sneak away unnoticed, leaving the commotion of the party behind us. He leads me into a poorly lit side corridor. The only souls we meet are guards and the weird robotic servants.

Diaphonus opens the first door on the right and steps into the room confidently, and I realize that he has probably carefully selected the place for our rendezvous.

The scarce light of the wall sconces reflects on glasses full of pickled vegetables lined up on long shelves, massive cheese rolls and crates full of fruits are stowed away, and giant sacks of grain lie on the floor, looking just like bean bags. We are in a pantry.

Before I can ask, the elven priest kisses me like a man possessed, his slender fingers impatiently lifting the hem of my silk dress.

"Oh, Celeste," he moans against my lips when he fills his palms with my ass and realizes that I don't wear any underwear by the strict order of Dairell. I still tremble remembering the spanking I got when he found out I dared to breach his order.

His warm touch feels like returning home. My body has missed him.

Our hips grind against each other, our bodies craving more than touches. I freeze when I hear the door screech open and whip my head, expecting to see a guard or, even worse—Dairell himself, coming to punish me.

Instead, my eyes linger on sun-kissed skin covered in mystical tattoos, thick dark hair, and a body to kill for.

"Tarcyll?" I murmur. Diaphonus doesn't cease his ministrations. He pulls down the neckline of my dress, revealing my breasts, and buries his face between them.

"You didn't expect me to miss the fun, did you? You don't mind me joining, Celeste?" the spymaster stalks toward us, his blatant erection straining his tight-fitting pants.

"Mmmmh," Is all I can utter between the licks and bites of Diaphonus.

Tarcyll wraps himself around my back, and I lean into his carved pecs. Realizing I was starving for him, I shamelessly rub my bare behind against his bulge.

"Oh, how I have missed you, Celeste," he inhales my scent like a madman, then starts fiddling with his pants. An instant later, his cock is between my ass cheeks, rubbing me while he grazes and sucks the sensitive skin of my nape.

I gasp when I feel the priest's fingers find my folds, spread them, and his middle finger dive deeply into my throbbing opening.

"She is drenched for us, Tarcyll," he declares hoarsely, smirking roguishly, and his friend responds with a low growl. I suppress a scream when the dark-haired male's finger slides inside me, too, joining Diaphonus, stretching me, and both wicked Fae start working me simultaneously. I feel the intense heat of their cocks—one pressed against my bare stomach, dripping its clear nectar, the other gliding between my cheeks.

"You are so ready, Celeste, aren't you? You were missing us, too," Diaphonus whispers in my ear before dipping his tongue inside it.

He's right. I missed them. The way they took me, the way they used my body and claimed all my holes, the pleasure I was able to provide and receive in return...

The Fae carefully lower me on a large bag of grain, and I feel the hot fingers of Tarcyll pressing my thighs open.

I lay completely bare, my folds spread and dripping before these two savage males starved for me. The high elf wraps his hand around my throat and pushes his enormous manhood between my lips. He moans, moving slowly in and out, and I choke on the hard flesh. He feels like steel wrapped in satin, and I am eager to take more.

My eyes open wide, meeting the cerulean heavy-lidded gaze of the priest when his friend presses his firm lips over my clit and sucks gently. I spread my legs wider, thrusting my hips into his hungry mouth. The way these Fae take advantage of my body, how they devour me, and how I respond to them, I have never thought it possible. All my life, I was obsessed with controlling and restraining myself sexually, too shy to share and live my fantasies. Too afraid to be ignored, ridiculed, or rejected.

And now I watch under my long lashes how Tarcyll rises in all his decadent naked beauty and agonizingly slowly buries his magnificent cock inside me. At the same time, the blond priest murmurs words of veneration while fucking my mouth.

"So wet and tight," the spymaster rumbles and switches to his own, melodious tongue. I can only speculate what profanities he mumbles while ravaging me. These words arouse his friend to a feral state, his length filling me to a point where I have to struggle for breath.

"You are so eager to eat my cock today that I see you were really missing it," Diaphonus growls. He grabs a fistful of my hair and angles my head to allow himself even deeper access.

Their moves are so vicious yet precisely calculated, aimed perfectly to deliver and receive the optimal amount of pleasure, that I don't want this to end. Ever.

"Our sweet little human whore, ne'hil thallané" Tarcyll pounds viciously inside me, "look how much she craves us." Somehow, the dirty talk sets me ablaze, and I whimper. He withdraws with well-measured cruelty, leaving me empty and throbbing, and spits in my slit. "Stretch that pussy for me, show me how you ache for me." I obey and pull my labia aside, revealing my throbbing, soaked, pink entrance. Both males drool over it like hungry wolves, then continue their onslaught even more ferociously.

"I was thinking about all the ways I would fuck you for days," Diaphonus breaths, "my cock was sore from touching myself while dreaming of you. "

"I must confess, I am addicted to you, too, Celeste. I ravaged many of your kind, imagining it was you," Tarcyll confesses breathily.

I'm not sure how I feel about this.

No time to ponder over it though. The spy rubs my nub with his knuckles, sending me over the edge. I shatter in pieces, my screams muffled by the blond elf's cock buried deep in my mouth.

Then I start doing the creepy stuff. My glow is more intense this time, and I feel like levitating, but firm hands keep me on the grain bag. The world around me falls apart in shiny pieces, yet I still manage to register the screeching of the door. I suddenly feel cold and empty and look around in terror.

Tall and terrifying, the prince stands in the middle of the room, his eyes glowing red in rage. Darkness pools around his feet and stretches its sticky tendrils toward the spy and the high elf.

"I told you, you can have her during the ritual and never again, you worms!" he barks, and I can barely believe this voice belongs to him, "She is mine! Now get out before I shred you to ribbons!"

They know better than to challenge the mightiest sorcerer of Faëheim in a situation like this. Steps hurry away from me, and the door shuts closed. We are alone in the gloomy room, and I suddenly feel claustrophobic.

He circles me with a casual, menacing gait, and I look down at my exposed body. My luxurious dress is rolled up to my waist, my pussy still stretched open and leaking Tarcyll's cream. He has filled me up well. My makeup is all smeared, and Diaphonus' seed drips from my lips to my bare, hard nipples. He halts before me and slowly unbuttons his pants.

"You disobeyed me, Celeste, and I will have to punish you," he rumbles, then his strong arms wrap around my waist and flip me over, "Oh, how much I will enjoy this."

I can hear him panting behind me, savoring the delicious sight of my creamed-up slit and bare ass.

"You humans are so filthy yet arousing at the same time," he dips a gloved finger in my cunt, slowly pulls it out, and drags it up my crack, "I smell them on you, "he spits with disgust, "yet I see they have missed one hole. "I stiffen when I feel his enormous, firm cock pressing against my rear, and the weight of his massive body is crushing me. His wings spread wide, and the whole room drowns in shadows.

"Open up, Celeste, and receive your punishment," he purrs in my ear, and I oblige. His thick tip spreads me, and he hisses when he slowly penetrates me.

"I heard everything, you know," he whispers, his forked tongue following the outlines of my ear, sending shivers of bliss down my spine. "You are mine, Celeste, and I plan to keep you forever."

He cautiously starts pumping, and I arch against his chest, drawing a low rumble, "You promised to let me go after all this is over!" I protest, trying to free myself.

"I did, didn't I? That was before I tasted all the pleasures you can provide, before I heard how enthralled these males were, ready to risk my wrath to have you again," another low growl, and I feel arousal heating my lower regions. "Do you think I didn't notice how every Fae in that ballroom was eyeing you? Oh, I know what they all were thinking." Another deep plunge, and I try to fight him again. He seems to enjoy it, because I hear him chuckle.

"You have to thank me, as I am the only one standing between you and that pack of rabid wolves that would feast on your blood while fucking you into a shapeless pile of meat." I feel his hard-as-rock abs press against my back and his breath in my ear.

"Did you like being taken by both of them at the same time?" the menace in his tone makes my hair stand on end. "Do not forget, little human, that you are mine, and I will fuck away the memory of them from your body."

He unleashes himself upon me, increasing the tempo, and I whimper. I feel stretched and full, about to burst, yet I crave more. My hand glides between my legs, and I try to touch myself. Bad idea.

Iron fingers close around my throat, and I claw and dig my nails into his forearm. "Oh no, Celeste, this is not about pleasing yourself. You got plenty of that just a minute before. This is punishment." he tightens his grip, and the pantry spins around.

"Breathing is a privilege I will grant you whenever I feel like it, Celeste, "his cold voice terrifies me, and I freeze. For an instant, the world ceases to exist. His hard cock shoved up my behind, and his fingers around my neck. And twisted as it is, I find this the most exciting thing I've ever felt.

Dairell loosens his grip, allowing me to suck in air greedily while mercilessly pumping my ass. "You felt this too, Celeste?" he asks, his voice suddenly warm.

Then the moment is gone. The prince presses his face against mine, and I feel his jaw tighten.

"Oh, they were right. This hot, tight flesh can provide such exquisite pleasures. And you are very eager today, little one."

His dark tone, the steel of his body, his dominance—it is too overwhelming. I feel my pussy twitching madly, craving attention, begging to be filled. Somehow, he notices it too, his elegant nostrils flaring, his eyes narrowing.

"Do you want to ask for something?" he mocks.

"Touch me," I rasp, "touch me there."

"Touch you there while you are full of Tarcyll's seed?" he spits again on the floor. "No. But I am feeling merciful today. I might touch you if you are a good girl. Will you be a good girl?" I nod weakly.

"Then tell me you were thinking of me when these two were taking you." A squeeze on my throat, just tight enough to remind me of the consequences if I do not oblige, urges me to speak. Fast.

"I was thinking of you," I breathe. The loud slapping of Dairell's hips against my skin reverberates beneath the tall ceiling.

"You might roll on the floor with low-borns, but you will address me with Your Majesty tonight. Now repeat it like a good girl," he demands, his aggressive assault intensifying.

"I was thinking of you, Your Majesty," I manage, and he climaxes, burying himself deeply, his hard body aligned with mine, his mighty wings reaching the tall vault of the chamber. Before I can come to my senses, he removes himself from me, turns me around so our eyes meet, and smirks.

"All filled now," he chuckles, "you have been a good girl."

His gloved hands spread my thighs, and his knuckles brush against my clit. I gasp, my slit twitching with desperate need. I whimper.

"You want that filled, don't you," he asks in a low voice and suddenly produces a dagger with a hilt encrusted with colorful gems. Its blade is hidden in a filigree golden sheath, yet it's terrifying despite its beauty.

Is he sick of my games and intends to punish me more seriously? Unpredictable and dangerous as this male is, I must be ready for anything. His knuckles still rubbing my nub, he grabs the tiny weapon by the sheath and slowly plunges the bejeweled hilt into my pussy.

Oh my...

"Here, it is filled, and my hands are still clean," he smiles darkly and starts sliding the handle in and out of me. I grind my teeth. It is cold, yet the sensation of the uneven surface and all the gems gliding in and out of my entrance is oddly exciting. My hips adapt to the rhythm of his moves, and soon enough, I grind against his hand.

Crystal sweat beads appear on his high brow, and when I shatter before him, a hint of awe peeks from the depths of those otherworldly aquamarine eyes.

I convulse, releasing a massive wave of energy, and he watches me.

"Will you let me go back home when all this is over?" I ask as soon as I am able to speak, determined to exploit the sudden softness in his gaze.

A cruel smile stretches his lips, and he looks down at me. "Let's see if you will survive this and if there will be a home to return to when this is over," he declares and leaves the room, leaving me cold, terrified, and alone.

I spend the following days idling in my room. Oddly, Dairell visits me every day, surprisingly talkative. He holds heated monologues about the strategies agreed upon with the other kingdoms. It seems that Tarcyll and Diaphonus have already left for their lands to build wards that would be activated by the arcane blast I will release, to prepare the armies, and to prompt the mages. They will meet us at the Sentinel in a week to perform the Ritual.

The Ritual, he calls it.

It has an ominous sound to it, but I know the hidden meaning behind it. It's more like the mating with these four feral Fae males. The thought of it sends shivers of anticipation and terror down my spine.

The plan is simple yet requires precise timing. We will tap into my magic at the roots of the ancient tree, and then Diaphonus and the prince, both the most skilled and powerful mages of Faëheim, will amplify and channel the energy down the roots of the Sentinel and the surrounding vines. If it works and the magical ecosystem springs back to life, enormous amounts of arcane power will shoot up the vines and release on the surface, powering the wards. The mages and soldiers of all Fae kingdoms will then join forces to push back the invaders.

Our weak hope is based on the surprise of our risky counterattack. The Siphons are mighty yet severely outnumbered, and a massive, coordinated attack from all sides should drive them out.

The noose around my throat tightens when the massive iron gates of the underground city close behind us, and we head back to the lands of Dairell.

The wheels of the black carriage leave deep trails in the shimmering inky sand, and I can't look away, a foreboding squeezing my chest. I cast one last look at the dark elves' stronghold, hoping to spot the tall silhouette of Cyrell mounted on Cerberus, yet my mysterious stalker is nowhere to be seen. I make myself comfortable in the bouncing cart and try to sleep.

An abrupt stop wakes me up. Something is wrong. I feel it in my gut. Horses neigh and gallop around, and there are other, more disturbing sounds. It's more like barely detectable vibrations that give me goosebumps.

"Stay inside, Celeste!" the prince commands, dismounting his horse. I hear him unsheathing his sword and shouting at his soldiers in the tongue of the Fae. My jaw drops when I look through the window.

Cyrell stands tall, a vicious lance in his hand, its tip pointing at Dairell. Cerberus` metallic plates reflect the dull light of the shimmering orbs floating above.

The Black Guardians around them act oddly; they run around or drop to the ground as if pierced by invisible blades.

What is the meaning of this pantomime?

After a moment of hesitation, I step out of the carriage. Death is written all over the handsome faces of both males. I am unsure about my role in this conflict, but I will do anything to avoid bloodshed.

"The mightiest warrior of the Lower Lands, allied with the enemy," Dairell spits on the ground. "Will you fight me or let your newfound friends finish the deed while you cower behind them?"

Newfound friends? What does he mean? I look around, confused. It's only us and the dark elf in the middle of nowhere.

Cyrell's glowing eyes spot me, blazing with sudden longing and sadness. The prince follows his feverish gaze and whips his head toward me.

"So it is about her, then? I thought you, stoic and disciplined as you are, could keep your cock out of the state's business." The tip of Dairell's long sword draws a half circle in the black sand. He takes a fighting stance, his mighty wings drawn up behind his back.

Shit.

"It's always been about her. I tried to make you see some sense, but you refused. I will not let you kill her. I claimed her first, Dairell. I drank on her, and she tasted me, too. She is mine."

Wait, what?

A roar escapes the prince, and he takes up to the sky, hovering over Cyrell before darting down, his blade aiming at the heart of the dark elf.

Dairell's bitter cackling makes my skin crawl. "And you think your magic-hungry allies will spare her the second they sense her powers?"

"I will make sure they will. I called them here for you. They will let me keep most of the Lower Lands in return for the favor. And most of your lands, too."

A deafening clang of steel cuts his words. Sparks shower from their blades. His battle instincts kick in, and Cyrell deftly leaps to the side. Their moves are so fast that I can see only blurry limbs and the lightning arcs of their steel.

I know I should do something, but what?

And what new friends does Dairell mean?

The air ripples around me like a hot day over a black road. I blink and rub my eyes, and then it hits me.

Is it even possible...

I sense a presence. I've heard from Diaphonus that my mortal eyes would most likely not be able to spot a Siphon, as these abominations are constituted of pure, unrefined magic. Yet I can sense them. And they are approaching. They will be onto us as soon as they finish off the remnants of our escort.

Both males are locked in a life-or-death skirmish, so no help is coming. Cyrell brought them to us? No, this cannot be. I try to wrap my mind around this. Then, suddenly, icy chills run down my spine. I feel watched.

Cold, eerie, unblinking eyes measure me up. I have drawn someone's attention, just like the retreating postman captures the attention of the guard dog.

I step away from the carriage and the whistle and clang of the blades. The horses panic, and gallop away. I look around for a way out or help. But there's nothing, just endless rows of dead vines on both sides of the road and two males consumed in their thirst for vengeance. Then, a shove by invisible hands throws me to the black sand. A caress of dead fingers, a curious brush of something other. Something that does not belong here.

Ice crystals form in my skull. I feel my mind violated, the pages of my memories flipped as if a careless child leafs through a book.

The sound of steel meeting steel behind my back fades, so does the freezing grip on my brain.

The landscape around me blurs, and I trip over something. How did I stand up again? I blink to adjust to a bright light and look down to see—

The body of my mother slumped on the three steps leading to our porch. I nervously pull the straps of my school backpack, startled by the loud voices and children's laughter. The school bus is parked just twenty feet away. The driver is already heading my way, worry and pity written on her face. The other kids find the sight of my mother passed out in her vomit rather amusing. She was probably out drinking again. I was so occupied with getting ready for school that I didn't notice her absence this morning. A swarm of schoolchildren follows the driver, who bends over and pulls down the indecently rolled-up skirt of my mother, then turns to me and grabs my shoulders.

"I think you should stay home today, Celeste," the driver murmurs, "Help me get your mom inside and open the door."

I try to move, yet my feet are glued to the ground. Why is it so cold here? Why is everyone staring at me? An icy grip squeezes my mind, and I'm being consumed. Something drains my essence, my life…

The first group of children reaches the steps where my mom's lifeless body lies among the stench of cheap liquor, vomit, and urine.

"My father says your mother is an alcoholic. AL-CO-HO-LIC. Is this what she is?" Becky from my math class asks.

"Is she even alive?" I hear a rumbling adolescent voice from behind.

"My mum is a nurse and says that it happens often with your mom," Diana confidently declares, "It is because she drinks—"

Life, my life seeps away from me. The coldness crawls up my feet, and I look down at the tiny hands of eight-year-old me.

"Does she beat you, or does she just lie there and puke?" a boy asks.

Breathing gets hard. Ghostly fingers close around my throat. All eyes are on me.

"Are you an AL-CO-HO-LIC too?"

"It is because her dad left them—?"

"Oh, I thought he left because of that—"

I start taking fast, shallow breaths. The laughter grows deafening.

I'm being drained, consumed. My life seeps away with each breath.

My older self recognizes the impending panic attack, yet I can't do anything to prevent it.

My vision blurs, and I'm hyperventilating.

"Celeste, are you okay?" the driver squeezes my bony shoulder. Laughter in the background. The air isn't enough. I'm suffocating. I will die here while they laugh at me. Tears roll down my cheeks.

"Told you she's crazy, just like her mom!"

"Alcoholic isn't crazy!"

"I can see her bum!"

A cruel blade pierces my chest and nape; cold sweat runs down my brow.

"Celeste? "the driver shakes me violently, "Snap out of it!"

I can't get enough air. This is how I die. The world around me spins and disintegrates, leaving me only with pain. Gut-wrenching, annihilating pain, the kind that rips my soul out and fills the void with alien nothingness.

I am empty, drained, squirming. Violent tremors shatter my body. I hit the ground. Not the rotten boards of our porch but in the fine black sand of the Underworld. I'm suffocating, the pain tearing me into pieces, yet the cold fingers around my brain retreat in panic like a child who touched a hot plate. The grip has loosened. Whatever has invaded my mind is running now.

No.

Not so fast.

You will pay the price.

You will suffer with me.

I've been living with the weight of these memories for twenty years. If someone or something is stupid enough to peek inside my head, they should suffer the consequences. I refuse to be a victim anymore.

The scorching tentacles of my pain lash out, twist around the fading entity, then squeeze. Tighter.

"Celeste! Celeste, snap out of it!"

I open my eyes and stare into the burning gaze of Dairell. His hair is matted with blood, and his black armor drenched in crimson.

"Celeste—" my breaths become more, even when he cradles me, warmth and care flashing beneath his thick black lashes, "How do you feel?"

The tremors recede, and the pain shrinks to a faint discomfort.

"What happened?" I rasp, my throat sore as if I was screaming for hours. Maybe I did. I blink around in confusion.

"I've never thought a mortal capable of this, Celeste," awe ripples his voice, "you just destroyed a Siphon."

It all makes sense now. The relentless grip on my mind, the feeling of being drained... And I managed to fight back. A sense of savage triumph flashes over me. Not only have I defended myself against a lethal magical entity, but I have also destroyed it. Made it pay for the suffering it caused.

It's short-lived, though. Dairell shoots up to his feet and pulls me along.

"We need to get you to safety, Celeste. They're everywhere." I look around, yet there is nothing to see, just a sense of dread hanging heavily in the air.

"Cyrell...?" I dare to ask the question tormenting me since I returned to my senses.

The warmth in his gaze fades and his regal face turns into stone. "The traitor who set this up has been punished."

In the distance, a slumped metallic figure and Cyrell's motionless body leaned against it confirm my fears.

Tears wet my cheeks, yet there is no time to grieve for the lonely, strange, dark elf. I feel that eerie tingle in the air around us. More Siphons approach.

Dairell whistles. His enormous off-white stud appears from nowhere, and he leaps into the saddle with a superhuman grace. Powerful hands wrap around my waist, and he pulls me in front of him, molding his massive frame to my back. Cyrell's blood soaks into the back of my dress while we gallop toward the castle.

Time blurs as the horse meanders between the thick vines, the magical wisps in the murky skies recede, and we move in almost complete darkness. I feel Dairell's chin pressed against my cheekbone, his arms squeezing me so tight that I must fight for air. His glowing eyes are set at the horizon ahead, scanning for danger.

I can see the outlines of the massive gothic building just when the horse stumbles for a second time. The prince hops off the saddle, helps me down, and I stretch my legs with gratitude. Then he pats the neck of the animal and whispers some soft words in its ear. He turns to me when it disappears into the vines.

"We walk from here."

My back is killing me, yet I keep up with his wide stride. Black Guardians rush to meet us.

Melancholy and fear consume me in the following days. I have experienced firsthand the suffering a Siphon can inflict. What if we become swarmed by these demons? What if they manage to drain me, to deplete my magic? Would I lose my mind, turn into an empty husk, or would they kill me on the spot?

How am I supposed to let three Fae males please me and reach the most intimate corner of my soul while I fear for my life?

I cannot get Cyrell's warning out of my head each night as I toss and turn, restless in my bed. *Gambling with your life... the plan will not work.*

I share my fears with the prince over dinner one night. I haven't seen him much in the last days, as he dedicates all his time to organizing the defense of the Sentinel. He is leading the drills to synchronize the Black Guardians with an army of dark elves who have joined our forces.

Dairell looks haunted. Something is eating him up. He stares at me when we are together with gut-wrenching sadness. He always looks away when I catch his gaze.

"I... I am not sure if I could reach out to my powers with so much at stake and such a danger around us," I confess, poking at my food.

His black wings flinch, and he runs his fingers through his midnight tresses. "You are the most precious thing Faëheim has, Celeste. Me, Diaphonus, and Tarcyll will gladly give our lives to purge the Siphons. The magic in your body is in harmony with ours—we are the Serpent's perfect match. Even in miserable circumstances like these, we crave each other. Trust the forethought of the Serpent, Celeste."

I know there is more to his words, yet I am too afraid to ask. "Trust your instincts, little human," he whispers, his eyes sparkling sapphires in the candlelight, "Whatever happens, don't forget we are brought together for a reason." The sudden need to close my eyes is so overwhelming that I immediately recognize the sleeping spell. Before I drift off, the last thing I see is his arms around me and the pain on his face.

I wake up in the morning feeling rested and calm. Ready to get it over with it and go home. A gentle knock on my door announces that it is time. The prince fills up the doorframe, dark circles framing his beautiful eyes.

"It is time, Celeste. Get ready and meet me at the courtyard."

And so it begins.

We ride to the Sentinel surrounded by the allied forces.

Desperate determination, faint hope, and mind-numbing terror clash inside me like the waters of three oceans. If Dairell is to be trusted, then I simply have to give in to the pleasure awaiting me at the hands of these three gorgeous males. After the Ritual is completed, I will be a normal human. Maybe then the Dark Prince's possessiveness will melt like snow in the sun, and he will allow me to return home. Back to Cathy and Jasmin, to my mother, who probably hasn't even noticed I am gone. I will say goodbye to this delirious dream I have lived in this last month.

But this is the most optimistic version, the outcome I hope for. The official plan. No one can foresee what will happen with so many variables at play. Maybe my arcane power is not enough to change a thing, and all we would achieve is bait all Siphons of Faëheim to the Underworld? Or perhaps it will all work out great, and then the Dreadful One will decide that he doesn't want to part with his human toy?

I've heard them discussing the possibility of a massive swarm of Siphons attacking us, lured in by all the magic. The prince himself suggested raising wards and keeping the Siphons trapped in the Underworld to save the rest of the realm. This idea raised many eyebrows; everyone in the room was surprised by Dairell's selflessness. Everyone but me. I knew about the guilt he was carrying around for ages, the suspicion that this all resulted from his failure to restrain his mother's lust for power. I knew the lengths he was ready to go to to make things right and the shelter he offered runaway slaves.

"If I could give my own life to make it right, I would do it in the blink of an eye."

We slow down, and I see the leviathan outlines of the Sentinel. Hazy silhouettes swarm the ghostly forest. The soldiers and mages have secured a perimeter around the tree.

Glowing orbs float around the mighty trunk. A luxurious canopy of airy fabrics stretches over a magnificent low bed, screens granting some privacy from the troops patrolling the dead forest.

The bed is massive, covered with tempting satin sheets. *Large enough to fit four*, I think, and shudder with horror and anticipation. Suddenly, I feel light-headed.

Dairell wraps his arms around me, his warm touch grounding me and helping me off the horse. I arrange the pleats of my risqué dress, raise my chin, and prepare to head to the tree. He grabs my hand and squeezes it in reassurance, a spontaneous act so unlike him.

"Celeste, I—"

Something in his voice makes me freeze. I recognize that sound of longing and desperation, I heard it just a few days ago from Cyrell. Turning around to face him, I see this powerful, winged warlord hesitant. His shoulders hang, carrying the weight of a mysterious pain. For an instant, I think he will grab me, fly away with me, and damned be the Ritual, damned be all Faëheim. Is this what I want?

"I... I admire your courage. You are the most precious thing I have in my life." His voice breaks and his eyes well, yet he reins himself in quickly. "It's time. The others are waiting."

I follow him with a sigh. My mind replays Cyrell's words over and over: *Remember that I am the only one who offered you a choice!*

Have I made a grave mistake?

It's too late now.

The grass around us and the silver bells seem to be thriving, little sparkles of hope. Green leaves cover the vines closest to the Sentinel. Life is blossoming in the little oasis around the tree. An oasis we have created.

As we pass, the foliage moves despite the complete lack of draft, as if the plants watch us with unnatural curiosity.

Diaphonus and Tarcyll are already expecting us, tall and heartbreakingly beautiful, dressed in matching outfits: flowing silk shirts and soft dark leggings, bare feet, hair braided up. The casual elegance of their clothes cannot conceal the blades strapped over their arms and thighs. They have come prepared, and for an instant, I see them for what they are: deadly creatures of light and shadows roaming the borders of the realms.

I literally salivate, enthralled by the inked images on Tarcyll's skin, glowing faintly in the magic-saturated surroundings, captivated by Diaphonus' golden hair, glistening in the cool light of the wisps. They welcome us, their faces solemn, yet I notice the burning need in their eyes. Will they still crave me after all magic is drained from my body?

I try not to think, not to feel. Instead, I focus on my seductive walk. Probably, I look comical, but it works. Their eyes are ablaze. Diaphonus parts his lips and licks them, leaning on Tarcyll's shoulder to steady himself. The spy crosses his massive, tattooed arms at his chest and smiles devilishly.

Oh my.

We enter the area, shielded by the silk screens. The tangled branches of the Sentinel above make it appear like a cozy treehouse, like one of those luxury eco hotels advertised on social media.

The priest reassuringly squeezes my shoulder when I join them. No words are needed. Tarcyll hands me a gilded chalice with a wink.

"I know you don't like wine, Celeste, but this is a strong one. A special one, it will help."

Taking the chalice, I look at Dairell, who nods encouragingly. I empty it in two gulps, feeling the intense, fruity liquid burn its way down to my core. Warmth spreads in my body, and I am suddenly less concerned.

The world around me fades into a kaleidoscope of sun-kissed skin, heavy-lidded glimmering eyes, razor-sharp fangs biting lush lips, and glossy hair strands casually tucked behind pointy ears. The three males surround me, and I am trapped between walls of rippling muscles, heat, and lethal power. They tower over me, and it's intimidating, but in a way that awakens the pulsating need between my thighs. I wonder if the drink or the magic inside me responds to their closeness and heat, and I bite my lip in anticipation.

Tarcyll trails the outline of my back. "I have always wondered if you can take three of us at the same time," his husky voice resonates in my ear, and my knees give in.

"We will try to be gentle," the high elf whispers, snaking his arm around my waist. His voice, dripping with dark desires, promises otherwise.

Dairell watches us; his features are hard to read. The flame in his aquamarine orbs is dangerous, and his jawline is so sharp it could give me a paper cut. He clenches his fists as if to rein himself in, when the high elf rips my bodice open and fills his hands with my breasts, gently twirling my nipples. Tarcyll kneels before me, rolling my transparent silk dress up. I moan when I feel his ragged breath on my folds.

"This little pussy is all soaked already," he breathes, and I squirm when his tongue darts up and down my seam. My legs give in, and I am grateful for Diaphonus´ strong arm around my waist.

How we reach the bed is a mystery. The spymaster gently pushes me down. He captures me with his midnight gaze and slowly unbuttons his shirt. Leaning on my elbows, I pant with need at the sight of his gorgeous, inked pecs and carved abs. The blond priest pins me under his weight while I savor the view and presses his enormous, erect cock against me. His scorching lips are on my breasts, sucking, licking, tormenting, and I arch into him, digging my fingers into his heavenly soft hair. Then I push him down, as I am craving to feel these lips somewhere else, and he obediently settles between my legs, his tongue slowly circling my clit.

I forget about the importance of the Ritual and all the risks. Sizzling waves of carnal need sweep away all my fears. It's just their bodies and mine now. My desire is stronger than all my insecurities and doubts. The magic in my bones sings, roars, and the males in the bed respond to its siren's call with the ferocity only Fae possess.

Diaphonus' slender finger enters me while he devours my clit. Tarcyll lunges onto me with a devilish smirk, capturing my nipple between his fangs, sucking and grazing, awakening an ancient rhythm in my body. I angle my hips toward the high elf's greedy mouth. He traces every line, tastes every rim, then gently sucks on my nub. Tender fingers brush away my hair, grounding me. Startled, I turn around to meet the cerulean gaze of Dairell. He has stripped down to his soft leather leggings, my God! A cascade of chiseled muscles narrows down to a tight waist, a dusting of dark hair descends from his navel to the low rise of his pants. The dents on both sides of his lower abs guide my greedy gaze down to the mouth-watering bulge in his pants.

The prince gently places my head on his lap, his gorgeous arousal straining to break free and pushing against my nape, and I cannot resist the temptation. I reach up behind me and set this beast of a cock free, then shove it into my mouth. With a low growl, the prince grabs a fistful of my hair and positions my head in his lap at an angle that allows him the deepest penetration possible. Our eyes lock. Oh God, how I enjoy the barely leashed madness in his otherworldly gaze! The rough thrusts of his rock-hard flesh stretch the skin of my face, and I realize, terrified, that he could indeed kill me with that.

Diaphonus lifts my thighs, spreading me wide. He props himself up and rubs his dripping cock along my throbbing clit. I try to pull away from Dairell's assault, to beg the blond elf to take me, yet my attempts to escape his grip are futile.

"I will fill that sweet little cunt now." Diaphonus rasps, the profanity in his words so not priest-like. The other males growl in approval. Dairell leans in closer to watch the elf slowly sliding his cock inside me, delivering the sweet stretch I have craved. Diaphonus starts pounding me viciously, my bouncing breasts escaping the gluttonous mouth of the Fae spymaster.

My eyes widen when Tarcyll straddles me, firmly grabs my bouncing breasts in his large arms, and slides his cock between them.

Oh. My God.

The spymaster moans and turns to Diaphonus, "You need to try this, brother, ma'chtariel, dò anne..." he says breathily while fucking my breasts. His actions and words set the other two Fae ablaze, and they resume their assault with brutal force.

My lips are stretched around Dairell's veiny cock, precum and saliva trickling down my face, yet I manage to catch a glimpse of Tarcyll's steely tattooed abs, glistening with sweat.

A possessive yank of my hair reminds me of whom I belong to.

"Eyes on me, Celeste," he rumbles. I wonder if he will hold back and let them have their way with me or lose it and shred the other two males to ribbons. Knowing his possessive nature, I wouldn't be surprised, yet common sense wins over, and he settles for the latter. He pulls out of my mouth, and I brush a finger over my swollen, wet lips to check for blood.

Tarcyll and the high elf exchange looks, and the world around me blurs. The muscled, inked arms of the spy wrap around my behind, and he pulls me into his lap. He lays down on the fine sheets, and I end up on top of him, my breasts at the mercy of his fangs, his hands roughly squeezing my ass.

"Let me stretch this pink pussy, Celeste. Let me fuck you like an animal." A note in his voice is certainly not human and makes me shudder. Terror and arousal are the addictive vitriolic mix that I often experience with these Fae. He sheaths himself deep inside me and roughly smacks my ass. Then he starts pumping me like a man possessed, just like he promised, the supple flesh of my breasts slapping his face with each move.

I need more. I am aching to be filled. All of my holes.

"Fuck my mouth, Diaphonus," I hiss, opening my lips invitingly. The elf smirks and complies, penetrating my mouth, and I can taste myself on him.

The dark prince shuffles behind me. He has undoubtedly a delicious view of Tarcyll's massive length stretching my slit to its limits. My walls clamp around the spymaster's enormous girth, and this position—me on top, gives me a maddening rub on my clit. I tilt my head backward, feeling the long strands of my hair tickle my lower back, serving my pebbled nipples to the spymaster's mouth. A low rumble vibrates down his strained abs when he takes my breast, nibbling on it, his tongue leaving glistening trails on my flesh.

"Your sweet mouth has suffered enough today, Celeste," the elven priest withdraws from my lips and moves away.

Suddenly, I feel the warmth of his muscular torso behind my back. Diaphonus closes his fingers around my neck, tilting my head up. He kisses me slowly. When he releases my mouth, I immediately sense his tip rubbing against my tight back hole; then he presses in.

"Let me have you like that, too, beautiful Celeste; let me experience this divine pleasure," he whispers hoarsely. The idea of being filled by both simultaneously is so arousing that it almost makes me orgasm. I spread my legs wider to give him access. He slowly enters me from behind. A moan escapes the beautiful elf, pure music to my ears. The sensation of being completely and utterly filled and stretched makes me mumble some incredibly indecent words.

Then I feel a firm pull on my hair.

I look up to see Dairell's magnificent, dripping cock just an inch away from my open mouth.

"By the Serpent, Celeste, look at all the delights you can provide," he thunders, pulling me up. His hands grab my breasts and knead them with a moan. Then he glides his cock between them, just like the spy did before.

"Bow before your prince, Celeste," he hisses, and I realize what he means. I bend my head, part my lips, and let his engorged head slide between them. I whimper, driven mad by the thought that he's fucking my tits and mouth at the same time.

He roars, his wings of shadows spreading.

The thought of the pleasure my body delivers while being claimed by these three breathtaking Fae males sends me over the edge. My scream is choked by the jets of hot seed filling my mouth.

Powerful spurts flood my other two holes, and I fear I might lose consciousness. Wave after wave of earth-shattering bliss causes my body to convulse. The glow of my magic pierces the centennial twilight of the dead forest around the Sentinel, and I feel the mighty rumble of an arcane force roll in the distance. Strong hands steady me while my body still trembles.

Spells thicken the air, weaving invisible threads of pure power.

Diaphonus and Tarcyll shout commands to the unseen soldiers and mages around us.

"Breath, Celeste, breath, that's it, good girl," I hear a husky voice and feel my surroundings shift. Long fingers stroke my hair, lips meet my lips, licking off Dairell's seed, muscular arms lift me and prop me against a rock-hard body like a tiny doll. The world still spins. I'm on my knees, and my back rests on the broad tattooed chest of the spymaster. My dizzy mind registers the firm fingers of the Dark Prince on my thighs, spreading my folds. My opening is still twitching in aftershocks of the devastating orgasm, still leaking cream from the powerful climax of Tarcyll that has filled me up to the brim, yet Dairell doesn't care. He stretches my labia open, his gaze hazy and mesmerized, starved. His forked tongue flicks over his fangs.

"That mortal heat, that passion!" he rumbles before diving between my legs. I shudder, feeling the gentle pressure of his tongue exploring me, licking me clean, before delving deep into my slit. I squirm, but the strong arms of the spy restrict my movements from behind, holding me just in the place the three males need me to be. I look away from the inky tresses of the prince between my legs and up to the chiseled bronze torso of the elven priest, holding his stiff shaft in his fist. Hard and ready to go again.

"Did you think we were done?" The deep rumble of Tarcyll's laughter behind me stiffens my nipples, "Oh dear, we're just starting."

I notice distant light explosions, probably the mages redirecting the magic waves that still linger around us.

Our bodies are slick with sweat; all my holes are drenched, twitching, begging for more. The steel of the spymaster slowly glides into my back hole while my pussy is entirely at Dairell's mercy. His fingers join the sweet torment of his tongue and curl inside me. He starts pumping me feistily while his forked tongue leaps around my throbbing nub. Sweet fatigue has softened my bones, and I open my mouth to beg for mercy, yet it is not granted. The steel embrace of Tarcyll still holds me into place while his massive cock slides in and out of my ass, and my only chance to catch a breath is cut short by the blond priest as he shoves his shaft into my throat with a feral growl. The onslaught continues relentlessly, and I comprehend why some mortals couldn't survive mating with Fae. I am locked, penetrated, kneaded, squeezed, consumed, and the savage passion of these males terrifies and arouses me simultaneously.

And we are just starting.

Maybe they will really fuck me to death.

I feel the tension build-up, and they notice the trembling of my body. Dairell withdraws his skilled fingers and swiftly replaces them with his thick veiny cock, spreading my walls with each rough thrust.

The wicked males work me in a savage harmony. It is almost too much to take. I try to free myself from their crushing grip, but my attempts are quickly thwarted, my resistance suffocated in their scorching embrace. I am completely at their mercy, I realize, their massive cocks buried deep in all my openings. The fine dark hairs at the base of Dairell's blade rub against my clit, and I feel the wave of the next orgasm swelling. The three males sense it, too, as they pause their onslaught, and the prince slowly withdraws himself from me. His eyes glow in the twilight, just like the deadly beasts roaming the emerald depths of the jungle. Intoxicated, he indulges in the sight of my open, throbbing pussy. I wiggle in protest and try to form coherent words, yet all I achieve is getting the elf's cock shoved deeper into my throat.

"I think she wants you back inside her," Tarcyll rasps, his dick still deep in my ass, his muscular inked forearms holding me steady, his palms full of my soft flesh.

"I want to hear her begging for it," the Dark Prince responds breathily, looming over me in all his mighty warlord splendor, his shadowy wings making him appear terrifyingly large. His fingers spread my labia open to the point of pain, and he looks me cold in the eye.

"Beg for my cock, Celeste."

I squirm and feel my eyes water, my pussy pulsating with mad need. I bet he can clearly see the convulsions of my walls. The other two males slowly withdraw, leaving me empty and desperate, aching to be filled. I lie before him on the bedsheets soaked with our passion. Seed and saliva drip down my lips and to my breasts when he captures my jaw and forces me to face him.

"Beg me to fuck you, Celeste."

Darkness pools around him, and the other two males retreat another step. Are these the sounds of a sword fight in the distance? Are the blinding explosions getting closer?

I am still sprawled before him. He inches closer, his enormous, engorged head within my reach.

His black wings brush the sheets with slow, hypnotizing sweeps. There is such a halo of might and supernatural beauty around him that I know I would do anything to please him.

"Please, Your Majesty," I mutter, the mad ache between my thighs blurring my mind, "please fuck me."

His beautiful lips turn upward, and he nods in approval. "I like it when you call me that."

I greedily open my mouth and reach for his cock, yet his firm hand grabs my hair and yanks me backward.

"Have you asked for permission?" he hisses, slapping my cheek.

I rub my thighs, aroused to madness by this game of power and control. "Please, your Majesty, let me suck your cock," I mumble, my fingers descending between my legs, desperately trying to relieve the tension. He nods and glides between my lips, and I devour him hungrily. He slams against the back of my throat, choking me.

"You are mine, Celeste," he growls. The gloom around us gets thicker, and I hear the distant clanking of swords and the thunder of spells. My head spins. It is so dark. Where are Tarcyll and Diaphonus? Have the Siphons discovered us? I am amazed to realize I don't care.

"Are you ready for me, Celeste?" he asks, his whisper dripping dark promises. I look up at the rippling curves of his abs and massive pecs, meeting his glowing aquamarine gaze, and nod. He lifts me like a feather, straps my legs around his waist, and I whimper at the deep penetration. His mighty wings beat the air, synchronized with each tantalizing thrust of his hips, and I suddenly feel heavier, all my body weight pressing me down to his shaft.

We are flying.

The distant thunder of the battle fades as he skillfully meanders between the mighty branches of the sacred tree.

"It's just me and you now, Celeste," his words caress my ear, his tone soft and warm. With his arms around me, his cock deep inside me, and the power of gravity working in my favor, I sense a soul-crushing orgasm building up.

Dear Lord, how will I survive this?

I don't even try to suppress my scream as the first wave of my orgasm nearly destroys me. Dairell's massive manhood claims me with powerful thrusts, and tremors seize my muscles, but he holds me tight, flying higher and higher, and the explosions of arcane energy I release color the branches of the Sentinel purple.

His mouth captures mine. Hot and hungry, desperate and relentless, his tongue caressing mine with firm, demanding strokes. I respond a little bit too late, dazzled and panting.

Another deep thrust releases a second climax, and I squirm in his strong hands, my body weightless, glowing.

"Remember that I am doing this only because I have no other choice, Celeste."

I don't know where the dagger came from. My eyes widen when I recognize it's the same one he used to please me in that pantry back in the Lower Lands.

My panting turns into hyperventilation as he lowers the blade, and I feel its lethal coldness against my chest. My brain seems to struggle to catch up with my body, because the terror hits me while I still orgasm. Surely this cannot be happening, right? Probably some sort of sick Fae game, I guess.

The panic attack hits me full force when the blade slowly and deliberately slides between my ribs; the unbearable pain, violating coldness, and fear petrifies me. I try to scream, yet no sound escapes me.

"I am so sorry, Celeste," he murmurs, shoves the dagger deeper, and releases me.

I feel the icy metal buried inside me, draining my life as he lets me fall.

I plunge to my death. Lethal pulses of raw, raging magic mark my fall. The tree absorbs my raw terror, my savage release of primal energy, amplifies it, and shoots it back. The vines around me glow up in fantastic colors of a supernatural spectrum.

Wave after wave, I release roaring cataclysmic magic and agonizing pain into this eerie, violent world. Far beyond the Underworld.

Cleansing, destroying, white-hot agony.

I hear disembodied screeches of pain and terror.

They depart.

Faëheim is safe.

The branches of the Sentinel painfully break my plunge into the abyss, yet the forest floor is so far away. Magic streams out of my body with each hit of the branches on my way down.

I hear my ribs crack, and my left arm twists at an impossible angle.

Agony cuts my body in half, and I gasp, unable to take another breath. My body squirms and glows, tossed from branch to branch by merciless gravity. Shimmering streams of pulsating energy, of life, are leaving me, and the sounds of the battle below fade.

Darkness closes me in, and the Crystal Serpent's glowing body, stretching into eternity, welcomes me.

And takes away my pain.

End of Book 1
Celeste's adventure continues in Book 2 of the Crystal Serpent series: The Pillars of the Firmament

Printed in Great Britain
by Amazon